D1707030

To Tony

Westward the Gods

The Answer

E. A. Isola

printed with createspace.com

copyright © 2013

To order online:

Createspace.com/4380404

Amazon.com

other retailers

ISBN: #149 121 7111

Printed with Create Space

Charleston, South Carolina 29418

USA 2013

"Phoenicia"

The picture of the reconstructed Phoenician ship seen

on the cover came from a blog by

Professor Ferrell Jenkins

"Name Is Aribaal" is the first volume of a

two volume set

To order online: createspace.com/3869029

Available from Amazon.com

and other retailers

Chapter 1

After losing my beloved Nikkal, calm in despair, I sat by the sea as one dead, refusing both food and drink even in the hottest hours of the day until my uncle and my friends began to fear for my life, as well. It seemed that my light had been stolen and I cast into a dark, deep well of pain from which there could be no release. In my agony I knew there resided a place within me that would forever remain empty and barren no matter what good things life brought my way.

After my period of deepest mourning the friends continued their lengthy preparations to debark. There seemed no reason to delay the departure any longer than necessary. I did not know if I had gained any wisdom from this terrible grief that stole my joy.

Time passed on crippled feet while I remained inconsolable even as I half-heartedly oversaw the outfitting of the ships and the selection of additional seamen. I stayed by myself most of the time playing the lute by the sea or walking hour after hour along the waterfront with my eyes either toward the ground or aimed at the distant horizon.

When gazing at the inner sea I contemplated what I would discover when I traversed the great ocean to the west beyond both sight and imagination. I considered the quasi-visions I had experienced, the feathers, the heat and the raucous animal sounds.

I tried to picture what people there would be like. Did people actually dwell there or was it a hallucination inhabited only by fantastic dream creatures? Sometimes I attempted to recall the visions. I believed if I could see and hear them once more I might understand them a little. But I could not. The visions were but a memory and an increasingly vague one at that. Finally, I gave up and involved myself in the preparations being made by others.

Smoke or cloud sometimes wreathed the higher

mountain tops and hid them from sight. At night, for a long stretch, a red glow showed from the bearded summit of one mountain and reminded me of the coals in Baal's fire pit.

I shuddered when memory blended with the present to impress me with a strong sense of danger. Even as I stood on the deck of Hiras' vessel answering an endless barrage of questions from Deidre I continued to have the uncomfortable feeling of some strange creature crawling on my body.

Unable to see, hear or identify the source of the sensation I chose to ignore it. Instead I pointed out to my daughter the new raw villages that had sprung up from the labor of men coming to this place seeking a new life and a brighter future. Some of these, the unruly ones, had been outcasts from their homelands because of their own wickedness. Others, such as freed or escaped slaves, and not a few men with adventurous spirits expressly sought new places and people.

Deidre delighted in the voyage. She clung to rail

much of the time, her eyes constantly searching the sea and the nearby coastline for whatever curiosities might catch her attention. After many days I decided to take Helen and the children and accompany my uncle north along the coastline. We sailed slowly, taking in the scenery. In places the mountains looked to have their feet in the water and in others wide beaches with grasslands appeared to the west.

"See, Father, there are dancing fish."

She clasped her hands in delight.

"They want me to dance with them. May I, Father?"

She began to climb as if to leap into the sea. The dolphins, weary it seemed of following us, dove beneath the water in a graceful arch, their shining bodies in perfect unison.

"They are gone."

Her face crumpled and tears formed.

"Yes. They are gone. But they will return when they are ready. However, you may not jump in with them. The sea is their element, yours is land. You could not survive as they do. But you can take pleasure in watching them dance and dive and show off for you."

She wiped her eyes and followed the tears with a damp smile.

"Yes. I will wait for them.

She returned to her scrutiny of the coastline. In some places where the mountains touched the very edge of the water sharp rocky promontories seemed to forbid access.

"You would not want to be shipwrecked in a place like that. See how sharp the rocks are on their sides. They can cut a ship in pieces as easily as I can slice a loaf of bread with my dagger. When traveling, it is imperative to sail farther out where the rocks cannot reach."

"Would I die then?"

"It is possible but do not concern yourself. These deceptive waters are like a lighted path to the captain and his crew."

She looked around as if to locate the lamp that lit the sea for the mariners. Not finding it she shrugged and turned her attention back to the scenery.

The dolphins that followed us part of the time and sometimes swam side by side with our ship continued to fascinate her and kept her attention for hours at a time. She continually darted from one side of the ship to the other, tracing the movements of the graceful swimmers and of the sea birds which accompanied us. Her antics made me laugh and I felt grateful for her light-hearted presence.

By the time we returned to my uncle's home my small daughter had already restored some small part of my joy in life. Excitement began to overwhelm despair and, while there was no doubt of my grief had diminished.

Before what now promised to be the most incredible journey of my life I had some small familiarity with the great ocean. I passed the pillars in my boyhood, but sailed only along the coast to the south. As soon as my father's cargo ships made the transition from the great inner sea to the vast ocean, the much deeper waters beyond turned dark and ominous while the vessels clung close to the shore.

The wonders of the hot wetness of the southern lands and their intriguing denizens could not quite overcome my increasing curiosity about the ocean. When possible I questioned traders from the exotic nations around the sea, but none had ever experienced the huge body of water to the west of us. I decided then that one day I would follow that mysterious water wherever it led me. Perhaps, I laughed at myself, the great adventurer of my youthful dreams would ultimately find himself back where he started, having travelled in circles. No one knew what secrets dwelt in and around those mysterious waters. However, even that enigma could not quench my thirst for knowledge of the ocean.

On that most auspicious day my uncle Hiras and his entire family gathered to see me off. Hiras made no bones about his skepticism. Ultimately, he lifted his shoulders in a final shrug and with a casual toss of his hand dismissed me and my folly. My friends and I would attempt to cross the great water beyond the strait that separated the inner sea from the more massive ocean and my uncle knew we would try or die.

As far as anyone knew no one before me had ever attempted such a crossing. If someone did, he never returned to tell the tale. There were, of course, legends and rumors of monsters that lived in its depths and came forth to devour those foolish enough to challenge the vastness. The expressions of family members who came to witness my departure told their story of doubt, fear and the conviction that I must be mad.

Just at the moment when I would board my flagship, Helen appeared, pushing her way through the gathered crowd of family and citizens.

"Ari", she called out, "wait for me."

She hastened to reach me. I could only admire the

loveliness and dignity her innate grace gave so vulgar an act as pursuing her husband bent on abandoning her.

"I want to go with you."

She lowered her voice as she spoke, so to keep our conversation as private as possible.

"You cannot." I kept my voice low but emphatic. "Wives do not accompany their husbands on voyages of this nature." I took her hand and bent closer. "Besides, there are the children who need you."

"They will be well cared for while we are away. The family will see to that. Should it become necessary, Hiras will send them to your adoptive family in Egypt. But, my husband, I cannot be apart from you any longer. I must go with you, wherever and for however long it takes."

Very gently, I kissed her soft lips then pushed her away.

"It cannot happen, Helen. I am sorry. Return now to our children who need you. For me, on such a perilous sea you would be a distraction and a burden to protect. I promise to return as soon as I can."

I pushed her a little more firmly and watched as she began to turn away. I had to admire her courage, both in challenging me and in pleading her case before the whole city.

From their expressions, it was clear the observers read the situation well enough and great pity spread over most of the faces. Reluctantly, Helen turned and left to join the others sending me off into the unknown. As I oversaw the last minute loading of supplies and personal goods aboard our ships, the family crowded the cothons. When at last we could board the ships, Helen was nowhere to be seen. It saddened me to realize how I had rejected her while at the same time, I felt grateful that I no longer had to cope with her presence and my guilty feelings about her.

With a powerful sense of adventure and an overwhelming conviction that I had seen and felt a visionary call to a new land, a place never before witnessed by civilized man, I ordered my sailors to cast off into the great sea which bordered the known lands of the world.

After leaving Helen and the children with my family at Etruria, my journey began on a peaceful note I could not have anticipated. Even the weather in that storm ridden area of winds that funneled along the rocky coast chose a benign path that augured well for the ships. The sea, ever mysterious and capricious, carried my flagship along quickly with purple sails in full bloom before a strong breeze.

For several days I traveled in sight of land, familiar land, places I had seen many times before, either from a ship, as now, or beneath my feet.

I called Men-el, my friend and erstwhile slave, to watch with me as we neared the great pillars of rock that separated the inner sea from the true ocean. This expedition, not the first he had undertaken with me, unquestionably must be the most precarious.

"We are about to make the trip from the great sea, only this time we will travel west, not south."

"Yes", he replied, in his confident way. "It will be an adventure."

He stared at the great rocks which seemed to grow larger and more forbidding as we got closer.

"None has gone this way before, have they, Ari?"

"Not past the coast of Africa, at least as far as I could learn."

I grinned at him; my heart leapt at the thought that somewhere far beyond any familiar land sat a great territory where I might learn who I was intended to be and why I had to be sacrificed on Baal's fiery altar.

Even though several years had passed since that fateful birthday when Theon's knife had only managed to cost me a very nasty injury and a long scar on my left side, I shuddered as I felt again the terror and pain of that day of horror. That day my sister Dido expeditiously rescued me from Baal's fire to thwart the priest's plan.

I turned around and watched as Theon's ship fell into line behind mine. Ever my nemesis, he presumed much on his questionable claim to be my natural father. Since his assertion could neither be proved nor refuted, it seemed expedient that instead of killing the priest, it seemed I must let him live. In case his words bore truth I could not murder my father. Nevertheless, my hands experienced an urgent desire to circle his scrawny throat and press the evil life from him.

Despite my need the fact that he had experienced some small part of the vision I had been given at Isaac's home in Byblos indicated the time had not yet come for me to rid myself of this devious priest.

His ship's purplish blue sail with its gold fish, emblem of the Baal of Byblos, challenged the sun itself in intensity of light as his ship slipped behind the supply vessel and the one carrying my soldiers.

"One thing I never need concern myself about is Theon's excess of modesty." I laughed. Men-el laughed with me.

Senmut and Rem-Na, my Egyptian friends from the military academy, joined us.

"What amuses you so much, Na-Amen?"

Senmut used the name I had been given during my sojourn in Egypt. Both my Egyptian companions claimed that Aribaal was too foreign for them to pronounce easily. I, however, thought they just liked the sound of my Egyptian name and the memories it invoked.

"I have been admiring Theon's great humility", I laughed.

In a grumpy voice, my friend replied, "Anyone who can imagine a humble bone in that priest's body has to have gifts far beyond those of a normal man. He has certainly shows no sign of it."

I laughed once more then turned back to watch our

approach to the deceptively smooth rocks that formed a gateway into the distant waters. As excited as I felt about passing between them, I realized how imperative careful navigation became as we neared those great sentinels. Though they were set far apart, the currents and the winds narrowed the safe distance for the navigator. A couple of times I thought I would have to instruct my seamen, but at the last second the ship veered away from danger.

Eventually the ship passed through the mouth of the great inland sea and entered the greater one, that vast, mysterious ocean which ended I knew not where.

Instead of turning south along the coast of Africa, where I had once traveled from Byblos with my trader father, Abishima, I now committed myself to the gods and continued to sail farther and farther from the land, from everything I had ever known. The color of the sea deepened until it became a blue-green that would make the lapis and turquoise of Egypt envious. The swells rose and fell rhythmically and still the ships sailed on as the great sentinels receded from sight.

The gods appeared to favor my decision. My whole flotilla proved strong, the sails able to carry the ships along with little demand on the rowers. Because this was the first time I had ever ventured so far from shore that I could see no land, even in the far distance, I remained on deck with Rem-Na and Senmut throughout much of the daytime. It seemed expedient to keep a close eye on all the waters that surrounded my vessels.

Senmut declared, "Rem-Na and I have decided to sleep on deck as the seamen."

"I, too, will join you."

I smiled at my friends much as we had ever done when encamped in the desert.

"The better to watch the stars and point ourselves in the chosen direction."

In some ways, it did not matter which way the ships

sailed, except that we should continue to the western ocean, which seemed right to me, despite no real reason to think so.

My Hebrew friend Isaac, on the other hand, whose life had so nearly been destroyed by plague, preferred to spend his time inside the cabin, studying the books he had brought aboard. His strength still evaded him, a circumstance I decided had much to do with his years and the grief he felt at losing everything he had built up in Byblos. That he lost it all through the sacrifice he made for me intensified my determination that I must, in some way, find a way to restore him to health, both in his body and in his mind.

The second day out, when the flagship had arrived at a place where no land could be viewed from any direction, even from the top of the mast, he joined me in the prow of the vessel. He had done this when we sailed from Byblos to Egypt on the occasion of my rescue from Theon and his attempt to claim my life. Though but a few short years, it felt a lifetime ago.

"There appears to be no world beyond this expanse. We stare out at the nothingness of water that constantly moves before us to stop at the horizon. Then, when we must have reached that ending, we continue on and see yet another horizon which tells us again that we have come to the world's final end. It is a never ending game we play with the sea."

He turned his head to speak against the rising wind. "Is this not a great mystery, Ari?"

I glanced at my Egyptian friends, seated side by side with their legs drawn beneath them along the port side of the ship where they could rest without interfering with any seaman busy about his duties. I wondered what they, desert denizens, thought of all this. The much shorter trip from Carthage to Etruria and Rem-Na's short term return to Egypt on my behalf hardly prepared them for so much water, such vast distances. Even their lengthy travels by horse or chariot could not begin to prepare them for this voyage.

"There have been so many happenstances in my life, so much mystery, that even the most outrageous situations seem normal after a while."

Isaac smiled at me. "I guess so, my friend. Sometimes, when I think about how little you know yet trust the gods, I wonder at your ability to continue on after so many untoward experiences. Perhaps that is why I feel safe with you. I cannot imagine any situation, however perilous, you would not survive."

He added, "Of course, I actually do not put my faith in you but in my God who, I am certain, has instigated all this to some end we do not now understand."

I laughed loudly at that. I called Senmut and Rem-Na to join us.

"My friends, do you find the days tedious? What do you think about as you huddle on the deck and watch the sea pass by us?"

Senmut replied, "As for me, I think of dry land and the battles we have encountered. I dream of beautiful women waiting for me on the other side of all this water. I flex my muscles and hope that if this journey lasts long so much inactivity will not weaken me beyond recovery."

"I think of Egypt and the home I have so rarely seen, the family stolen from me by those who would destroy my life."

Rem-Na's voice sounded husky, as if it had grown sere before the breezes from the sea.

He grinned. "Enough of this foolishness."

We all laughed together this time and I felt grateful for these faithful friends who had accompanied me from fire pit into many battles both of mind and body to arrive at this moment. I stood and stared off in the southern distance, where the sails of our supply ship and that of Theon's personal vessel could be sighted minimally along the horizon line.

Not for the first time, I wondered what the Baal priest, so clearly my enemy despite his words, hoped to get from this journey to an unknown destination. I feared I might have a glimmer of understanding. Unfortunately, his lust for power might demand he inflict his cruel religion on a new population. I shrugged as I realized that I had no control over the priest and his ambitions. If I must oppose him at some future time, for now all I could do is keep a canny eye on his ship and continue my vigilance.

Isaac, seeing me watch Theon's ship, said, "You can do nothing at this time, Ari. We will all help you should a crisis arise with that man. I do not believe he can vanquish all of us despite his powers."

Even so, I believed there had to be more he sought than a journey into an unknown place, one so fraught with the inevitable hazards of ignorance, that it was folly to undertake it. At Carthage, he enjoyed great power and influence, which he surrendered in order to sail with me and my friends to an alien place where grave danger and even death could await us. I had a sense that he enjoyed a mystical insight that I could not fathom. I tore my eyes from that distant sail, with its boldly shining gold emblem, a challenge to the damp sunshine of the afternoon.

Should I hope to flourish as in the past, I recognized I must arrive somewhere new and unexpected fairly soon. But for now I contemplated my most recent history when I bade my goodbyes to Etruria and my family there.

We now sailed west, farther into the great ocean that awaited us, the unknowing ones who cast our lives into the precarious hands of the gods of sea and land. With no one having gone before us, we set our minds to enter that new territory beyond the great pillars that separated sea and ocean.

After many days of glorious sailing, we sighted land. I had known we soon would, as our water grew sparse and brackish, and all the portents told of good fortune to come. Just the day before sea birds had soared above the ship then away and a great spout of water could be seen afar. Soon we saw what had to be an island, seemingly uninhabited by any but beasts, and few of them from what we could observe.

And yet, as somewhere to settle, the place appeared hospitable and pleasant, with great hills beginning a short way from a natural deep water harbor and covered with foliage we had little time to investigate. My Phoenician training made me wish to remain for a time and send back representatives to establish a colony there. It seemed that so lush an island must surely have people somewhere on it already, and it was possible they would accept a new culture rather easily, or simply establish trade with our people. But I knew this was not the place of my destiny.

Theon's ship, those carrying our troops, and the supply vessels that traveled with us had fallen half a day behind our sleek vessel. We watched them come in, the gilded bow of Theon's ship aglint in the brilliant sunshine, his sail of deep purplish blue a sharp contrast. All our ships anchored along the perfect harbor formed by a massive underwater rock outcropping. Theon, as we had done, stepped off onto the natural dock that would have been the envy of many a port city.

"Perhaps I am foolish to set out with you on this voyage to nowhere." he said in a weary voice, obviously in discomfort from the crowded conditions aboard. "But there is something...yes; decidedly, there is something I must do wherever it is we are going."

"You were not enticed to join us on this voyage, as well you know. I do not even know why you came. It cannot be pleasant for you. You have never told me your motives." I watched him carefully for any reaction. None was forthcoming and his expression remained unfathomable.

"I, at least, have a vision. What do you have?" I challenged him. "If you were a military man, I would suggest you were seeking a new world to conquer. But you are a priest. What possible need does a priest have to discover a new place?" I hesitated, and then added, "And you are not even a true believer but, rather, a charlatan, a manipulator of other men's faith."

"I have you, Aribaal, and you have, as I know well, a vision. Perhaps I could share in yours."

I laughed. "That might not be wise, as my vision first came to me when I was very ill and in the form of a horrible nightmare." I paused, remembering. "It was hot, hotter than I have ever known, before or since, even in Egypt when summer grew full. And the sounds and the smells and the feel of the place were different from any other. Exotic birds flew and roosted, strangely colored, such as no man had ever seen before and trees bore fruits so unusual that I believed no civilized man had ever encountered them."

Even now, as I spoke of this vision, my heart leapt within me. And yet, I thought, despite my fear I must try to find this place.

"Yes. I do know, if you recall, having shared some

small part of this experience of yours."

I remembered that time when Theon, himself, entered my vision for a brief moment. Perhaps, I thought, the gods really intended him to accompany me, despite my reservations.

That night we set up tents for sleeping on land. Their bright fabrics fluttered in the breeze which had joined us ashore. Senmut, Rem-Na and I scouted the immediate area around the landing site and were grateful to bring back fresh meat in the form of wild boar. It was good to hone our hunting skills again and we were like young boys when we returned to the tents.

When the game had been roasted we ate heartily, all the men surrounding the fire, laughing, singing and telling tall tales about the life of a seaman. Even my Egyptian friends, no seamen, joined in with tales of battle. They told of my prowess against the Libyans and how I had received the accolades of great Pharaoh himself.

I joined in until they began to come too close to my marriage to Nikkal, my beloved, mother of my son, Ben-Namen. When their talk edged near her, I stood and walked away from the fire, suddenly unable to withstand the memories they evoked. My emotions still carried the bitterness of recent experience and my heart felt as though someone had taken a rasp to it and shredded the verges of my life.

My sudden restlessness affected the others, many of whom had no knowledge of that part of my life. Our small party broke up then while some sailors stayed behind and salted the remaining meat to take aboard with us. I could not estimate how long it would be before we tasted fresh meat again.

Later, as I sat alone in that dark night beneath the stars, I played my lute and sang. Men-el accompanied me on his small flute with its high sounding trill. Words seemed to come easily, words of hope and encouragement, words to honor a god I did not even know. I did know that something or someone guided me to wherever I headed, even if I knew not where or what it was.

Chapter 2

The hour grew very late before I slept. Uncertainty unsettled my mind and left me agitated, tugging me this way and that and stole my peace of mind. What did I really seek? I knew no way I could answer my own question. Merely, I sought. I had no assurance, even, that I would recognize it if I found it.

Finally, fitfully, unconsciousness came, but it was destined not to last. Suddenly, from the darkness surrounding my tent a loud commotion arose, several voices raised in conflict. I leapt up, startled, and reached for my sword to defend myself against marauding beasts or men. But it was neither beasts nor men responsible for my interrupted sleep.

Helen, her arm held tight by our watchman of the

night, stood at the door of my tent, her head held high in defiance of the soldier who restrained her. When she saw me, she jerked away from the man's grasp.

"I told you this is my husband's tent, did I not?" she demanded of the bemused warrior, who was one of those lately recruited from my uncle's regular army. "Here he stands before you, your lord and mine."

With a great sense of shock I realized that I was not in the midst of a dream but that Helen stood there before me in her flesh.

"She speaks the truth", I stammered at her guard. "She is my wife."

I dismissed the bemused man and pulled Helen into the tent.

"How did you come here? And why?"

"I slipped aboard one of your supply ships while everyone so busily prepared to sail. I have hidden there ever since, among the fabrics and foods." She sat on the rugs laid out for my sleep. "I had adequate to eat. And plenty of water."

"But why, Helen? What has become of our children? Are Deidre and Ben-Namen protected?"

"They are safe. I left them with your cousin Ribbida and his family. If we do not return within a year or two, the children will be taken to your family in Egypt."

She stopped, swallowed twice, and then went on, "I could not let you go without me. What if you did not return? How then could I go on?"

I dropped down beside her and put my arms around her, concealing from her the aggravation I felt at her sudden and unexpected arrival.

"Now what can I do with you?" I asked her. "If I send a ship to return you to Etruria, we must remain here until it makes the two way trip or lose whatever goods it contains. That alternative is not a welcome one."

"But I wish to travel with you, Ari. Why else would I

have done such a thing as stow away on your ship."

Her expression turned desperate, her suddenly tear filled eyes meeting mine.

She said, "Do you hate me for Nikkal's death, Ari? Do you wish I had been the one to die and she to live?"

Her words carried her too close to the rocky shoals of my fantasy life. How many times had I asked the gods why they chose Helen to live and my moon goddess Nikkal to die?

I did not hate Helen, whose care and devotion after my rescue from the fire pit of the Phoenician Baal lifted me beyond the gate from which no man may return. So why then did I continue to reject her?

Despite my contentment with Nikkal, I had married Helen to give our daughter, the fruit of my healing sojourn at Isaac's house in Byblos, a family and a name. Little Deidre immediately managed to steal my heart as is the way with small daughters, especially ones as beautiful and charming as she.

However, in the totality of my love and fascination with my wonderful dancer, Nikkal, I found little place for Helen. Now, as is the capricious way of the gods, she alone remained, while Nikkal lay in her elaborate Etruscan tomb to await the day I would join her there.

I laughed, with no small touch of bitterness. "I see no alternative to taking you with me, but I warn you it will not be a pleasant journey. No Phoenician woman has yet traveled with her husband on one of his journeys."

Her eyes lit up and their new found warmth appeared in them to dry the tears. "Then I shall be the first." She rested against a bolster of rolled up blankets. "Besides, you are not a true Phoenician any longer, but a man of many nations. How can all that matter now?"

I laughed again, heartily this time and in true amusement. Her decisiveness and determination to stay with me proved infectious.

"I think you have the right of it, Helen. But I warn you that I cannot predict what might happen to us. I do not know where we will end up, how we will get there or what will befall us. Not only am I unable to know how long we will be separated from our children but even if we will ever see them again."

I paused to give her time to think about my words.

"And life aboard ship leaves much to be desired. Ships rarely travel as smoothly as ours have done thus far on this trip. It could become very uncomfortable for you."

Tossing her tawny hair with a shake of her head, she said emphatically, "I do not ask comfort of you. I am content to be your companion wherever you may go. Since the first day I saw you, in the temple during Elissa's novitiate, I loved you. And I have never stopped. If anything, my love for you has grown immeasurably since we were reunited at Carthage. And we will return to our children. I know it in every beat of my heart. Further, I am convinced not a long time hence."

How could I resist so caring and resolute a wife? I held her in my arms all night, happy and at peace in her presence. For a short while I could almost forget that she lived while Nikkal was lost to me forever.

And so Helen became a part of my adventure. My sister's former slave and my wife, Helen came originally from a land of the sea people. Her father had been the king of an insignificant country who had by unfortunate happenstance got caught up in a battle between great lands, a situation neither of his own making nor to his taste. When armies from across the great sea overran his small nation, Helen became a trophy of war, taken by an Assyrian military officer, and eventually sold to my sister.

By the time I learned about Deidre's birth I had already married my lovely Syrian dancer, Nikkal, named for her nation's moon goddess. It was only right that I wed Helen as well, to give legitimacy to our beautiful little daughter. Fortunately, my two wives became friends very quickly, despite the fact that it was always clear that I preferred Nikkal. How could I not? She was the woman of my dreams, the possessor of my heart.

And now, here Helen lay in my arms, determined to join me on this precarious voyage to I knew not where. I had no idea what else to do with her. My emotions bounced around resentfully because she had placed me in this unwarranted situation.

"It is too late to return you to my Uncle Hiras' home, or to my family in Egypt. Our vessels have already passed the gates between the great sea and the greater ocean."

I saw no choice but to keep her with me.

Soon it became apparent that we had passed into very different waters. The waves grew larger and more aggressive. The wind blew stronger and our vessel moved farther and farther from the landfall where I had rested, renewed myself and my crew and refreshed the supplies.

Several days of clear sailing followed while the winds, somehow able to convey a sense of the great distance they must travel to reach me, continued to tempt me to believe anything possible. No more powerful than many I had experienced thus far, they presented us with a benevolence I had not expected. The ships, appearing so much smaller out here than in the harbor at Etruria, held their own nicely in the vastness of moving water. It filled me with pride and confidence in my shipbuilders.

I felt carried along by the hand of some sea god I had never before encountered. In that time of calm sailing and firm breezes, it seemed that nothing could stand against me and mine. I spent many hours entertaining myself by conversation with Isaac and my Egyptian companions.

Helen, for the first time since I had known her, could now claim a fair amount of my attention without me being ill and needful of her ministrations. She made herself indispensable aboard, as she cared for any injuries suffered by the sailors and assisted the cook from time to time, which he accepted as if she were a goddess come to earth just to aid him. It took little time before she won the hearts of all aboard.

"How do you charm them, Helen?" I asked. "At first I thought it was just the fascination of lonely men for the sight of a woman, but what they see in you is vastly different than that."

"Perhaps it happened that my years as a slave, especially the ones before I got purchased by Elissa, gave me a deep compassion for the lost and the hurting."

I recalled how smoothly she became my caregiver after I suffered the altar of sacrifice in Baal's temple. She anointed my burns and worked with a renowned healer to encourage the mending of my side, just below my heart, where Theon's blade failed to cut me unto death.

I laughed shortly at her words and my memories. "I hope your compassion does not extend toward the hurting sailors as it did to me in Byblos."

Even as the words escaped my mouth, I wished I could call them back. I watched as her face, even more beautiful as she flourished in the sea breezes and sun, crumple into weeping.

I grabbed at her and pulled her into my arms.

"I did not mean that, Helen. I know better. I ask your pardon for my untoward words. If I did not have you to comfort and nurse me at Isaac's home, I might have died as much from despair as from the wicked wounds."

"It was much more my desire than my duty, Ari. I loved you already from our first encounter."

"How could I forget the pleasure and comfort you provided me as I feared what must become a bleak future with no home, no family and no fortune? Your steadfast conviction that there actually could be a future for me influenced me greatly, encouraged me to hope,"

I thought of Deidre, whose existence I never

suspected until the day I sailed from Carthage to Etruria. I recalled the shock that knifed through me when I recognized Helen that day. Then, when she turned to welcome a small girl from the palanquin, I could not believe what I saw. As soon as Helen introduced her as my daughter, I knew it was the truth. Our encounter during the healing time at Isaac's home in Byblos had brought this child into the world. I could not deny her.

Helen and Deidre came aboard at Carthage, sharing a cabin with my wife Nikkal and our newly born son Ben-Namen. All of us, including my warrior friends and Isaac, wore the disguises of Syrian traders as we fled Theon's knife once more. This time the threat was to my son.

Later, when I left Etruria to enter the ocean beyond the rocky coast, Helen pled with me. "Take me with you, Ari." She hiccupped a couple of times and fought to contain her tears.

In my selfish desire to love only Nikkal even after her

death, I turned away from her, unwilling to look her full in the face. My imagination brought Nikkal's countenance to overflow hers and waver back and forth, so that at times Helen's face took precedence and at others Nikkal's did. I blinked and looked behind us at the members of my extended family who had gathered to bid us farewell.

From their expressions, it was clear they read the situation well enough and great pity spread over most of the faces. Reluctantly, Helen turned and left to join the others sending me off into the unknown. As I oversaw the last minute loading of supplies and personal goods aboard our ships, the family crowded the cothons. When at last my friends and I boarded the ships, Helen was nowhere to be seen.

It saddened me then that I rejected her while at the same time I felt grateful that I no longer had to cope with her presence and my guilt feelings about her. Evidently, I now thought about her intense determination that led her to this place and this time. I had misread the depth of her love for me. Now aboard the flagship with Helen as companion, I accepted the truth.

With our travel going so well and as always very capable of amusing herself, Helen became engrossed in fine needlework. I wondered how she had smuggled the fabrics and other accouterments aboard. It made me smile to think of how carefully she must have planned and organized her escapade while hiding her intentions from everyone. It must have been a challenge, especially in so extensive and closely knit a family as ours at Etruria.

Chapter 3

We were many days out, bearing both west and south, when Rem-Na leapt to his feet crying out, "Look, Na-Amen, there are monsters!"

He threw himself onto the rough boards of the deck and reached for his sword, so to do battle against the leviathans he saw swimming near our ship.

Senmet and I, who had been seated in the bow, watching the colors change from green to blue to gray and back again, rushed to the side and looked where Rem-Na pointed. There were indeed monstrosities, not far from our ship. Their massive bodies, sleek with water and glittering in the sun, rose and fell with the rhythm of the waves, then water spouted from their colossal heads and they suddenly disappeared beneath the sea.

Fear like a spike entered my heart as I watched the great animals. I had seen them before as, I was certain, had most of my crew, but only from a great distance. These whales, kings of the seas, had a reputation among some seamen as killers of sailors. Fear of unknown, possibly murderous, beings clearly much more powerful than all of us put together sent spasms throughout my body, as I geared myself to face the possibility of sudden death.

"Sheath your sword", I instructed Rem-Na. "And you, Senmut, lower your lance."

As Senmut's arm came down from its throwing position, I made an internal bow to whatever power had sent these mighty fish.

Were these beasts sent by Dagon or another sea god to destroy us? Or did they come to guide us where we should go? I told Rem-Na to forget about his sword and

Senmet to lay aside the lance he still held ready to fight the huge creatures. Fighting them would be the greatest folly, as clearly our weapons could have little or no effect on them.

"We must seek the gods right now. Call Isaac, who sleeps in his cabin, and together we will ask mercy of the gods."

Isaac came on deck, rubbing his eyes. Helen, who had gone below deck a few minutes earlier, followed him, her work still in her hands, her eyes huge in her suddenly pale face.

"What is happening, Aribaal?" Isaac demanded.

Without speech, Rem-Na pointed to the monstrous whales still diving and surfacing around us, with great gouts of water emanating from their foreheads. Some came so close to our ship that we could feel the spray from their heads.

"Yes, I have heard of these things, but never before have I seen one of them. They are great fish sent by God to accompany men on their journeys." He glanced at me. "Surely, you are familiar with dolphins, as well?" When I nodded, he went on, "But, indeed, I have not seen anything quite so huge as these before now."

He leaned forward over the deck rail and might have fallen had Senmut not been quick to haul him back.

From his expression, Senmut, that scion of the desert, felt terror when looking at the great creatures though he struggled not to show it. I recalled his immense courage when the great cat attacked him in Egypt. Torn and bloody, he yet stood his ground against the much stronger leopard until his damaged body could do no more.

"Among the sea people there are many stories about such creatures. Most of the stories tell of the large creatures appearing near ships to guide sailors, but some say that they are known to wreck vessels as well." Isaac shrugged. "Who knows where the truth lies? Anyway, I look on this visitation as a portent of good, not of evil. Is that how you see it?"

Intrigued by his positive words and with a certain excitement, I replied, "I agree with you. Let us continue."

With my friends standing close, I watched them for a long while as they dove then rose to the surface, marveling at their grace in the water. Then, as suddenly as they had arrived, the great creatures left. All sign of them, the outpouring that gushed from their heads into the air, their huge bodies that wound in and out among the waves, the agitation of the waters near the ship all ceased. They were gone.

I searched as far as I could see of the ocean with my strong eyes alone, but all I saw was waves and Theon's ship as it hove into sight behind me. A desolate feeling overcame me and I felt rejected by these apparently friendly and welcoming denizens.

We sailed on, westward, and the days took on a pattern that seemed might continue forever. Most of the time, Theon's golden ship with its purple sail adorned with its gold emblem was out of my vision, but sometimes I could see it gleaming in the sunlight as it followed us.

The great beasts continued to shun us and I could only wonder why. We had done nothing to offend them. The only unusual event had been the arrival of Theon's ship as he chose to sail near us. Could it be that the great sea denizens sensed his murderous heart and fled his presence? Since I had no answer I decided to carry the question in my heart for later perusal and concentrate on finding a place to land our ships and supply them with food and water, both of which had become scarcer by the day.

Instead of growing very hot, as I had expected, the air became colder as we traveled west, and the color of the ocean grayer. The winds grew erratic and we would have days when no air moved at all, even though the sky filled with clouds that made us expect wind. Then, just when we began to succumb to discouragement and fear for the lives of our rowers, a breeze would rise once more and push us before it, our sails at full as we bobbed along atop the waves.

It had been many days since we felt land beneath our feet and even I, the lifelong sailor, grew weary of shipboard life, which became dull and unexciting. In order to keep the men active, I made up jobs for them. Never before had our ship been so clean and in such perfect repair while at sea.

Helen alone among us expressed satisfaction at the pace of so confined a life. I had to admit it seemed to agree with her. The sea breezes and her moments in the sun enhanced her skin color, giving her flesh a vibrancy that made her lovelier than ever.

"You never seem to find the days onerous, Helen. Do you not miss the company of other women? And what of the children? Do you not worry about them?"

She set down her hand work and appeared to think for several moments.

"I will speak of our children first, Ari." She paused again. "I have little concern for them, despite my longing to see them and hold them in my arms." She smiled across to where I had seated myself on a pile of spare sails. "I would not have left them had not a great calm overcome me before I left. I was desperate then, torn between a need to accompany you and the alternate need to remain with the children. One thing I understood from my prayers was that they were safe with your family. Another certainty offered itself. I knew they would be safe as long as Theon remained with us."

"But what could you do if he decided to finish his work of sacrifice?"

"I do not know. I did not receive anything else from my prayers but that I must sail with you. That has given me peace, even in those times when I have to shut myself away for a while and let my tears flow. I never wanted to have to leave Deidre and Ben-Namen. It tore my heart to do so. But I knew I must."

I looked at her with fresh eyes. How could I despise what she claimed to have learned from the gods when I myself had entered on this precarious voyage with no assurances other than that some unknown god must be directing me? My respect for her courage grew mightily at that moment. Reluctantly, I left her to visit with my Egyptian friends.

My desert warriors had the most difficult time. They longed for battle, the return of the sea creatures, or anything else to relieve them of the tedium of the days and the restrictions forced on them by limited space. They were familiars of the desert, accustomed to endless sand and mountains, and the sea did not hold the same fascination for them it did for me and the other sailors.

Finally, Senmet established a routine designed to keep all of us in trim. We warriors began a regimen to practice our martial arts, using sea birds to improve our archery and each other to keep our sword arms strong. We improved our wrestling holds and tossed one another about like children at play. While these seemingly unending war games distracted us somewhat, it became clear that they did not truly satisfy our needs.

Instead of growing very hot, as I had expected, the air became colder as we traveled west, and the color of the ocean grayer. The winds grew erratic and we would have days when no air moved at all, even though the sky filled with clouds that made us expect wind. Then, just when we began to succumb to discouragement and fear for the lives of our rowers, a breeze would rise once more and push us before it, our sails at full as we bobbed along atop the waves.

It began to look as though we would go on forever, sailing to the west and keeping ourselves fit by war games. But the gods' plans challenged me and mine.

Chapter 4

The great gale came upon the ship so suddenly that I could not doubt the sender to be some malevolent god, determined to destroy us before we could accomplish our mission to discover a new land. Was this Dagon, jealous of these mere mortals who dared to travel the breadth of his sea? Or had some strange god or gods, angry at us for our temerity, attacked us? Fear like dark demons darting among us attempted to take over our minds and our souls and we looked at each other in confusion.

After the peaceful days of gentle winds and calm seas, we found ourselves in the center of a maelstrom that threatened to rend us and our ships apart. When the winds began and before the full fury of the storm hit I recognized the meaning of the coming change in the weather, and signaled our ships together. As the storm gained strength, we stowed our goods and firmly battened them against the coming attempted wrack of our ship. Now we sailed in good sight of each other, the others afloat beside and behind us like fledglings around their mother.

We wrapped ourselves in heavy wool against the fierceness of the wind and the pelting of rain. The storm increased in intensity moment by moment until the waves became walls of water many times higher than our little ship. I lost sight of the others almost immediately after the full fury of the tempest hit. I could see nothing but the high waters around my ship.

We all grasped at anything which seemed strong enough to hold us and then there was nothing left to do but lower our sail and beg the gods to keep us safe while the storm slammed us up and over giant waves and back down into what seemed deep as the pit of Hades. Helpless to comfort them, I heard my desert friends cry out in despair and fear.

Each of us asked all the gods he had ever known to forgive us for whatever we had done to offend them. I could hear Isaac as he cried to his Hebrew God his words of repentance and ones hopeful of forgiveness. I could but hope his god listened. After having done all, we merely clung to our ship and waited.

Of us, the most patient and relaxed was Helen. It seemed as though she refused to entertain the thought of death. Although she, too, grew afraid as the ship groaned and her timbers made cracking sounds as though they had rent apart at every seam, she continued to emit a mood of placid acceptance unlike any of the rest of us on the ship.

I felt very grateful that Theon sailed aboard a different ship, as I assumed that he almost certainly would claim a life in sacrifice to Dagon or some other god. I knew I could not abide that. I had already experienced too much human sacrifice with the memory of his sacrificing me to his Baal, and I could find no stomach for more of it. His sacrifices had become totally anathema to me.

Waves tossed us about with a kind of contempt that made us akin to tiny ants clinging to a twig and thrown into a river by a careless hand. Our ship, so magnificent and powerful she had seemed at Carthage and again at Etruria, crashed through wave after wave, her now puny sail nearly shredded by the force of the wind even as it lay along the strut, her hull shuddering as it fell helplessly to the bottom of each fierce swell.

It seemed as though the waves transformed themselves into mountains of water that alternately permitted us to climb them then dropped us from the crest into a great trench formed by receding seas. As the ship shuddered and threatened to come apart completely, I trembled with it, almost more afraid to show my fear before my crew than before the gods. Helpless, unable to offer comfort to anyone,

I clung like a terrified child to the unraveling threads of hope for survival.

I could not tell in which direction we went. In its fury, the ocean sent us this way and that, sometimes in great circles until it seemed that my head would drop off. Nothing remained where I expected it to be. I could not determine where the water stopped and the heavens began. They were as one, gray and cold and in constant motion.

As the hours passed and the storm continued to rage and torrents of rain threatened to swamp us, I began to doubt myself. Perhaps, I thought, I have grown so proud that tradition and traditional wisdom seem beneath me. Was it possible that Theon's concept of human sacrifice to appease the angry gods might be right? Just because, with the assistance of Elissa and her husband Accroupi, my friends were able to save my life, it might not mean I had the right of it and Theon the wrong. If this be so, then surely the gods were angry.

I wanted to talk to Isaac, but we were separated by too much space on the deck and my voice had no power against the wind, which pushed the words back into my throat with such force that they nearly choked my life away. There was nothing to be done but pray that our ships could survive and we with them.

Then, after two days and a night, as unexpectedly as it had come, the tumult ceased. In what seemed like moments, the wind changed from a raging beast seeking our blood to a placid friend with a gentle touch. I looked about me, fearful that some of us might be missing. Thankfully, all of us on our vessel survived, much bedraggled and banged about from the tossing we took, but everyone present nevertheless.

I loosed myself from my bonds and walked a few steps. My reluctant legs bore my weight, though my body trembled all over, whether from fear or exhaustion, I could not tell. After a few moments, however, I could stand straight and walk again.

I laughed. "It seems we have again cheated the nether world, my friends." I said, in a shaky voice. "It must be that the gods have work for us yet."

Senmet, who appeared to have regained himself the best of any of us, brandished his sword and said, "And I am ready for whatever comes."

He laughed loudly in what I recognized to be joy that he still lived, tempered perhaps by a touch of his customary bravado.

Rem-Na was ill, unable to stand alone, so I sent him to his bed below. I knew he would recover quickly, but also that he needed to rest while healing. I had expected Isaac to be the sick one, but he had ridden the storm very well. Helen, not surprisingly, survived with a minimum of effect.

"I am so glad you made it through," she said, as she grasped me about my neck. "Had I lost you, I would have tossed myself into the ocean to join you." She laughed lightly and fearfully. "Perhaps we could have joined the court of Poseidon."

The only reply I made was a huge grin intended to encourage her.

We worked together, seamen and warriors, and soon had our ship cleaned up and ready to travel. Some of our oars had broken before we had opportunity to draw them up. Some we could save, others were cut up and set aside. Our sail had sustained some damage, but not beyond our ability to repair it. Our sail maker came from the east and his work was so fine it was difficult, when he completed the job, to locate the patches.

Senmut and I searched the sea as far as we could see for some sign of the rest of the ships with our supplies of goods and foot soldiers. We watched for Theon's, as well. We saw nothing but the still calming waters and clouds gilded by the sunlight behind them. Already large patches of blue could be seen between the clouds and, as we watched and time passed, the waters turned from cold gray to a beautiful bluish green like turquoises on a queen's crown.

The air was much warmer than we had felt it since we left our landfall many days hence, so we spread our wet garments and blankets upon the deck where they dried quickly.

We could not hope to estimate how far we had traveled and in what direction until the stars came out and we could read them for signs. As for the rest of our crew members and even Theon, we could only hope they had survived and would find their way to us.

We sailed peaceably for some time. The sea gradually returned to its former placidity. Slowly, the day waned and the sun set. Because so many clouds continued to hover over us, scattered, I could not be certain how soon we would be able to read the stars. How else, I thought, can we find out our location?

When at last night fell, most of the clouds had

dispersed and stars stood strong overhead, but I realized in growing horror and distress that I recognized none of them. Every one appeared strange to my eyes. It was as though the heavens themselves had been re-arranged by the storm and the stars had shifted all over again into shapes and symbols strange to me. They looked like intruders into our firmament. I searched and searched the heavens, but everything had changed.

I called Isaac from his berth where he had rested ever since the storm abated.

"I do not know where we are or whether we will ever find our way back to our old home, but I would like you to draw a chart of the stars as we see them now and compare it to the chart we carried with us. At the very least, we will recognize these stars if we ever come back this far."

"I am convinced, Ari", he replied in a calm voice, "that we will go back home one day, and when we do, these stars and others will guide us unfailingly."

I clapped him on the back and left him at his spot on the deck, wishing to respect his need for concentration.

He bent to his task as the ship rolled with the gentle rise and fall of the ocean. A lamp over his improvised desk swayed with the movement of the ship, its burning oil threatening to overflow the sides, but never quite doing so. Above us, the strange stars glittered jewel-like against the obsidian of deep sky. He worked late, until the oil no longer moved in the lamp, but had been nearly consumed by the flame. Then he sighed, bent backward to stretch his spine, and declared himself finished.

"We will be able to come back here, at least. By then I trust we will find our old stars and our way home."

I nodded and wished I had his confidence. I moved around the vessel and stared out to sea, my eyes seeking, hoping, for some sign, however small, of our accompanying ships. But none was to be seen.

Senmut came over to me, Rem-Na and Isaac with

him. The three of them stood around me closely, as if to comfort me with their presence. Helen, quietly seated in the background, remained where she rested.

"I have brought you here to lose you in the great scope of the ocean, far from your homes and with no way to return there."

I knew my voice sounded filled with despair, but I could not prevent it. Had I been younger, tears might have come, but I was a man grown who already had met and overcome many challenges, so there could be no question of tears. I girded up my mind and my soul to face what must follow.

"We will go with the winds where they carry us and trust in the gods to keep us safe and rejoin us with our other ships."

"We will. And we do trust ourselves to God." Isaac replied, in the way he always distinguished his God from all others.

Hearty nods from my other friends testified to their acquiescence. As I gazed into each of their faces, I detected fear but not fear alone. Beside the fear there was determination and hope.

I turned away, made small by their friendship and confidence in my vision. Even as I stood there, leaning against the rail of the ship, comforted by the presence of Helen, who had left her seat to stand by me at the rail, I felt the air change direction and temperature, and become weighty with water. I wondered where we were being led and to what fate.

Chapter 5

Daily the heat and the wetness about us increased until it seemed every breath we took in consisted more of water than of air. We were bathed in sweat and our movements grew sluggish. I had not felt so strong a heat since I had traveled with my father along the coast of Africa and experienced its alienness. We still traveled blind, as men who had a film over their eyes. By day, the sun and the breezes carried us south and west, and by night we began to learn the strange stars.

Senmut, Rem-Na and I continued to flex our fighting muscles against each other, with swords, wrestling holds and bows. Isaac studied the manuscripts he carried aboard.

We had sailed for several days since the storm and still not found our missing comrades. I grew worried about our supplies. Though the storm had robbed us of very little, we had no access to more and our store began to run much lower than previously. Without any contact and no way to locate our supply ship we faced the possibility of starvation.

We had no way to determine how soon we would reach landfall or even if we ever would. I felt old beyond my years and heavily burdened with the lives in my care. If we did not find some place, wherever it was, would we sail about endlessly, finally to succumb to death on board our ship? I pushed such thoughts away as unworthy and unsolvable, and kept my eyes on the reaches of the sea for sign of our ships. Still, there was none.

Interestingly, the whales, those curious water-blowing creatures, returned at last. They stayed close to us and often before us, and now were accompanied by a number of the smaller dolphins. These latter showed themselves frequently and gamboled about like lambs in water.

They were wonderful to watch as they dove and leapt and made shining paths before our ship. Were they from the gods, I asked myself, to guide us? Surely, creatures so entertaining and so beautiful could not intend our destruction.

After spending part of a day watching the comings and goings of these amazing sea denizens and breathing in the now stronger smells of the sea, I called Isaac to the rail.

"Are these meant for our good, or for evil, Isaac? Would the gods send them to lead us astray, when we have prayed many times for mercy and guidance?"

When he replied, his long face grew grave and thoughtful, "We cannot know the mind of God. He is unfathomable. We can but do as we must and follow him to our best ability then leave all the rest to him."

I laughed. "Truly, Isaac, you are becoming more and more Hebrew the farther we get away from your native land. You never used to be so insistent about your one Hebrew God."

"Very true, Ari." he said in a plaintive voice.

"Perhaps it is the result of being so far afield. I have been away from my country a very long time in the soul but now I am far distant in the body, as well."

I shrugged impatiently. "I still do not know if we are following those creatures to our sure destruction."

"It may be that they trail behind us. Or that they are here just to give us other life to offer company and comfort. Or that they are a protection from something we know nothing about." He turned around and leaned his back against the rail. "I have always heard there are very vicious monsters in the depths. It is possible that the presence of these which dive and surface and circle us give notice to the predators that we are not fodder."

A sense of comfort accompanied his words. Now, as I watched the great animals swim and disappear, then re-appear, their huge heads astream with blown water, instead of being threatened by them I felt reassured. We continued to watch for the rest of our company, but nothing showed visible from our decks or our mast.

One morning, the air currents turned around and new odors assailed our senses. Instead of the constant salty, damp sea smells, we began to notice the hint of a heavy, sweetish odor, as of fruits and decay. To the west the atmosphere grew hazier than previously, with mists rising wraithlike from the sea. It was an eerie sensation to feel transported by a foggy atmosphere imbued with exotic scents to a new and invisible location. Our watch woke me with the cry "Land. There is land!"

He waved his arm and pointed toward the place I might expect to see land eventually. Now my imagination conjured up new odors so to locate a beach which might or might not actually exist.

I leaped up and into my tunic then ran to the rail. I could not yet see the land announced by the watch. However, there flew a company of the kind of birds which travel equally well over earth and sea. These travelled toward a smell of growing things wafting toward us enticingly across an invisible distance that informed me that the watch had it right. I found it difficult to contain myself for excitement.

"Helen! Isaac! Senmut! Rem-Na! We have land to port!"

They all dashed from their resting places, faces alight with eager expectation.

Isaac cried, "We thank Thee, O God!"

He threw himself to his knees in thanksgiving and I felt gratified on his behalf to see his prayers answered.

Senmut rushed to the rail. "I do not see any land. Where is it?"

"Only the watch has seen it as yet, from the mast. But it is surely there, my friend. My seaman's nose tells me so."

The rowers began to pull on their oars more vigorously and the ship plowed rapidly through sluggish waves in the direction pointed out by the watch. Suddenly, everyone on board began to scurry around, eager to help prepare the ship for landing.

As the men hasted around on board, Helen, my friends and I stayed at the rail to await our first glimpse of this new land. Around us now leapt several dolphins, who seemed as pleased as we to make a near approach to the shore. They remained with us for several hours, while the land mass before us emerged from the haze and grew larger and more distinct to our eyes. Then, as unexpectedly as they had arrived, they left us.

We saw nothing then we saw much. Afar off, as though beckoning us to draw near and nearer, the branches of palm trees waved. A beach, white and gleaming in the pale sunshine, spread itself like a silken carpet inviting our tread. And just off shore in a line reminiscent of soldiers on review, were our missing ships.

Theon's vessel still shot forth rays of gleaming light

from its curved bow. From this distance it looked untouched by the great tempest that had separated us for so many days. As we sailed ever closer to the land, we could see a camp set out just under the shade of the verdant forest, with Theon's purple and gold flag on a hut in the very heart of the encampment.

"He has ensconced himself, has he not?" Isaac's question was tinged with both humor and irony. "One might take him for king."

"Perhaps here, in this strange land, he plans to become king." I replied.

My heart thumped like a drum, whether in anticipation of a new adventure or chagrin at Theon's unwelcome presence I could not say.

"Well, we shall soon learn what has happened, for landfall is upon us."

We had reached the shallows, beyond which we dared not demand our ship proceed. I called out to drop anchor and prepare to disembark.

When our feet touched the beach, every man of us began to dance about like victors after a great battle. Only Helen remained still, holding herself slightly aloof, as though reluctant to draw attention to her presence. Truly, we felt like victors, even if the victory was not of us, but of the gods.

Theon came to greet us. "So, Aribaal, you have survived, after all. We had decided you were lost."

He reached out and embraced me as a father might a son. I stood passive in his encompassing arms until those arms fell from me.

"I am pleased to find you well", he went on, turning toward the palm thatched huts behind him. "As you see, we have been here some days already."

I nodded at him then turned to order the men to unload our cargoes and establish a camp. I wondered where here might be. Looking into the forest, which grew almost onto the beach, I could see almost nothing beyond a tangle of greenery of all kinds, in which birds and small creatures flitted and ran and jumped. Once or twice, I caught a glimpse of what might have been a much larger creature, but whatever it was appeared shy and did not leave its protective screen of leaves and grasses.

The great heat, wetness and brilliant colors assaulted my eyes and my senses with an intensity that was almost painful. For several days I had felt strange heat in my body accompanied by pain in my head. I decided it was nothing but a reaction to the fear and sense of responsibility that pervaded my inner being. I looked about me at the land we had reached.

Surely, I thought, I have been here before. Surely I had seen this place, felt this heat, smelled these lush odors and heard the raucous bird cries before now. In my mind, I could recall all this, but nothing that could produce such a memory.

My head began to swim with the pain and the

remembering. My legs shook and were found wanting. Without volition, I sat down swiftly on an outcropped root and waited for my head to clear and for the excess heat and pain to leave my body.

This was the place of my vision, of my dreams, of my fears.

Senmut and Rem-Na appeared, one on either side of me, as if to protect me from an attack from an unknown threat.

"Are you unwell, Na-Amen?" Senmut cried. Men-el, my former slave and always friend, who had been supervisor of the unloading, dropped an armful of goods and ran to me.

"I will care for him", he cried out, "I know his need."

Like a child, I allowed him to lead me to a shaded spot, while he signaled a man to lay out a cloak for me to lie upon. When I was down, he bathed my face in clean, cool water from the sea, and loosened the wide belt around my waist, which held my sword in place.

The heat, both within and without, grew unbearable. I heard myself cry out for water as a sudden fever burned inexorably inside and on the surface of my body. Men-el, the faithful, found fresh water for me and had me carried into one of the huts.

There, for some days I lay as one dead, while the fever raged in me. In my delirium, I was unsure if I were dreaming or actually in the land of my vision.

I awoke suddenly, without knowledge of where I was or how I had arrived there. And then I remembered. Men-el, who sat near me on a carpet, rushed to call Helen then came back to me.

"You have returned, Ari", he said quietly. "Will you take water and food?"

"Water only", I croaked from a mouth that felt crammed full of cloth.

He brought me drink and I took it.

"I dreamed I was lost in a place of much blood and death and disease. There was no way out. I knew that I must die a horrible death in pain and exile. Everywhere I turned there was more death, more ugliness, hatred I could neither imagine nor believe. Despair possessed me entire and I was ready to embrace death as the only hope. Then, a great light came and with it came deliverance and freedom, and I woke up to find you here."

I shivered as the memory of the dream's terror came again. My body felt very light, as if I floated on water, though I knew I did not. I needed to get up and about my business, but great lethargy had overtaken me, and I found I could not rise. I felt wet all over from both the air around me and the release of fluids from my body as the fever fled. All strength was sapped from me.

"You have been very ill, Aribaal" said Helen, as she leaned over me, concern on her face.

"Yes, Aribaal." Men-el hovered about,

straightening my clothing, changing my position on the bed of rugs beneath me. When I looked around, I learned that I was in one of the lean-to huts I had noticed when I arrived on this shore.

Beyond the entrance, partly covered by a curtain of cloth, I could see nothing save an empty strip of sand facing the ocean and a group of people gathered a short distance from my tent. In front of them, Theon sat on a chair elevated above the others, his priestly garments flowing about him, his freshly shaven pate agleam in the brilliant sunshine.

I pushed aside the curtain and tottered toward him, feeling like an infant just learning his legs. As I attempted to garner strength to query the priest about this new circumstance, he raised his hand in an imperial gesture.

Two of my soldiers rushed to me, bearing a chair even grander than his. They lifted me as easily as if I were the child my weakness made me feel, and set me on a seat covered with elegant rugs and fabulous fabrics. These soldiers, most of whom fought by my side in Libya and chose to travel with me to these strange shores, now raised the chair aloft and placed it before Theon. Confused, I looked around me wonderingly, in search of some clue to what was happening.

Besides the men who had come with us, there were many others who stood near Theon. These were very small men with dark flesh, some nearly as dark as Africans. In their hair, they wore feathers so exotic that the colors shone out against the deep greens of the forest behind them like flowers in the midst of a garden. They wore little beyond the feathers, just aprons over their loins.

The sheen of their bodies was nearly gold, whether from sweat or oil, I could not tell. They all bore long lances with vicious looking points, but I sensed no threat in their posture. Rather, they gave the impression of an honor guard formed between Theon and me. As my chair moved toward them, the whole group fell on their faces before me, their lances stretched out on the ground in front of them, tips in their direction, butts toward me. They looked to offer me their weapons.

I turned toward Theon in puzzlement. He pulled forth my cloth-of-gold cloak from somewhere around his seat. He dismounted from his elevated chair, advanced to me and threw the cloak over my shoulders. Then he bowed low before me as to a ruler or a god. After this the same men lifted Helen onto a chair nearly the size of mine and all of them now bowed, though slightly less deeply, toward her.

"What is this, Theon?" I asked petulantly.

I did not understand what it was all about and felt convinced I did not want to know.

"Receive their homage, Aribaal. You have been immortalized. They have declared you their god. And your wife has become a goddess they call the White Lady."

I looked askance at the group of men surrounding me, their faces expressive of something I could not comprehend. I turned to Theon.

"Are you mad at last, priest?" I cried. "Has your great power finally unhinged your mind?"

Very coolly, he replied, "Not at all, Aribaal. To the contrary, I believe that it was for this that your life was spared in Byblos. It is your fate to be a god to these people. It is mine to be your priest."

Full of anger that made me strong even in my weakness, I started to leap from the seat, determined to put an end to this farce. I could not imagine what situation the priest had now arranged for me while I lay desperately ill and helpless.

But, even as I attempted to stand, Senmut came close and whispered, "Hold steady, Na-Amen. You must cooperate for a time. Do not push against what you do not yet understand."

I sat back, my body shaking from conflicting emotions. The small dark men remained prostrate a moment longer then rose as one, picked up their lances, and stood at attention again. As I watched them, I realized that one of the men was clad in a cloak of the same feathers they all wore on their heads. He stood slightly apart from the rest as if isolated by choice. Then he advanced alone, removed his feathered garment and offered it to me.

Almost without volition, I received the donation from his hands. I ran my fingers over the brilliant feathers, soft and delicate, harsh and rigid at the same time. Beneath my hands the colors glowed with a life of their own and seemed about to leap into the air and flutter away.

That man, who appeared to be the leader of the dark men, spoke words that were an enigma to me. I looked at him and nodded gravely, accepting the gift. The man smiled at me, his mouth wide and full and his teeth very small and covered with gold inset with gems. He bowed respectfully and backed away slowly, as if to savor his time in my presence.

At a gesture from the leader, women came forward carrying a cloth robe with the same colors as my feathered one, and placed this on Helen's lap. Helen accepted it and slipped it over her head, letting the rich colors encase her.

Our acknowledgement of the offerings broke a tension I had not previously noticed, and my friends let out a concerted sigh of relief. Senmet and Rem-Na drew near together and took up stations on either side of my chair. At a soundless signal from Senmut, our soldiers picked me up and carried me to a hut farther along the beach. Another group followed with Helen's chair, which they bore to the hut beside mine. The one allotted me was larger and more sumptuously decorated than any others in the compound. They bore me inside and set the chair on the amassed rugs.

I stepped out and asked nobody in particular, "What is this all about? What is happening? Who are these people and why do they think I am a god and Helen a goddess?"

Isaac's voice, from directly behind me, replied to my

question.

"It seems that the color of your skin and hair is the reason, and they believe it is confirmed by your arrival in a golden ship with flying sails. As soon as the first native men arrived and saw you, asleep and ill in the hut, they became agitated. They ran off then and quickly returned with a colored sculpture of a man with gold hair and flesh, whose round staring eyes were the blue green color of the sea in summer, and who bore wings of gold. They pointed at it and at you and began to jabber in their language."

He paused, looking at me if as to gauge my reaction. Fortunately, I was too stunned to react immediately, so he went on.

"Soon the men left for a while then reappeared with a figure of a white painted woman with copper hair which they held aloft near Helen. They apparently discussed the likenesses for a few minutes."

"They, all of them left again, shortly to return with

others, including the one who seems to be in charge. They exhibited the greatest exhilaration, almost bouncing up and down in their enthusiasm. Then, as one man, they genuflected to you and remained so for several minutes. When you turned and murmured in your sleep, they ran from the room, clearly frightened. These activities continued for a time, before we realized that, although the rest of us were mere curiosities to these people, you and Helen were much more meaningful."

After a brief pause, he continued, "In the end, it was Theon who determined the truth of the situation. It was he who compared the image to your living selves and realized that the people here believed you to be the persons of the sculptures. He further surmised that these people did not think of you, Aribaal, only as the personification of an art work, but the as the god whose arrival they had anticipated for many generations."

"Ah, yes", I said sarcastically. "Theon would come

up with such a concept."

I felt frustration as I listened to his hasty words. If only my strength had not failed me. If only I could communicate with these strangers. I could explain that the unusual color of my flesh resulted from some mysterious transformation when I got thrown into the fire pit of the Baal of Byblos.

Unfortunately, in the light of Theon's ability to gain supremacy in any situation, more than my illness drained me of energy and I felt like a child, at least for the moment.

"What do they expect of me if they think I am a god?"

Theon, who had come close to my chair while I was speaking to Isaac, replied for him, "I think they just want you to be there for them to look at and talk to, when they wish. I expect they will see that your desires will all be fulfilled, as long as you remain where they can find you."

"And, if I choose otherwise?"

"They will most likely kill you and set up a statue to you, which will receive the homage they would have reserved for you as their living god. And, of course, Helen would have to be destroyed with you, as your spouse".

He yawned, as though the conversation bored him.

"It probably does not matter a great deal to them in the end, now that they have seen you. There is doubtless something in their religion that would explain the coming and eventual death of their god."

"So, what you are saying is that I have two choices: either I remain here, almost certainly under guard, until I die, or they will kill me in order to set up a statue in my honor", I said exasperatedly.

"Quite possibly they might even cover your dead body in gold and set it up in the temple for eternity. Not a bad ending, Aribaal."

Had I been less weak, less in shock, I might have grasped him about the neck and put an end to him right then.

Instead, I lay back in the chair and closed my eyes, which were about to close anyway, with or without my consent.

Isaac broke in, "This is not the time for such talk, Theon. Ari needs rest. Where will he be living? We will take him there."

Only vaguely did I hear their voices, which faded quickly from my mind. Whether I fainted or fell asleep, I do not know.

Chapter 6

The next time I opened my eyes, I lay stretched out on a bed in a strange place, once again covered with sweat. I still felt hot and damp, but the all pervading discomfort had ended.

"Men-el", I called, "are you there?"

"Aribaal, you have returned."

Men-el came to my side, a pale colored robe in his hands. He assisted me to dress then helped me to a chair.

I looked around me at the room. The walls appeared made of rough, dark gray stone. Hangings of many colors softened the harshness of the stone.

"Where am I?"

"This is the home assigned you. It is part of the compound of the temple where these people have worshiped for many years." His face twisted in contempt. "These are primitive people, Ari. Very warlike and undisciplined." He shook his shoulders. "But time enough for that. You must be very weak and hungry."

He clapped his hands and through a doorway covered by light draperies came a procession of servants bearing food. Men-el, ever the servant, plied me with good, strengthening things to eat. I took what he offered, and ate with fervor usually observed in one who had fasted a long time.

I wondered how long the fever had possessed me. I shuddered. It frightened me that I had lost control of my life for a long time. I did not even know what had occurred while I slept the weighty sleep of the near dead.

Before I could question him, Men-el offered me some strange flat bread filled with exotic vegetables flavored by spices I had never encountered before. At first, I distrusted the food, but Men-el's nod of encouragement overcame my trepidations. Surely, I thought, these people would not proclaim me a god in one breath then poison me in the next.

After eating the folded, vegetable stuffed bread, I finished my meal with fruit of a kind I had never encountered before, round and soft, with a yellow skin. It was all delicious to my flavor starved appetite. After many weeks of shipboard fare, everything tasted so good that I had to stop myself even as my desire for more continued to increase.

When I completed the meal, a servant from the native people entered with a goblet full of a steaming liquid.

I looked askance at Men-el.

"This is a drink reserved for gods and royalty. It has sacred qualities which they prize above all other foods." He looked sidewise at me. "You would do well to accept it."

I did, and was amazed at the taste of it. Thick and dark, in itself bitter and also sweet from some kind of honey, it was like no other food I had ever tasted. The smoothness of the drink, hot yet not unpleasantly so, the silky way it flowed down my throat, the aftertaste that lingered wonderfully, all conspired to make me wish for more. It managed to be both slightly cloying and refreshing.

"What is this called", I asked Men-el.

He replied, "They called it chocolatl, but the name means nothing to me."

"Or to me", I said, "but the taste of it and the feeling of relaxation it leaves with me makes it delectable."

I nodded my pleasure to the servant, who had been awaiting my reaction with considerable anxiety. I wanted to comfort the woman, explain that I was not a monster determined to destroy her, but I had no idea how to do this, so instead I settled for a brief smile of encouragement.

After the food and that spectacular drink, I felt much improved as strength returned to my body.

"I would like to look around this new world, Men-el, now that I have recovered from the fever and have regained much of my strength. Have you seen much of it yet?"

"We have been watched and guarded closely,

Aribaal. It seemed wise not to be too free about roaming in the city and its near environs."

He paused and his voice echoed the contempt I saw in his eyes.

"They are a primitive people without much culture, as far as I can determine. Basically, they grow exotic fruits and vegetables on the farms that belt the town or they engage in the selling of them and crafted items to each other. Their government appears to be equally primitive. A king, a chief counselor and a large bevy of priests seem to be the entire government. It was the chief counselor we saw on the beach."

He waited a few moments then continued. "They seem involved in incessant warfare against neighboring towns and tribes."

"Let us go and investigate the area. I always prefer to see for myself. Have you seen my wife and friends and our crews?"

"The crews either remained on board the ships or have established homes in the city."

He told me where the men could be found, and we set out to seek them. We had taken but a few steps when Theon abruptly appeared before us.

"Where are you going, Aribaal?" he demanded.

"To locate my wife and friends then to care for my crew", I replied.

I started to walk around him, but he sidled over into my path.

"You cannot." he said.

"Why not?" I asked, with some acerbity.

It galled me that the priest felt he had the right to order me around. He may actually be truthful in his claim to be my natural father, but there had been nothing between us to bolster the claim. Again I tried to walk past him and once more he blocked my passage. I grasped him by the shoulders and moved him out of my way.

Breathlessly, he replied to my question.

"Because you are a god, Aribaal, and you are in your temple. From now on, those you wish to see will be brought to you, as you must not be allowed to go to them. It would be unseemly for the living god to walk among men as a mere mortal."

I laughed, hopeful that Theon might join me in my attempt at a humorous interpretation of his words. But his face remained somber, the lines of his advancing age drooping into deep folds like crevices in a rock face.

"You may not leave." he said gravely. "There is ample space within the temple confines for you to gain your exercise and keep your body strong. Around the exterior of the temple building are extensive grounds, gardens and walkways where you will be allowed to come and go as you please. Your wife is in her apartment and readily accessible. Your friends have been given their own apartments in the temple. You will, of course, have guards nearby at all times to protect you. But you may not leave the temple precincts."

At first, when he began to speak, I nearly burst into fresh laughter. But very quickly, I realized there was no mirth on Theon's countenance. He spoke exactly what he intended.

I felt my face grow hot as anger rose in me. "Protect me from whom or what? And who are you to decide this for me?" I demanded through tightly clenched teeth. "I am no god and you know it full well."

I stood before him, prepared to vent my outrage through physical contact. I advanced toward him, covering the short space between us with one step. To get rid of this pesky priest seemed my only hope of deliverance from the horrifying situation that had befallen me.

Suddenly, Isaac was in the room with us. I had not heard him coming and he was like a wraith able to pass at will, unhampered by walls. I knew it was not so. I thought it must be an effect of the fever I had suffered.

"Aribaal, you must listen to him." The desperation in Isaac's voice cut through my anger and need to destroy the Baal priest.

"These people will never permit you to wander around as the rest of us are able. To them, you are the personification of their god, sent to live among them."

He spoke soothingly, as to a belligerent child.

"For the time, Ari, for the time only. Soon we will find a way to leave this place. But, for now, you must cooperate."

As he spoke, I felt the fire go out of me and I was left spent and weak.

"Stay with me, at least, Isaac, and have Senmut and Rem-Na brought to me, as well."

"I will remain and soon your other friends will join us."

He gestured me to a bench of a dark stone which rested against a wall of the room. I walked with him and we sat side by side on the cushions provided, soft and seductive, soothing to bones that still ached from whatever sickness had seized me.

Theon left as he had come, soundlessly except for a tiny rustle of his garment. Isaac and I sat without speaking for a few moments.

"How did this happen, Isaac? What is the meaning of it?"

Then, after a lengthy silence, I added, "What have the gods brought us to now?"

At last I had asked the important question.

"I cannot say, Ari, but I have given it some thought. I remember the dreams you suffered even when you were still in Byblos. You dreamed of heat and exotic colors and strange experiences among unknown people. From what you told me at that time this sounds very much like that dream."

He stopped for a few moments. "I wonder if God has a reason for this. If there is not something he wants of you."

"Now have you gone mad as well as Theon?" I waved my arm to include the room where we sat. "If I am now a god, of whom then do you speak?"

"I am speaking of the one true God, the Yahweh of my people, the one who is the chief of gods. He is the only one who could so dispose the affairs of men."

I laughed bitterly. "If you are correct, then this God of yours has arranged some peculiar and dangerous things for me, for us."

"That, Ari, is why I suspect his hand in everything that has transpired. We arrived here, the place of your previous dreams, in an unexpected manner and in a most mysterious way, impossible to predict. The natives of this strange world, with Theon's connivance, have decided to make a god out of you. All of these occurrences cannot be coincidence, without reason or purpose. And there is no other who can cause all this to happen, save Yahweh."

I stomped around the room like an angry, petulant child. My head swirled with memories of the short time when I took on the persona of a slave boy with Isaac as my master. I recalled how frightened I had been when the realization hit me that no one around us knew the truth about my apparent slavery. They could not know that it was but a disguise to help me flee after Theon tried to sacrifice me in Baal's fire pit.

Had Isaac been unscrupulous, it would have been very easy for him to alter the illusion of slavery into truth. He could have sold me long before I could get in touch with Elissa and Accroupi.

With lingering feelings of relief tinged with insecurity, I replied, "Then this god of yours must be a most capricious one. He seems bent on causing trouble."

"Mmmm", Isaac murmured, "I do not think he is whimsical and unreliable. He has his plan, and may well decide to manipulate events to bring that plan to pass."

Solemnly, he shook his bald head, denuded by the fever of plague. "But fickle or impulsive are not words I would use to describe him. Contrarily, he has planned your life and all of our lives from the beginning. He simply chose to permit us to discover that truth piecemeal, rather than in a moment of revelation. I suspect he realizes that, given too accurate a prediction of our life paths, we would rebel and try to avoid his plans."

I shrugged impatiently. "I do not care a fig for your God and his plans. If I must remain here for the time being, however, I may as well take advantage of all this luxury."

I leaned forward toward the door. Soft padding sounds could be discerned from the corridor as servants passed by, intent upon their duties.

Frightened by a future I could not imagine, stifled by what I envisioned as a lifetime of inactivity and angry at finding my life manipulated by a conglomerate of gods, kings and priests, I said, "If I am a god to these people, surely they will be eager to keep me mollified, is that not so?"

"I expect it is so. What do you want, Ari?"

"Other than keeping my friends around me, I have not decided, but I will find something they can do to keep me happy." I looked around, at the servant who hovered near the door, at those people who walked outside the room in the corridors. "Are there no women in this land, Isaac, save the servants?"

"Yes, there are women. I am certain companionship will be provided, if you so desire."

"I do so desire."

"What of your wife?"

I turned away from him then, angry at my situation, and determined to take advantage of my position as a god to these people. Why, I thought, should I pay attention to Isaac and his talk about his god, when I was one myself now, with all the benefits of a god? Why bother to spend my time with Helen, who was already mine and available whenever I wanted her, since there were many women at my beck and call? As lovely and delightful as she was, in my anger and frustration I turned against her entirely. And on that day, I chose not to honor her as my wife.

As I rested against the plush cushions tucked at my back by my newly acquired servants, my mind drifted to the incidents that brought me to this place at this time. Had my beloved Nikkal survived the disease that so terribly ravaged her after the birth of our son, Ben-Namen, all would have transpired differently. I and my friends most likely would have remained either in Etruria with my uncle and cousins, or at Carthage, where my sister Dido at that time reigned or in Egypt with Accroupi's family.

Instead, in my grief and despair I listened to an unknown voice and set out across the great ocean beyond the inner sea with no goal or location in mind beyond the remnants of a vision from the gods. This vision the gods shared in part with my Hebrew friend, Isaac and the priest.

The discovery of Helen on board my flagship changed everything. Although she proved very brave and calm throughout the terrifying journey over the water, a part of me continued to resent her. Why, I asked, should she continue to live when my Nikkal was gone from me forever?

As soon as Theon realized my situation and his as my supposed spiritual leader, he made his move. He hoped to obtain power and influence with these people, using both Helen and me as alleged conduits of his spiritual power.

"You see, do you not, Aribaal, that had Nikkal lived none of this could happen? With her dusky flesh and black hair, she could never be taken for the White Lady of their prophecies. But the very moment when the temple priests brought out the tiny figures of the expected god and his wife, it was obvious that they fit you and Helen perfectly."

Unwilling in any way to agree with the hated priest, ever my enemy, I replied, "There is a slight resemblance, mainly in the coloring of the figures. The male's coppery flesh and yellow hair combined with the pale skin and red hair of the woman could be taken for representations of Helen and me."

I waited for his response which did not come immediately, then added, "Unfortunately for your interpretation, the figures, being so crudely formed could be construed many ways, even as accidentally painted in the style they used."

I shrugged impatiently. "My concern is that you want to use us to advance your influence among these unsophisticated people."

"Do not let your stubborn anger at the gods and at me as their proxy lead you to make foolish and dangerous decisions. I strongly suggest you accept what the gods have brought you and relax in the sunshine of this nation's approbation."

Isaac, who sat silently on a nearby bench, now interjected, "I must concur with Theon in this, Ari. Until we know more and can understand their language enough to communicate with them, it would be best to go along with this performance as god and goddess. A refusal to cooperate could lead to true tragedy."

He stood and moved toward the entry to my apartment. "Right now you are watched constantly, both by the guards assigned to protect you and Helen and by the servants who minister to your needs."

Feeling trapped in a situation I could not control, I decided to play the game with a vengeance, taking full advantage of all that these people offered me in luxury and decadence.

Chapter 7

At the beginning of my ascendancy to god-status,
life proved most exhilarating. The native people, who
called themselves Olmec, evinced great eagerness to
supply my every want and did so, sometimes even before I
knew I wanted it. There was no dearth of food, drink and
women. While they did not possess the gracious wine of
my country and its neighbors, they did have a drink, made
of a native plant, whose potency I deemed even greater.
From the earliest hours of most days, my Egyptian friends
and I remained drunk with this new wine.

Theon, who by some trick of mind known only to
himself, very quickly grasped the native language with its
peculiarities unfathomable to my ears, and served as
interpreter between us and the local population. My friends,

who filled their lives with as much revelry as I did my own, had never experienced such a dedicated pursuit of pleasure, even in the sybaritic palaces of Egypt.

The flavors and scents of this new land constantly excited my senses. As quickly as one experience cloyed I discovered another. After a while, I began to think it possible to forget that our temple of gratification was in reality a prison for me.

Slowly, I picked up bits of the native language and actually achieved a trifling degree of conversation with the king's chancellor or 'ku', known as Ku Po, who seemed less fearful of my trumpeted powers than others who hung about me. I might have learned much more had I less anger and resentment toward the ku, whom I regarded as the embodiment of the conspiracy between the natives and Theon to keep me subject to the benevolent slavery of my new life.

However, I sensed that even the few conversations I

had with him and with the women sent me for my and my friends' pleasure would prove beneficial to me at some time in the near future.

Isaac questioned me about Ku Po. "Can you determine how much he has the king's ear? Is he close to him? Can he be used by us to help find a way to get out of here?"

Unfortunately, my friend chose a moment when I had succumbed to so much despair that I had totally filled my body with the potent liquor of the place and my soul with an indifference born of overindulgence and despair.

"I do not know about him. He comes and talks to me and most of his words are meaningless to my ears then he leaves. I do not know whence he comes or where he goes. He appears then is gone."

Exasperatedly Isaac replied, his voice forced through clenched teeth, "It is your wantonness which causes you to lose the information and opportunities the chancellor makes available."

He hissed like a cat frustrated at the escape of its prey.

"Perhaps you have reconciled yourself to a lifetime of captivity, but I have not. And I suspect the day will come soon when your Egyptian friends will rebel against your captors and be killed trying to escape. If that happens, the blame will be on your shoulders, not on theirs."

His voice taking on the hardness of sarcasm, he added, "You are our leader, the great gift to us from God, whether you like it or not. What happens to all of us including Helen is in your hands. God help us if you are the only pillar against which we can lean for our support."

I leapt to my feet and threw my goblet of precious Phoenician glass so carefully transported from its home hard against the dark stone wall and watched it shatter into myriad shards of sparkling glass then fall dead as its parts scattered at my feet.

"Leave me", I screamed at him as I hurled the goblet.

At that moment I totally resented his long time role as my conscience and I might have let resentment flare into hatred and hatred to murder had he not fled before my rage.

Even as he disappeared beyond the door, I regretted my reaction, but my drunken pride would not permit me to recall him and seek his forgiveness. Instead, I sent for Rem-Na and Senmut so that they might join me in my dissolute practices. Together, we tried during the next several days to drink the city dry and to entertain as many girls as possible.

Many lovely young women dwelt among the natives. Very small and somewhat stocky in build and faces broader than the women of our world, with dark skin of a reddish tint, they were quite beautiful despite the differences. Since they were there to serve the god even as do the priestesses of Ashtoreth, my friends and I had no occasion to be lonely.

When at last I began to come out of the near coma my licentious activities of the past several days had produced, more days of sickness and pain followed. My head felt swollen to unimaginable proportions and filled with creatures pounding on me from within. My body servants kept busy cleaning up behind me and when sanity began to return shame accompanied it.

I watched as my young friends joined me in the consequences of our debauchery. Even as ill as I became I recognized that my leadership had brought a curse upon them. Despite this I was not yet ready to acknowledge my perfidy and turn my life around. Selfishly, I continued to lead them into dangerous activities.

I just began to recover my strength and equilibrium when once more the servants arrived to transport me to the temple proper.

Theon joined me to instruct me.

"You are too sodden yet, so I want you to lie back on the chair and not speak. The people do not care about what you might say, anyway. They want to look at you and reassure themselves you are among them."

I started to nod, but the pain in my head intensified so I did not respond. From the expression on his face I concluded Theon preferred it that way.

During these ceremonial times when I entered the city, strong men carried me on a sedan chair like Pharaoh. Because the native liquor was so strong and its effects so intense, I saw nothing clearly as my chair passed through the city. Everything became a blur of color, movement and often raucous sound without vivid form or substance. Borne to the sacred precincts of the temple, I sat through long wearisome rituals while priests led by Theon performed their functions, frequently accompanied in their gyrations by the strange flute music of the temple. Then, before I entirely recovered from the drink I had consumed, the bearers returned me to my apartment to begin all over again.

I saw Helen rarely. The temple area was extensive and her apartment well separated from mine, so that we had contact with each other only when we chose. I had little desire to be with her. Her presence pricked my conscience with tiny darts of awareness which her background as princess then slave and the obvious precariousness of her new life prevented her from mentioning. Only her eyes spoke and I refused to accept their message.

My needs, at least my physical ones, were well fulfilled by the revels with my friends. Any spiritual needs I quickly repudiated before they could gain access to the depths of my soul. After making sure her external needs were met as well, I convinced myself that I successfully managed my obligations to her.

It was not Helen's fault that she still lived and remained with me while Nikkal had left my side forever. Yet each time I met with Helen, I missed the beauty and the elegance of my Nikkal, my graceful little Syrian moon goddess. Perhaps, I thought, I could one day come to accept the reality that I would never see her again.

I had not yet reached a place where I could relinquish my passion for her. In fact, if anything, that fixation appeared to increase since I arrived in the new land. I did not understand it, but neither would I let it go. I even had moments when I sensed her presence holding me to her memory.

When Helen came to mind I shunted her image aside and refused to think about her. Her only support came from Isaac on those rare occasions we were together.

"When are you going to cease your abusive ways toward Helen? You don't treat her even with the thought you give your slaves. To you, she is a piece of debris you picked up as you sailed the great ocean. But never your wife."

"I forbid you to speak of her in my presence unless I bid you to do so. She has her own life and it is one of great luxury."

"Ha", he exclaimed. "Death from loneliness is a

luxury now, is it?"

He offered a sarcastic laugh.

In my passion for forgetfulness it never occurred to me that her way of life engendered far more loneliness than mine possibly could. As the White Lady of the local religion she had been forced into an existence totally unnatural to her. Constantly attended, watched and served, she had no friends or companions to help her pass the days. She spent much of her time learning the language and ways of the natives from her maids.

I refused to concede anything to Isaac and sent him from my apartment in a rage. I had no intention of apologizing to him or to Helen. I liked things as they stood.

I put both them from my mind and made another attempt to speak the strange tongue of my hosts, my captors. My tongue had trouble with their strange words filled with oddly placed harsh sounds. Finally, I gave up. I could not see any real need to communicate with such primitives, even though I thought I might enjoy more of Ku Po's presence.

Their architecture and mosaics I judged extraordinary by anyone's standards and I would later learn that they had remarkable engineering and mathematical skills as well. Even their music, so strange to my ears in the beginning, began to make some sense to me and I learned to pick out many of their sounds on my own instruments.

The arts turned out to be my avenue of contact with Ku Po, however narrow it might be.

I asked the counselor about the gigantic heads that populated parts of the area.

Forced by my ignorance to encourage my ears to hear and recognize sounds of the ku's conversation I learned a little. They had come as great blocks of stone to the area where the heads were sculpted by local artists.

"That happened a long time ago, Lord. Long before you came to us." He hesitated. "I believe they were done in honor of early kings, long, long ago, long before you arrived."

"Perhaps by the same means the figures of the 'White Lady' and me came. Is that possible?"

He shifted uncomfortably in his chair. He appeared unusually nervous around me.

"Is there something wrong, Ku Po?" I asked.

"No, Lord. I just have little experience of talking to a god I can see with my own eyes and talk to as if you are but a man."

That account unsettled me. I could hardly explain that I had absolutely no experience of being a god.

"I promise not to use your words against you, Ku Po. Do you worry about that?"

His eyes widened. His face paled.

Rising from his seat he prostrated himself before me. I gestured him to come to his feet. Suddenly wearied by all this posturing and prostrating, I waved Men-el to me.

"I believe Ku Po has become distraught. Please

escort him to his chair."

To the counselor I said, "We will meet again another day. I believe I have wearied you enough for now."

After he had gone I was left with my thoughts. For some unknowable reason I learned I could understand the ku's words when we conversed about the arts. Could that be because we shared a mutual interest in these things? Could such a tie transcend ignorance and offer understanding?

I shrugged away those thoughts. My edginess increased and I considered calling my Egyptian friends to me but in the end chose not to do so. They needed some time to recover from our last orgy, as did I. Even as foggy as my mind continued I wondered how I had managed to cause so much pain and heartache to those I cared for most.

My relationship with Isaac remained distant and uncomfortable and I could see no way to mend the rift which had grown between us. In past times, I would have sought his counsel on a broken relationship but, since the explosive problem existed between us, I did not know where to turn.

When we met in a corridor or were forced to join together for diplomatic reasons, he would bow and say something like, "Good day, My Lord Aribaal" then move on as if in the presence of a stranger.

At last, in frustration and confusion, I decided to talk it over with Helen. Feeling forced by circumstances to consult her did not please me, but even more I did not want the friendship with Isaac, now hanging by a mere thread of our shared historical experiences, to sever completely and irrevocably.

It was late in the evening and the day's heat had begun to abate when I approached Helen's apartment. All along the broad corridor leading to her door, torches set strategically on the walls illuminated the way with intense, intermittent light which wavered and failed after a few steps. Only Men-el accompanied me on this, my first visit to my wife in weeks.

She stood on her balcony with her arms resting on the balustrade which overlooked a different aspect of the city than mine did. A slight breeze ruffled the soft, sheer white fabric of her gown. Near her hovered her personal maid whose hand held a fan, adding coolness to the balcony. With her regal posture and her elegantly wrought head crowned by great coils of honey russet hair Helen looked the part of a goddess.

My heart lurched when I saw her. I had forgotten just how perfectly her lovely face and figure were formed. Possessiveness flooded me as I gazed at her. I knew I could enjoy her favors if I so desired. Yet, something held me back. Perhaps it was shame for the way I had treated her.

Her smile, palpably forced, wavered as she said, "It has been a long time, Ari. I feared you had forgotten me."

I bent to kiss her cheek. "That would be impossible." I peered closely at her. "You grow lovelier all the time."

She permitted a genuine smile to animate her

features.

"Perhaps", she said, "becoming a goddess has proven good for me." A small giggle slipped out as she spoke. "It certainly is preferable to life as a slave."

I grinned at her words. I had forgotten her charming and delightful ways. I recalled my own brief experience of slavery when Isaac helped me escape from Byblos to Egypt, however spurious it may have been, and I could only agree with her.

Then, my mind clouded by the realization of the limits placed on my life and hers by this elevation to deity, I said, "Perhaps there is slavery and, again, slavery."

Thoughts of temple guards, of spies who watched for any deviation from expected behavior, of worshippers who daily demanded miracles, now mitigated my pleasure at seeing Helen. I thought of the times when I wished to cry out during an audience against the ludicrous hopes of those who pressed against my chair or held their ailing children before my eyes. I knew I was no god, and this knowledge goaded me with its many tiny pricks of reality. I shook my shoulders to free myself of the burden of this perception.

"Helen", I began, "I have need of your abilities."

Embarrassed by having to acknowledge my need for her skills, I glanced only briefly at her then let my gaze move around the balcony and to the view beyond. Instead of city streets, what she saw below and before her consisted mainly of nearby farms and distant mountains. From her eminence, the noises of the city became muted and sounded only as an indistinct hum in the background.

She waited quietly after dismissing her servants with a wave of her hand.

"I have no special abilities, Ari. You must realize that."

"You have knowledge of the local language."

"Only a very rudimentary one, I assure you. My conversation is limited to the necessities of daily life." She stopped and laughed. "I do not enjoy deep philosophical discussions with my maid."

She stretched to peer into my face, let her eyes move up and down my bloated body.

"You have changed, Ari. And in so brief a time. You look more like a dissipated old man than the young warrior I accompanied to this new world."

I felt the heat of anger rise in my face. My first reaction to her scathing words was an intense desire to slap her, to wipe that expression of contempt from her face. Fortunately, before I could strike out in rage the inner discipline, learned so painfully at Nyto's war academy in Egypt, took over and dissipated much of my natural response.

Pulling my breath in sharply, I said, "While I can offer no reasonable rebuttal to your statement, I suggest that this is not the time for me to seek it. I need someone who can help me understand what the ku is saying." I looked full into her face. "Will you help me?"

The bones of her face appeared to sharpen as she heard my request. "How can you even ask? As your wife, I am available to you any time you need me."

Abashed, I stammered, "Yes. Yes, of course. I did not mean to imply…"

She waved away my words. "Just send for me when this ku arrives and I will gladly present myself to you. I will listen and do my best to help. Did you really doubt me in this?"

"No. No, of course not."

Suddenly I needed to leave her apartment. Shame hovered too close in there.

"Thank you. I will send for you."

I swiveled away from her and strode into the corridor, not even remembering to offer her a kiss on leaving. I could feel heat rise on my face as I ruefully accepted the implied rebuke.

At that moment my apartment seemed a place of refuge where I could escape my conscience for a time, however brief. I gestured at Men-el who had stood sentinel during my visit. As he moved into position to guide me with his torch among the shadows of the less lighted corridors I thought I caught an expression of dismay on his dark countenance.

He did not speak but walked ahead of me as he had done when he was still my slave, with his head lowered. I wanted to address him, that friend of my youth, who had always accepted me just as I presented myself, without qualification, but I felt afraid of what I would learn in his eyes. Instead, I followed him voiceless.

Chapter 8

Almost immediately after our arrival among them
and under Theon's directions and plans, the priestly
inhabitants began to re-build their city the better to suit their
living god - me, as interpreted by Theon. The devious Baal
priest, who claimed to be both my natural father and part of
an ancient priestly family of Knossos, used his remarkable
powers of persuasion to nudge King Tu Topiltzin in the
direction Theon wanted him to go. I never believed that the
priest's influential gifts came from his nature alone, but
certainly must have been instilled in him by some god,
possibly his Baal he carried with him from Phoenicia.

Under Theon's leadership all the streets became laid
out like a structure unknown to these people, spokes of a
wheel completely around the projected new temple. They

had already begun to erect the massive building itself on a newly terraced hill in the heart of the city. The mound now became the focal point of the capital, as a sign that their god actually lived with them..

"Never", Theon told me, "has a god enjoyed so magnificent a temple as yours will be when completed."

His long bony face lit up as though he had transported to another world and his eyes seemed to gleam with a strange dark light.

"Together, Aribaal, we will bring the totality of the greatness of Phoenicia, Egypt and Greece to this beautiful, primitive world. We will transform all of human history and be remembered as long as people remain in this place. No power will be able to stand against us, Aribaal. We will rule our own world."

I realized then that, though I had long suspected that much was amiss with him, it now grew clear that his fanaticism had carried him over the threshold of sanity. This knowledge frightened me as much as it could penetrate the fog caused by the potent liquors and other excesses of my life in this enigmatic new world. I sensed something important hidden in Theon's words, something ominous and fearful that I needed to understand. Whatever it was managed to elude me as if it were able to fly away, however, and it caused an increase of pain in my head. Confused as well as frightened, I shrugged off my trepidations and let them slide back into the general haze of my life.

For some reason it pleased Theon to have me there by his side part of the time as he watched the construction of what would be the new city.

"Watch, Ari, how cleverly these great monoliths come together. My pyramids certainly will rival and even surpass anything the pharaohs built, do you not think?"

My response always had to be a nod, slow and painful to my head. My befuddlement from the use of alcohol and other less easily defined substances precluded any real understanding of the priest's bragging. I concentrated on the few things that managed to penetrate the foggy obstacle in my head.

It seemed obvious to me even in my current state that the construction of their holy city had already advanced greatly toward its final phases. The native king, Tu Topiltzin, clearly beneath Theon's influence, made quick progress with the restructuring project. He employed the labor of many slaves to bring about the city's transformation with speed his major impetus. Ku Po alone of the ruling council appeared edgy and uneasy as he watched the rapid assembling of stairways and the temple at the top of the man-made pyramid.

Great gray stones, quarried many miles away, tugged to a waterway and floated down river to a suitable landing site, became the fabric of the temple. Distant workers removed the huge slabs of quarried stone onto massive sledges which were pulled and hauled overland by vast numbers of laborers, pushed up ramps and dropped into position.

Snippets of understanding managed to get through my self imposed wall of resistance. As I watched, strong apprehension grew in me. Clearly, this would become a great construction, my new home, even more restrictive than the one where I now resided. Resentment tried struggling through apathy to alert me to a future threat. The mind dulling orgies I experienced daily kept apathy foremost.

I continued to live in the old temple while the new one remained under construction. Ku Po visited me frequently, for what reason I could not fathom. I sensed he was trying to alert me to a need in the city and country, but I could not comprehend it. When my frustration level rose high enough that I could no longer sustain my patience, I sent for Helen.

Her acquaintance with the language had progressed amazingly. She could fathom the intricacies of his language well enough to discern that the ku worried at least as much as I did about how Theon had gained the king's confidence and became his guide.

Still uneasy in my presence, Ku Po spoke more readily to Helen than to me.

"I fear that your priest has cast a spell on the king that keeps him in darkness and thrall. Tu Topiltzin acts like a man whose mind has fallen under a powerful influence. Can the priest truly be the cause of this?"

I glanced quickly at Helen, unwilling to offer an answer to the ku's desperate question.

Helen said, "He promises to consider your question and give you an answer soon. It is never his wish that anyone suffer from the machinations of another."

Ku Po nodded his acceptance of her reply. He bowed deeply before me.

"Great Lord", the ku asked me, "will you release our king from his condition?"

I began to lose my hold on time and place and I grappled with the ku's problem. His words began to scramble in my ears. I could not understand what sort of danger he feared for his king.

Tu Topiltzin looked the picture of health. Granted, I rarely saw him up close and then only in the temple and after I had more than my fill of various exotic intoxicants. Even so, Tu Topiltzin was young and strong. I could attest to his strength, having watched him in the temple yard engaged in mock battles with his warriors or when he entered into athletic pursuits that would challenge many an Egyptian warrior. Since I was the god to whom Theon ostensibly owed his allegiance it was to me Ku Po appealed.

It horrified me that this man with his worried eyes and strained expression depended on me to save the king and the nation. I accepted that from his point of view such an appeal was logical, even called for, but I also knew that my god status was a sham. Even through the miasma of drunkenness, I recognized both his need and my inability to help him. Sometimes it took all my resistance to avoid striking the ku and putting an end to his pleas.

Helen, who understood my dilemma, watched with stricken eyes as I tried to bring my mind to bear on the ku's need. Finally, after she realized how greatly Ku Po feared Theon's influence over the king, I told her to assure him I would take his request under consideration and let him know later what I decided. Bowing deeply and reverently Ku Po, a man of great import in that nation yet humble beneath the power which assailed him, left my presence assured that all would be well now that he had made me understand the urgency of the situation.

"What are you going to do for him, Ari?"

"What can I do?" I replied. "I am not what he thinks I am." I laughed a sharp, sarcastic burst of sound. "I am a prisoner of my own god life, and nothing is under my control."

Perceiving a glance of mixed dismay and contempt on her face, I said harshly, "Go back to your apartment, Helen. I will send for you when I need you again."

I turned my back on her and waited until I heard her light step on the stones of the floor before I permitted myself to look around. As I suspected I stood alone in my room. Even Men-el had left.

Days passed before I called on her again. I settled back into my routines, Helen and Ku Po both exiled from my mind as if they had ceased to exist.

When I questioned Theon, demanding some contact with the outside world, however minimal, he responded.

"You may do so under certain conditions. You must be carried on your chair, clad in your feather cloak and headdress."

He eyed me in the suspicious manner that seemed endemic to him.

"You must never attempt to speak to or otherwise

communicate with any citizen of the city. Should you wish to do so, I must arrange a meeting in your audience room and it must be for some spiritual reason alone."

Theon's words hardly added any comfort to my life. Such a complicated set of rules sounded too difficult to follow and I knew myself too lacking in initiative to try. The strong restrictions effectively sliced away my expectations and the whole concept of travel beyond the temple left much to be desired. Also, I appeared to have lost my interest in adventure.

On a few occasions when boredom overcame curiosity and my head cleared slightly from its drugged fog I actually did instruct my servants to carry me out into the city and even into its environs to observe the changes made so rapidly by Theon and the workers. This I could do, as such an outing could be interpreted as a survey of my realm as titular god. It would be safe as long as I did not dismount from my palanquin.

At times, I felt tempted to demand I be lowered to the pavement so I could walk among the people but each time caution overrode desire and I restrained myself. I could not see how it would be of benefit to the people should I end up a dead god rather than a living, false one.

Surrounding the urban zone, farms and orchards flourished, cut out from the great forest that constantly threatened to recapture them should the farmers relax their vigilance. They fought an unending battle against the encroaching trees and grasses.

Over all there was the prevailing odor of the ubiquitous vegetable called chili in its several manifestations. Its potency when added cooked or raw to other foods frequently caused tears to overflow my eyes as I ate. The natives consumed this strongly flavored and burning hot fruit as if it had no greater heat than any ordinary vegetable.

I thought how easily a man could form a trading company to carry this chili into my world. The unusual strength and taste would be desired by the wealthy residents of Egypt, Carthage and Etruria. Unfortunately, no trade could be established if no route were discovered.

I remembered much of what the area looked like despite my early desire to know as little as possible about the city, its environs and people. Most houses of the city were thatched with the same fronds that topped the high roof of the original temple where I resided. The homes of the nobility, large and elaborate with their stone carvings of ferocious beasts and fabulous birds, served as a tribute to the civilization which spawned them.

However, I paid them only small and intermittent heed, most of the time concentrating instead on my persistent pursuit of pleasure. Despite my hedonistic ways I could not prevent some degree of curiosity from invading even my hard acquired indifference.

The natives denied me, and by extension my friends, nothing. Rem-Na and Senmut participated wholeheartedly in my orgiastic life but Isaac continued to remain isolated from me as time went on. I would see him moving wraithlike from one part of the temple to another, his long face more and more drawn as the days passed. Sometimes in a feeble attempt to restore the depth of friendship between us yet without a true apology for my cruel insensitivity, I would call out to him and invite him to talk with me. But unwilling to do what was necessary to bridge the gap my stubbornness had excavated between us ultimately I would soon let him go his way as I went mine.

How long this state of affairs might have continued I do not know. But they were fated to stop when one afternoon, during a drinking bout, Senmut cried out in his intoxicated voice, "Na-Amen, we have not had a good joust since we arrived in this benighted land! It is time we fought again!"

I was not quite sober and in my half-drunken state it sounded an excellent idea. I sent Men-el to fetch our swords and pikes.

Men-el's face wrinkled with concern.

"Is this wise, Ari?" he asked in a troubled voice, as my friends and I exited to the temple courtyard to engage in a contest. "Caution might demand you wait a few hours until you have enjoyed some rest."

Even as inebriated as I managed to be, I could discern the fear in his words.

"Nonsense, Men-el. Senmut and I have much experience with our weapons. We are not amateurs."

Men-el shrugged a very Isaac-like shrug, making the muscles of his wide black shoulders ripple down into his back and did as I asked. I inspected my sword. There were no nicks to be found and the edge exemplified the skills of the sword sharpener.

Stripped to a loincloth, I challenged my friend and received a laughing response. Senmut, ever the aggressive one, jabbed at me, lunging and tripping as he attempted to attack me across the expanse of floor. We circled each other, made a couple of feints and stumbled clumsily into each other's arms. We pushed apart, cursing, and then clomped across the ancient stone floor like hippos on a Nile bank.

As we feinted with our swords, he touched me enough to make a slight nick on my fighting arm. Finally, we fell down, laughing at each other.

"I think, Senmut, we have let our skills lose their edge. What do you say?"

"I think we would have trouble fighting our way out of the women's quarters, let alone through an army."

My attendants dashed to me and began sopping the small amount of blood that spilled from my cut. A female maid rolled up the cloth and tucked it somewhere within her garment. Senmut and I continued to laugh at our clumsiness.

"So much for the great warriors of Egypt", I proclaimed.

At that moment Isaac entered unannounced, his face

troubled.

"Perhaps you might look closely at yourselves, my friends. You have grown stout and slow in your captivity."

He hesitated as if uncertain of his reception. "Do you wish to hear what information I have obtained for you?"

I frowned at him, willing my wayward mind to stay itself on him and his words. It proved a great struggle but I succeeded. Apparently, some of the fog had dissipated under the force of combined mental attempts to hear Isaac's words and the intense physical stress of our bout.

"Yes, please, Isaac", I replied as humbly as possible, ashamed of my recent treatment of this good and faithful friend as well as of my repulsive condition.

"I have overheard things that will interest you, Aribaal."

Could it be possible that his face grew graver? He waited until my nod assured him I actually listened attentively.

"Theon has set up an astronomical station as part of the new temple." He paused for a moment. "Very cleverly made, I must admit."

His eyes lit up briefly in admiration. Then he continued, his face solemn.

"He has studied both the astronomical and astrological signs and concluded that in a very short time the sun will turn to darkness and that this will signify the coming of a time of great evil on the land. He has expressed fear that this time of darkness will cause many to die and the sea to rise in powerful waves while the land breaks apart like a melon dropped from a great height. I heard that he claims that the only thing that can save them from this calamity is the shedding of blood."

Isaac stopped then, after a pause, went on. "He intends to introduce Baal sacrifice into the religion of this land."

I felt heat rise into my face at his words. Far off, I

could hear the beat of drums and the blast of trumpets as the faithful were called to worship. Any moment now the bearers would arrive to carry me to the holy place.

There I would be seated on a golden throne resplendent in a cloak and elaborate headdress of iridescent feathers while the people came and implored me in a language I had chosen not to learn properly and still barely comprehended. Then they would leave, thanking me for the audience. For the first time I felt revulsion at the cynicism of my part in the ritual.

Daunted by Isaac's information and shocked into attentiveness, I asked, "How was this received by the people?"

At that moment, my mind felt clear and my ears grew attentive. "Did they argue, refuse to consider it? Surely, they did not accept Theon's words as from the god?"

"No one offered a decisive repudiation of his claim. In fact, if anything, the priests appeared to agree with him.

You may not know that they have named Theon 'Pe Gyo', the wonder worker. Whatever arts he learned many years ago in Greece have been amplified by his studies in Egypt, Byblos, and other places. I do not know whence he receives his powers, but they appear to grow almost daily. The new astronomy center is part of it, although I do not know how it fits into his plan."

Isaac remained thoughtful for a moment then continued, "The power of life and death is very seductive, Aribaal. It is a rare man who can resist it."

Angrily, I threw my feathered headdress on the long couch, loosening a number of the luminescent bits of fluff.

"I will not have it. We left all that behind and I am more than grateful to be free of it."

Suddenly, I recalled the deep well that sat just below the new temple mound. Did that figure into Theon's plan? Did he expect in some way to make it a part of his ritualistic murders?

"Where will he get his sacrificial creatures?"

Isaac's face grew more troubled. "It appears that when the captive slaves grow too weary or ill to work they become expendable, a burden on their owners. When that happens Theon will have them killed on the altar to invoke the god's favors."

"Perhaps", I said, "that is a practical way to dispose of two problems at once."

Even as I spoke my words sickened within me and that was before I saw the tragic expression that came over Isaac's face at my callous comment.

In a choked voice he said, "There was a time, many years ago, when my people were slaves to Pharaoh in Egypt. They, too, were expendable and frequently had to work until they dropped from exhaustion. Those who fell were permitted to die as being of no further use to their sometimes cruel overseers."

Tears formed in his eyes as if the sad things of which

he spoke had befallen his people just yesterday. Once again I felt confusion at his strange way of thinking.

"But what has that to do with us?" I queried him.

"This land is far from your people's experience both in time and distance."

"Have you grown so apathetic? Do you not realize that the people living in this place are now your people?"

His eyes, usually so placid and soft, sent out reddish sparks of anger.

"They have elevated you and given themselves to you, asking little in return. A few words in a language they do not understand, a gesture of acceptance or forgiveness, an occasional appearance in their midst are all they hope from you. But they give you everything."

I felt the need to defend myself. "We are not speaking of the people, Isaac, but of their captured enemies. Why should any of us care what happens to them?"

My voice sounded pettish and childish even to my

own ears and, despite my unwillingness to acknowledge the cruelty of my words, I felt their ignominy.

Without affording him time to reply to me I conceded, "But you are exactly correct when you say we have grown lazy."

I turned away and called out, "Senmut, Rem-Na, we must recapture our fighting form." I signaled them to me. "We begin today. No more drunken nights filled with gorging and women. From this moment we become warriors again."

I grabbed at Senmut and pulled him toward me. Sobered by Isaac's information I knew I must act immediately to restore my physical and my moral strength, else I would be helpless to combat Theon's mad plan, whatever it might turn out to be when it got established.

Isaac, cut off from further converse by my frenetic activity, shrugged and left the room, his expression sorrowful. Part of me wanted to call him back, to apologize and admit how mortified I felt not only about this new incident but by the earlier one, but my pride got in the way. Instead, I resolved to restore my strength, both moral and physical and then deal with the other issues.

Chapter 9

On that day when the temple guards carried me into the midst of the people my mind was clearer than it had ever been on any similar occasion. However, I pretended disinterest in my surroundings to maintain the appearance I had fostered. On this occasion I permitted my eyes to open at last and I watched slyly through the feathers of my carefully repaired headdress as we crossed the city and reached the plaza of the new temple. For the first time, I looked around me with interest rather than with the bobbing head ennui of previous trips.

The crowds of people conducting business along the way in stalls and lean-tos raised their heads then bowed to the ground as my chair passed. Succulent smells from the open ovens faded as the merchants covered them then began, almost as on a signal, to disperse in the direction of the new temple. Panels came down across their store fronts to shield merchandise although the protections seemed flimsy as seen from my lofty eminence.

An air of urgency tinged with growing excitement saturated the very fabric of the streets. Mothers hauled small children by their hands toward the great building, still so raw, that dominated the entire city.

As the people moved away dogs arrived to clean the area around the stands of any bits of food that fell from the counters. I suspected some of them managed to get at food stored inside as well. After very quickly disposing of the garbage, the dogs disappeared again into the dark forest that inevitably pressed close to the inhabited areas.

Residents of the city for once moved quietly as if they already entered the precincts of the temple. The raucous cries of the many hued birds and the squeals of monkeys provided the only sounds beyond that of the soughing fronds and grasses and the quiet footsteps of the people.

There was a sense of suspended human life as if everything were drawn to the imposing edifice on the mound. The temple area looked striking to be sure, equal to almost anything I had seen in the rest of the world, though not quite up to the standards we encountered in Byblos and Carthage.

The stone impressed me. It looked heavier, darker and crude, its deeply incised carvings more threatening in some subtle manner. Ferocious cats and serpents with wide-open mouths appeared ready to consume any unwary stragglers who might stray too close. At the center of the front façade of the pyramid rose a staircase of a slightly different stone, wide and paler in color, which led straight to the altar and sanctuary at the top.

It was clear even from below that the new temple was incomplete. Nevertheless, I instructed my bearers to carry me all the way up, not an easy climb. Left to my own devices I should never so much as approach that temple.

Everything within me prodded me to flee that place, turn from the pervasive and increasing sense of threat waiting to be loosed.

An ominous atmosphere surrounded it, perhaps an aura of corruption, possibly even an actual smell. The odor of death, perhaps, so palpable that it hovered like a dark cloud over the building. I shuddered in my chair as a sudden chill passed through me. It required great effort on my part to remain seated as if all remained as usual and as though I felt content with the ambiance.

The building covered a large plot of land, the entire plateau, which had been reshaped to form a flat, smooth plot for the new sanctuary proper. Its top floor had been inlaid with gold and silver intermixed with gaily colored tiles fired and painted right in the city to honor the god. The whole structure, temporarily roofed, still looked raw while its ultimate glory already showed itself obvious to the discerning observer. There could be no doubt that Theon had planned this religion to survive long past his lifetime.

I despaired of my ultimate ability to re-direct his followers should they choose the way of human sacrifice. Already, the cries of the people resounded through the temple. Without their words being translated I knew that they had received Theon's announcement and awaited the first incident of sacrifice of a living human being.

After I had looked around carefully I stored in my memory as much information as possible. This proved frustratingly difficult, considering that my mind still suffered from the haze of my overly indulgent habits. I struggled against the continued influence of the liquors and drugs I had introduced into my body. I resolved to absorb as much as I could before I would have to instruct the bearers to carry me back to the old temple.

My thoughts constantly in turmoil, I attempted against all recent habit to fathom Theon's thought processes and his plans. I experienced much the same distraction as ever when I held my audience. Since this had become my usual condition it aroused no suspicions even in Theon, as a rare and obvious attentiveness might have done. I went through the customary motions, waving a languid hand over the head of each petitioner, speaking a few words in Egyptian which none but the few of us understood, all the while fighting a battle within myself.

Never since I had met him had I so desired to take Theon's scrawny neck into my hands and twist it like a fowl's. It made my gorge rise to think of the possibility of his being my actual father. Surely, I thought, the gods could not have been so uncaring as to permit me to be sired by this monster in priest's clothing. If it were true, did that reality doom me to repeat his wickedness? Could I hope to avoid becoming as he had become, a self seeking charlatan using every means available to gain and keep precedence over a whole nation of innocent people? My time in the temple passed quickly as I continued to speculate and try to conquer my own demons.

When the audience ended at long last without the addition of human sacrifice and the chanting of the worshipers died down, I returned to the old temple. There, Men-el divested me of the robes of state and washed my body of the perspiration accumulated beneath them. Suddenly, I was just a man again, and one whose life had become most confused and useless.

As soon as possible, I dismissed my temple retainers and called my friends to me. I sent all the servants except Men-el as far away as I could to ensure our privacy. When my closest friends entered, Isaac's face creased with concern which mingled with the still obvious pain of our separation. Senmut and Rem-Na looked expectant, like warriors anticipating a good fight.

"I don't see how we can hope to turn Theon's religion from the evil path of human sacrifice. If we fail to thwart him he will turn to the murder of children and infants."

I shuddered. "He has most of the priests, at the very least, entirely in his thrall and I do not know how many other influential citizens support him. Some who were present may oppose him secretly while they wait for the dust to settle."

I added, "Seated in the precinct of the new temple, I studied the area as well as I could without being too obvious. There can be no doubt that Theon's plan already has advanced very far. The only way this temple differs from Baal's is the statue of the god himself and since Theon has the living god in his hands a statue would only become necessary if I should die or disappear."

I spoke quietly, in case any of Theon's spies should continue to hover nearby despite Men-el's vigilance.

"Also, I made a point to examine the deep well as we passed. I took the liberty of having my bearers stop for a moment while I studied it for as long as I dared. When I gazed into its depths, it seemed the waters began to swirl and I saw bodies just below the surface, their arms raised in supplication. I recognized that these were the sacrificial ones chosen to initiate Theon's new plan. Understanding came to me as other visions have come, with an overwhelming power. Had I been anywhere but in my sedan chair, I might have collapsed. As it was, the horror of it and my helplessness caused me to be bathed in sweat more abundant than even during our most athletic jousts. I believe I could never abide having to witness the sacrifices Theon has planned for this temple."

I stopped as I began to tremble even from the memory of the vision then I continued after waving away an overly anxious Men-el.

"We will make plans to leave here as soon as possible and we must keep those plans secret from Theon. Should we remain in this new and increasingly violent world, we will have no choice but to give tacit agreement to

Theon's plot."

"We can keep him from learning what we expect to do", Rem-Na burst out, "as long as we speak of it only among ourselves."

"Perhaps so", Isaac interrupted, "but we must never underestimate the power that man can command. His strength comes from a source that we cannot comprehend and it is very great. Our hope is to become stronger than he is."

"It is true", I admitted "that he seems able to anticipate my moves even before I have completed my plans. Look at how he arrived in Etruria just as we reached there from Carthage. And again, he returned when were about to embark on the voyage that brought us here."

I shook myself free from hopelessness that abruptly washed over me.

"But we must not give place to fear. I suspect that much of Theon's power comes from the awe others sense in his presence. We must look at him as a man with a man's limitations or we will surely fail."

"I agree with Aribaal", Isaac broke in. "We cannot defeat Theon's attempts to control our lives if we ascribe omniscience to him."

Senmut had been silent thus far, but now spoke up. "How will we find our way back to our homes, even if we do escape from this strange world? We do not know how we arrived here in the first place."

Isaac replied, "I have been thinking about that. I realize that none of you believe in my God, but I am convinced that he it is who guided us thus far. For what reason, I cannot say, but I am certain it is he at work here."

He paused and looked around at all our faces.

When no one leaped in to contradict his words, he continued. "If it is truly he, then he will take us where we must go. If not, we are no worse off."

The words of Isaac left little to be said. To argue

with him would be fruitless, for he had as much chance to be right as any of us did. And I certainly could not claim any great wisdom in this matter. The only questions I must answer dealt with 'why?' Does Isaac's god approve of Theon's blood sacrifice? Or was the priest never intended to be a part of the venture from the beginning? Did he, through his persuasive forces alone, inject himself into the plan of my life? Did he use me as the means of arriving at this new world that he intended to capture for his own purposes?

Instead of either argument or question, I said, "We must forge our plans, speak and act only when we can be certain Theon's spies do not hover nearby."

I turned to Isaac.

"You more readily learn things, Isaac, since you have been permitted to come and go freely. Nobody feels threatened by you because of your reputation of a scholar. And here, as most places, a scholar receives certain respect and privilege."

"Senmut, whose size and scars clearly label him a warrior, is the best able to learn about the natives' prowess and their weapons. Rem-Na can stay near me and practice warfare skills with me whenever none of Theon's spies is around."

I added, "When our plans come closer to completion, we must let some of our men in on them. It will be their responsibility to provision our ships and inform the sailors."

Without argument they all nodded acquiescence. Because we were of one mind in this matter, the plan was established. As I watched them prepare to leave my apartment, Isaac hung back. While I might not have instigated an apology if he had not made himself so available, I determined to humble myself and take advantage of the opportunity.

"My friend, please forgive me for my unjust actions and attitudes toward you. And for letting the breach widen and remain for so long a time. I am without excuse."

"I do forgive you, Ari. I, more than anyone, have shared the terrible things and the good ones which have happened to you. Sometimes, I question how you have managed to hold onto your sanity in the light of these many tragedies. Yet, you have found a way."

He took a step closer to me then put out his arms and embraced me as a father might do.

"I see the unaccustomed actions you have taken in this place as a working out of painful inner turmoil. But now, with a real goal and a plan to expedite it, you have returned to your true character. All will be well, Ari, I am sure."

Chapter 10

Outwardly, our lives seemed the same. A daily round of temple visits for me followed by bouts of eating and drinking, modified greatly in order to restore clarity to our minds and strength to our bodies. When we practiced our martial skills, we did it with much merriment and shouting, so to give my captors the impression that nothing had changed. But in my private precincts we continued to discuss how to prepare the ships and their crews. We had to find a way to get past Theon and his watchers.

It was surprisingly easy for the three of us to return to our fighting form. It was good to use my body again, to feel the pain of stretching it beyond its diminished limits. I thought frequently of Nyto, our teacher and trainer in Egypt, who had taught us so much that now made it possible to overcome the effects of consistent overindulgence. Toward

Nyto I felt extreme gratitude for the rigorous way he forced us to bring our bodies under the control of our minds.

One great grief I experienced daily was my inability to practice riding and driving my war chariot. I missed my courageous horse Leopard, who remained at Etruria with my Uncle Hiras during my absence. As far as I could determine, these people of the new world had never so much as heard about a horse or a chariot. Their methods of transport seemed strictly limited to their feet or the rivers, although I heard rumors of a mountain dwelling people far away with beasts which worked for them. I saw that the lack of swift transport could be an advantage to us when the time arrived to leave this exotic, appalling place.

Without being insistent about it, I began to instruct my bearers to carry me along the beach frequent days, even sometimes getting down from my chair to walk briefly on the sand. To the eyes of any observers, I paid scant attention to our ships where they floated at anchor near the shore.

I could not trust Theon with even the smallest advance knowledge of my plans. If I showed any interest in the ships he might well burn them as they rode the waves, just to ensure I remain with these people.

Despite the danger of Theon's suspicions, when travelling the coast, my eyes managed to take in the condition of the ships. They looked well cared for, as far as I could determine from my circumscribed viewpoint at the water's edge. I could see men aboard doing their regular maintenance tasks and the sight of them warmed and encouraged me. Whatever else had happened, my seamen had not forgotten their priorities.

I watched as long as I could, from different distances and with all the discretion I could muster. The sun's heat intensified from warm to very hot, even beneath the canopy of trees beside the water. My feet caressed the white sand that flowed beneath my steps, hotter within the time it took me to cover the short stretch of beach. My heart longed again for the feelings I had submerged in my memory, my way of coping.

I began to compose songs as I walked free on the shaded strand, my voice muted as if singing about my god life.

I chanted of Nikkal the beautiful, my wife for so short a time, and whom I still mourned deeply. I sang of the many colored cloak of feathers I wore when I held court and of the people who came to me for judgment and to worship. Slowly, it got spread about that the golden god now sang his words in an equally golden voice, accompanied by a strange instrument no native had seen before.

Ku Po began to hover near me daily, as if enchanted by my singing. I suspected he understood more of my words than I did his.

"Lord, of what do you sing?"

He offered the question hesitantly, as if uncertain of his reception.

"Of my memories, of the beauty that surrounds me, of the people", I replied, deceiving with truth.

He smiled and showed me his teeth, with their precious stones imbedded in gold.

"If it were not impossible I would want know you better, as if you were but a man. But, unfortunately, a god cannot be friends with a mere mortal."

I smiled and nodded, my heart longing for friendship with this good man.

I dared not show my ignorance of the place and people and neither could I express my wishes. Gods do not need wishes. They need only to make things happen. Surely a man of such intuition and understanding cannot be deceived much longer. Or was he deceived at all? I dared not put that question to the test. Pu Ko had the ear of the king, even despite the influence of Theon.

We continued to converse briefly and cautiously then Pu Ko asked to be dismissed. With a nod I acquiesced. He bowed his way from my presence, leaving me with a sense of loss.

The next morning, when I traveled to my audience in the new and incomplete temple, the bearers carried me past a whole series of freshly carved faces and figures in the stones leading up to the sanctuary itself. I turned my head in fascination, for there in profile and repeated many times along the way, appeared a rough representation of my face, crowned by my headdress of multi-colored feathers with a strong dominance in yellow and green. I could only admire the artist's ability to produce colors that so nearly matched the originals.

Mounting the grand staircase and bobbing about in my elaborate chair on the strong backs of my bearers, I kept my eyes averted as we passed by the massive well or pool which I dreaded was intended as a place of human sacrifice. I entertained no wish to peer into its depths again lest I see things I could not bear to acknowledge.

When we reached the still roughly constructed precincts of the new temple, I heard the voices of many people and the trill of flutes. Worshipers lined up on either side of the temple floor, beneath the newly thatched roof, singing as I entered on my sedan chair. When I passed they ceased to sing and play, bowed deeply and began to chant words I did not know. My bearers carried me between the rows of worshipers until we reached the altar, set high above us on its platform of stone. As soon as I dismounted and, helped by an acolyte, seated myself on my throne the singing began once again.

The voices were lovely and my hands ached with desire to play for them. Since a god must not accompany the singers to his praise, they continued uninterrupted and I allowed the strange, sweet sounds flow over and around me for many minutes. Then, very slowly, the notes died.

When the music stopped, Theon stepped forward, his shaven pate covered by a skullcap of Egyptian design.

Besides the skullcap he was clad only in a loincloth with a feathered cloak about his shoulders. His cloak was less fine than the one I wore, but only just.

He spoke out in the native language. I understood very few words but I had the greatest admiration for Theon's accomplishments. That he had so captured the strange language in such a short time amazed and shamed me. He could speak confidently in this tongue which I had been far too self-involved to learn, except for the most rudimentary conversation.

After Theon spoke his plans he threw off his feathered cloak which an acolyte deftly caught with practiced grace. Now unencumbered, he stalked to the high altar with its bowl shaped center. He cried out once again in the new language. His strong voice reverberated from the dark stone of the walls and rushed back to my ears like a prophecy of doom.

I felt my body quiver inside my own cloak of feathers

as if I had become an overstretched string on a musical instrument. Horror of what might come flooded my entire being and I had to force myself to remain seated in my elegant chair and wait for what would happen next.

Suddenly from a side chapel came several priests clad in feather cloaks less grand as Theon's. They surrounded a young woman, who wore a long cloth draped over her shoulders that reached to the floor. She walked placidly with the men, as if keeping an appointment with friends. I sensed no trepidation in her gait, no hesitation as she neared the altar. When the procession arrived at the foot of the altar the men removed her cloak then lifted her high and placed her on the table with the area of her heart just over the lips of the shallow bowl.

Without the slightest hesitation and using a sweeping gesture, Theon drew from a crevice on the side of the altar stone a long knife with a viciously sharp edge. He thrust the knife into the girl's chest so suddenly that she had no time to protest nor had I time to make a move to prevent the knife's entry, even had I hoped to do so.

With a ripping movement, part slash, part twist, Theon opened the chest and pulled the heart out of the girl's body. The ravaged heart continued to beat, while its life blood poured down Theon's arms. Even in my chair, somewhat distant from the activity, I could see it pulsate. It lasted several moments then ceased. The girl had not uttered a sound, neither when she entered or when the knife removed the living heart from her body. I did not know, but hoped she had been fed a soporific and had felt no pain.

Acolytes grasped the girl's bloody remains and carried them ceremonially on a wool blanket of brilliant colors which mocked the feathers of my cloak and headdress. Along the length of the hall, down the long stairway past the profiles of my face and the fierce jungle cats with predatory birds interspersed among them, and dropped her body into the deep well at the base of the mound. A few gurgling sounds as the water laid claim to the body, then silence fell over the pool.

Theon then strode to my chair and bent his long body in a deep obeisance to me with the still dripping heart held before him in his bloody hands and he held it out to me as a sacrifice. Horrified, I gestured him and his prize away wordlessly.

My gorge rose as I realized that Theon had presented me as the apparent author of this new rite. He had most cleverly placed me in the position of a bloodthirsty god who demanded sacrifice. And, because I had so little common language with the people, I could not even protest.

Disgusted and remorseful after that show, I had the bearers return me to my home in the old temple as soon as Theon completed his ceremony. I felt relieved the older temple at least remained unsullied by the blood of innocents. As they bore me past the well I turned my head away, fearful that the girl's carcass might still float on top of the water.

Immediately, I sent for Isaac and my Egyptian friends.

They rushed to my apartment, clearly concerned by the urgency of my summons.

"It has begun." I told them in a strangled voice.

"Today, Theon implied my culpability by presenting to me the still beating heart of a captive girl he had cut from her body as I watched."

I bent my head to hide as much as possible the horror I knew showed on my face.

"There was nothing I could do either to prevent it or to let the people know the deed was not at my instigation. Theon felt quite safe in doing whatever he chose as long as he attributed his actions to my wishes."

I grimaced in shameful memory. "I do not know enough of their language to explain the truth to them or even to protest effectively."

Several minutes passed in silence as each man coped

with the news the best he could.

Finally, Isaac said pragmatically, "Nothing can change what has occurred. However, we must try to find ways to circumvent his future plans."

I dared not trust any god and unable to pray to any of them, I could only fret inside and hope to recover my life soon.

All my appetites failed and I did nothing but sit and nurse my soul in the hope of finding a way to deter Theon from the path he had chosen. When my friends visited they, too, remained mostly silent before the reality of the priest's evil. We could have little conversation since the only topic in our minds proved anathema to all of us.

Two days later the sun disappeared in the midst of the day, covered by a black pall as in a funeral rite. The only indication that it survived at all beyond its pall consisted of a rim of light surrounding the blackened orb and a few rays and pulsating fountains of fire that managed to struggle from behind the dark curtain.

Although the phenomenon lasted many hours while the light destroying pall slowly pulled away from the sun and exposed its glory once more, there was no massive rush of sea, the land did not crack open like an overly ripe fruit and except for a few elderly people whose hearts failed them in fear, no deaths ensued.

As the main result Theon's reputation as priest and soothsayer grew in stature and everywhere he went the people pointed him out to each other and made signs with their hands to prevent his eyes falling on them. They melted away from his sedan chair as it passed and streets emptied before him. It might be I whom they venerated but from this time it was Theon they feared. Even the man sized ferns seemed to bend away from him as if afraid to touch him with their fronds.

The day of the great darkness after Theon's prediction of the sun's disappearance had come to pass without the terrible upheavals and storms he made the

people expect. He now claimed that his sacrifice had

fended off the disasters he had predicted. Overcome with a

great desire to escape from that place as soon as possible I

determined to make it happen.

Chapter 11

The next night when the city quieted down from the hustle of the day and with Men-el to accompany me, I approached Helen's apartment. The day before, when the strange darkness fell, heat intensified over the land and for many hours not even a flutter of air crossed the city that seemed held captive in a miasma of the wet and smoky smelling air that surrounded it.

Then as though stirred by a benevolent hand, a breeze came up just as I entered her apartment. Once again, in the evening cool she reclined on her balcony to catch the slightest wafting of air. Now, the breeze quickened and Helen signaled her servant girl to leave the balcony.

"Why did you come here tonight, Ari? Is there something you need from me?"

"I have not forgotten that you are my wife, Helen, even though my actions might belie my words."

My bantering tone did not appear to amuse her. Her face looked strained even beyond what could be expected after the peculiar natural phenomenon of the sun.

I felt uncomfortable talking to her as though I had done her an injustice. Surely, I thought, she has much to be grateful for and nothing truly worthy of complaint. I realized suddenly that whenever I got close to her I tended to act like a petulant child who cannot be pleased.

I did not understand that sensation, but I determined not to be guided by the unpleasant emotion. Perhaps, I thought, the surliness was a natural outcome of being deified. Could it be, I wondered, that a human being is incapable of sanity in such a circumstance? As it appeared unlikely I would ever be able to answer my own question I forcibly put it from me.

"My reason for coming here tonight with only Men-el

to accompany me is for your ears only. Please send away anyone within the reach of our voices."

Helen dismissed the servants who still hovered in her apartment. I hoped they would assume that our visit was to be purely an amorous one and would suspect nothing more. Looking at her loveliness made it more than possible I might want to take advantage of the opportunity for a bit of dalliance with my neglected wife. However, I feared that she might not agree this was the time for that.

I nodded to Men-el, who inspected the premises carefully for any lingerers then signed that all was clear. When he felt content he took up his station just outside the door to her apartment in order to discourage any potential interlopers.

"We will have to leave this country very soon, Helen. That is why I had to talk to you tonight."

I watched her eyes widen as I spoke. Then an expression of joy spread like a ray of light across her face.

"How I have dreamt of hearing those words", she cried. "To see my Deidre again and little Ben-Namen! When? How?"

I shushed her with a hand lightly held across her lips.

"That is what we must discuss, and in secret" I said softly. "If our plans became known it could be very dangerous for us all."

She glanced about her cautiously, as if expecting to see people standing like statues in every corner.

"Then tell me", she whispered.

"For some weeks, my friends and I have been making preparations to leave. It must be done quietly as I am convinced that Theon would prevent us if he knew. That is why the secrecy."

Quickly, I gave her such information as would help her to prepare.

"How will we get back, Ari? Do you know the way?"

"No", I had to confess. "I have to trust that the gods who led us here will see us safely away. And why would they not? It was they, not our own wills that found this place. And having carried us so far from familiar shores, they must surely guide us back."

"Yes", she replied doubtfully. "But I do not understand who would wish to keep us here. And why."

A slight frown appeared on her brow and I reached over to smooth it away.

At first, I was amazed that Helen did not know about Theon and his coterie of priests. And then I thought that it was not strange at all. In no way had she been made aware of the inner workings of the two temples and the plots of their denizens.

She had been carried about like a queen, elegantly dressed in the finest garments, available to be seen while the people prostrated themselves before her. She had been cosseted, coddled and catered to ever since we arrived in this world and, except for the loneliness of a woman without her husband and a mother without her child, her life appeared ideal.

Unexpectedly recalling the tender feelings I experienced when first I saw Deidre and when I had held the tiny body of Ben-Namen in the crook of my arm I suddenly felt a flood of grief that must have come directly from Helen's heart to my own and my heart rocked and swayed within me like a ship on a turbulent sea. I looked at Helen with new compassion.

I took her hand and gently pulled her into the circle of my arms.

"My poor Helen, have you suffered a great deal in this place?"

She did not reply but my bare flesh felt the wetness of silently shed tears.

"No matter. Soon we will leave and trust ourselves to whatever gods carried us here in the first place. Then if all is well and we are not found wanting, our children will be where they belong, in our own home."

"That is my hope, Ari". Her voice emerged quiet and choked and not completely steady. "They may have forgotten us by now."

"Perhaps," I replied, "but we will make ourselves known to them again. You will see."

I held her closely for a moment longer then gently pushed her away.

"For now everything must appear unchanged. You must never permit the tiniest glimmer of excitement or anticipation to show on your countenance. To the contrary, you must appear completely reconciled to life among these people with no thought of leaving. Even your maid must not be aware of any change."

"It will be difficult, indeed, but my years of slavery will stand me in good stead. For no slave ever dares expose herself completely to a master or a colleague. Such would be folly and leave the slave open to every sort of betrayal and cruelty."

My heart wept at her words. I realized how little we who own slaves consider their feelings and their hopes. Even the brief time I had spent in this land, so new and distant, as a slave to the godhead attributed to me, convinced me of the joys of freedom. The thought made me long anew to feel the deck of a ship beneath my feet, that incessant motion that bore witness to the life in the bottomless sea beneath the ship.

As I was about to reply, Men-el suddenly appeared just inside the doorway.

"Theon is on his way to the Lady Helen's apartment, Ari."

Even as he finished speaking the words Theon brushed past him and entered the room, his long stride confident and sure.

"I hope you will forgive this intrusion into your

privacy, Aribaal." He bowed low to me then to Helen in token recognition of our declared positions in this society.

"A matter of great urgency has arisen which requires our presence in the temple."

"What", I demanded, "could require us in the middle of the night?"

"It has to do with the matter we discussed recently."

"The movement of the land? The earthquakes?" I asked, puzzled at his secretive ways.

He cast a sidelong glance at Helen. "Yes. Have you not felt it much more strongly today and again this night?"

Until he asked I could not have said so but now I recalled a kind of shuddering movement I had felt once or twice in my apartment. One of these motions caused the draperies within to sway.

"I have felt it a little but that is not so unusual. These sensations have been fairly constant in the past several days. Why, all of a sudden, has it become an urgent problem demanding our presence in the temple?"

He looked again toward Helen as if to indicate reluctance to speak before her.

I frowned at him. "Helen may hear what you say."

"I suppose it doesn't matter", he replied in an irritated voice. "A citizen of the city, who has been down country a while, working on the carving out of large rocks from the mountain sides, has returned and reports that a river of fire now flows from the great cone shaped mountain not far south of us. He believes that this river causes the earth to quiver as has happened. He says that the fire is very heavy and strong and that the weight of it makes the ground shift beneath it. He also says that the fire god is making angry sounds from deep inside the mountains." Theon shrugged. "We do not know the truth of it but the time has come when we must assemble at the temple to query all the gods about this."

I digested this information for a few moments, reluctant to give credence to Theon's fears. When I looked again at him, his face bore a tightly drawn appearance, as if its scant flesh were pulled hard by an unseen hand and the wrinkles pressed out. Long I had puzzled over the reasons for Theon's actions, and now I wondered if I might get some degree of answer to my questions.

Why, I puzzled inwardly, did he feel constrained to continue the use of human sacrifice as a form of worship? Why, even, had he been eager to sacrifice me, whom he clamed as his own son, to the fire-god, Melek and his brother, the Baal of Byblos? These questions arose again and again in my mind, leapt about like startled cats then got flung aside by my inability to find answers.

And now... did I finally have my answer? Was it as simple as a fear of death and punishment, of banishment to the nether lands? Could this man, so impressively tall and imperial in his priestly garb, his graying hair shaved to the shiny scalp, his thinly elegant hands moving to unheard music, after all be just a frightened mortal goaded by the mysteries of life, trying to stave off death and judgment?

"I shall join you shortly", I replied. "It takes some time to prepare a god for an audience, especially with other gods."

He nodded solemnly, seeming unaware of my ironic tone. Once more he regained his stern and arrogant mien. He bowed perfunctorily to Helen and to me then swept from the room, his loose robe aflutter behind him.

I looked at Helen, who appeared unaware of my new found understanding. A renewed surge of affection rose in me as I watched her watching me. Tenderness, almost of a father for a beloved child overtook me and I leaned toward her, my cheek touching hers.

"I believe that our schedule may have to be hurried. Please prepare yourself for the possibility of an abrupt departure." I looked at her critically. "Have your servants prepare you for the temple in case I have to call on you at a moment's notice. Be discreet so as to arouse no interest in your activities and put aside valuables and clothing items you might need for a long and uncertain journey." I smiled at her. "I never doubt your cleverness and your ability to rise to whatever occasion presents itself."

"Yes. I have been helpful to you in the past, have I not, Ari? And it would be my joy to assist you again."

She rose from her seat and crossed the few inches separating us. Her arms went about me affectionately. "Your slave always."

I was about to reprimand her, remind her of her status of wife, when I noticed the humorous play of her lips and knew she teased. So instead of issuing the retort I had planned, I bent my head to place a small kiss on her sweet mouth then turned and left the room quickly.

Men-el waited for me just beyond her door. His questioning glance disclosed that he had heard all that we spoke within. But he chose the way of discretion and said nothing aloud. Our return passage to my apartment was rapid and we walked in a meditative silence.

Once back there, he began to direct the servants to purify me and garb me for my visit to the temple. As the feathered robe and headdress were laid on my shoulders and head, a new seriousness of purpose came upon me. At last, all the licentiousness and indecision fell from me as if a skin sloughed from me and got cast away. I did not know what awaited me in the temple, but I did know that my direction would come when I needed it.

I called Isaac to meet with me before I mounted my palanquin in the courtyard. Sending away every servant but Men-el, I said, "You must check all our preparations right away. It probably will not happen tonight, but I am certain things will reach a crisis point in the very near future. Vigilance aboard the ships has now become mandatory. All our fighting men will remain aboard until we sail."

I hesitated while Men-el adjusted my headdress then continued.

"As soon as I leave, go instruct Rem-Na and Senmut that they must find a way to alert our ship captains and the leaders of our troops to increase their preparedness. They must be subtle as they prepare our people for whatever eventuality while still maintaining the appearance of permanence and stability."

Men-el nodded gravely. He, clearly aware of the possible results should Theon discern our plans, would be the very soul of discretion.

He asked, "And what of those who have taken wives in this place? Do they go away and abandon them forever?"

"I leave it in your hands and those of Senmet and Rem-Na to decide this question." I shrugged the problem from my shoulders. "They, especially, have remained close to the men and know much about their living situations. They can help you decide which if any of their wives should accompany us. There is space."

Isaac replied, "Some will want their wives, others

not. Do we warn the wives?"

"We dare not. They will have to be gathered at the last minute."

So it was that I left for the temple for the first time ever with some degree of assurance and confidence that finally I had true direction from whatever god worked behind the scene.

Chapter 12

Even in the middle of the night people lined the streets as our procession made its circuitous way from the old temple to the new. Numbers of lighted torches upheld by the hands of many slaves illuminated our path to the steep stairway, past the dark stalls where in daylight items were made and sold. We passed the humble residences of the common people and the richly adorned ones of the wealthy, skirted the pool of sacrifice with its mysterious dark depths.

Despite the lateness of the hour and a weak breeze from the sea, an unpleasant atmosphere of heat and oppression lay over the city, even in its northern outskirts which tended to be much cooler than the lower levels of the city. Almost, it seemed as if the very air were held in the middle of an inhaled breath, made captive there by the weight of anticipation.

The trumpeters and the arms bearers who immediately preceded my palanquin showed themselves exceptionally impressive on that night. More and more people slipped from the doorways of houses and shops as we passed, and many of them joined our procession. Solemnity appeared to engulf the city with a weight nearly equal to the heaviness of the increased water in the atmosphere.

To the south of the city, far away, a new luminosity, reddish in color, had altered the darkness of late night like a halo between us and the mountains. I had heard stories of these rivers of fire that had been a part of the distant past in this place, but they did not prepare me for the awesome power of their reality or for the fear they engendered.

Those people who had joined me in my journey to the new temple began to sing simultaneously and synchronously an ode that sounded more chant than song. Drums, previously silent, began to throb, their cadence setting the pace for the marchers. We seemed more like an army headed for war than a group of worshipers on the way to a temple. Without any organization, the mass of humanity had formed an honor guard for my chair, and my bearers moved with the rhythms of the chant.

The steps leading up to the sanctuary seemed to have grown steeper than ever before and the chair bearers bent as if beneath a great burden far weightier than usual. When Theon greeted me in the door of the temple, I looked at him more closely than I habitually did. For the first time, as though a veil had been lifted from my eyes, I saw real fear on his countenance, showing forth as vividly as a scar. I remembered that he told me he had been exiled from his homeland as a youth because of a great cataclysm which many years previously destroyed his home and his people. Perhaps, I thought, fear caused him to perform all the frightful actions I found so strange and sinister. This was something to be contemplated later at my leisure. There was no time for it now. All I could think at the moment had considerably more to do with survival than intellectual curiosity.

After the pomp and ceremony which accompanied my journey to the temple, the service which followed seemed anticlimactic. A few priests, looking slightly disheveled from their unexpected night awakening, incensed the altar then sang a song or two of supplication while standing before my throne. I bent my head toward them and again toward the people who had joined us on our advance to the mount. Most of those who had joined us at the sanctuary came from the ranks of the common people but scattered among them were some of the local gentry, their status indicated by the gold they wore plugged in their ears and around their necks in plated pendants. Ku Po was present but he did not sit beside the king. All of them watched me closely, waiting for some sign that I would protect them from whatever disaster might come upon them. Because I knew I had no means to protect them I turned away quickly and permitted none of them to look directly at my face.

All the while, I observed Theon out of the corner of my eye. At first, he stood to one side as an observer rather than a participant then suddenly he raised a hand and all singing, incensing and movement ceased. He spoke briefly and sonorously in the strange tongue. From what I understood of his words it appeared that this rite was a preliminary to a greater one, almost a rehearsal for one that would occur later. How much later I could not tell but I sensed that the near crackling of the air in the temple indicated a remarkable degree of tension. It would occur soon.

Even as I pondered these words and their import I felt it urgent that I must remove my people and myself from this land very soon. Especially, I thought of Helen whom I had rediscovered and of my closest friends and servants, Isaac, Men-el, Senmut and Rem-Na. I could not, must not, permit harm to come to any of those faithful ones if it were in my power to prevent. And, I determined, I would make it within my power. I sat there, pretending to strength I knew was not mine, and suddenly I felt within me a rising confidence I could not comprehend.

Theon continued to speak a few minutes longer, his voice increasingly vibrant as the frequently impossible to understand words issued staccato from his lips. As he talked his eyes strayed toward the side of the main temple opposite the altar away from where I sat cloaked in my splendorous feathers.

There, nearly across from me, sat the king, Tu Topiltzin, on a dais only slightly lower than my own. Occasionally he threw me a speculative glance and, as I ever did, I wondered if he saw me as a threat to his supremacy. Would he resent me more or less if he knew the extent of my eagerness to escape his land forever?

As the lengthy speech spun out I heard a name repeated several times in concert with my Olmec name of

Quetzlcoatl. This name was Tezcatlipoca. My grasp of the language was not great enough for me to comprehend in what way this Tezcatlipoca related to me in my god persona. Was this a new name being given to Helen? Had some strange god come on the scene while I plotted my journey back home? From the import Theon gave to the name and from the emphatic gestures he made I suspected it would be to my advantage to learn about this god or goddess as quickly as I could.

For the middle of the night the whole ceremony seemed excessively long to me, seated on my uncomfortable portable throne, but most of the people appeared riveted by Theon's words. They bent forward and up with their eyes wide, mouths slack. I wanted to yell out in frustration because I could not hear what they heard.

I wished that Isaac, that incredibly able learner of languages, had accompanied me but I had no time to roust him out of his bed before being carried to the temple and I did not think to ask Men-el to listen for me. Perhaps Men-el, whose competence had grown as he associated with the natives of the land, could learn enough from the Olmec people he spoke with to inform me on the import of Theon's words. The attitudes and expressions of his listeners convinced me that they were important.

Just when it seemed I could restrain my impatience no longer the priest's talk ended and he raised his arms to point toward the mountains far away. Suddenly, there was a deep rumbling that seemed to extrude from beneath the temple butte like a massive belch, and the whole building shuddered at the sound. Then noise appeared to issue from beneath our feet as it fled upward and into the ether. It was as if earth called to sky and they melded together above the roof of the temple.

Many people, shouting and screaming with fear, threw themselves to the ground before my chair crying piteously for my intervention. The redness of the distant sky intensified until I could almost recognize some of the people's features in the glow.

Theon, his face agleam with the bloody light from the sky pointed to me and bent his back at the waist with his face lifted toward mine. The priest's expression was so intense, so fierce that I nearly drew away from it in shock. Try as I would I could not read the information it offered. Was it fear? Anger? Triumph? He held the position for a minute or so longer then he straightened and looked again toward the mountains. The red glow lessened as he turned as if the mountains responded to his pleas. Then the rumble ceased entirely.

A murmur went through the gathering as the temple mount began to settle back and all the people looked toward me with great joy on their faces. Then as one they knelt and held their arms out, their bodies bent until their faces nearly touched the rough mosaic of the floor beneath us. I nodded at them graciously, recognizing that it mattered not at all whether I accepted the credit for the deliverance or refused it. However, it seemed expedient that I receive it.

All around me I heard their voices rise and intensify as the people began to sing to me. They sang of Quetztlcoatl, their Star of the Morning, of my goodness, of my loving protection of my people, using many of the few words I understood. Their songs reminded me of those I once sang to honor the Baal of Byblos and inside me I quailed at the comparison. Anger escalated in my breast as I considered my helplessness to aid in any way these people who looked to me to stem the flow of fiery rivers, to calm the mountains that moved, and restore the land to its peaceful status.

A silent cry went from my soul to those gods who had deceived me and so many others into believing that they cared and that they had our interests at heart. Was there no god, I questioned silently, who bore these attributes? Were we men just a kind of flotsam on a sea of existence, bobbing senselessly upon the waves, going nowhere in the end?

I frightened myself with my thoughts and I tried to pull my mind back from that strange land of doubt and faithlessness where it spent so much time. I made an inner obeisance to Baal and to his brother and sister gods hoping just in case that they could not hear those words I did not utter.

Slowly, the singing died away and Theon waved an arm in my direction. I lifted my hand over the heads of the congregation and offered them my blessing. Though there was no genuine value in the gesture, perhaps the blessing brought comfort to the beleaguered people. They rose and bowed to me as if they truly believed I brought them deliverance

The musicians, acolytes and priests who had joined us in those early hours re-formed their original lines and processed from the temple, followed by the king, Theon and then my chair. As my palanquin moved slowly down the steep stairs and through the city I could not help but notice that the glow from the mountains rivaled the sunrise in beauty and intensity. In some manner, it seemed prophetic, but of what I could not say.

Men-el waited patiently when I returned and then he assisted me from the chair and removed my ceremonial robes from my back.

He said, "I have sent for Isaac, Aribaal. I thought you would wish it."

I sighed. "Sometimes, Men-el, I think you know my mind even before I do. Yes, I wish it."

I continued my toilette until I felt cleansed and able to think clearly again. The true sunrise had become fully complete now and the sounds of day drifted up from the city below. There was a peculiar aroma in the air. Smoke, but different somehow, hotter and unpleasantly heavy. Can an odor smell hot and then hotter? I wondered.

The stench seemed to travel on the wind from the mountains, and smelled more like what could be found around the potter's shop or that of the maker of arms with a metallic quality that was curious to most but common to those professions.

As I stood on my balcony overlooking the city with the new temple and the mountains far away at the bend of the river I also discerned an unusual haze that came from the far distance and engulfed the city with its tendrils, like the arms of the ropy vines that grew in the jungles outside the city. There was an ominous quality to the haze, as if it bore more meaning than the usual early morning fog. I watched it for a while, musing, then turned and went back inside.

Isaac, when he arrived, looked tenuous. It appeared that his essence was not quite poised in this world but on a cusp between this world and the next. This frightened me and I hurried to him.

"Are you ill, Isaac? You look like your health has suffered a blow."

"I am well enough, Ari, at least in my body. It is my

soul for which I fear." He moved to a cushioned bench and Men-el rushed to guide him down onto it. "I slept little last night because my whole body and soul felt fitful and nervous. Then when I woke, I was full of foreboding that has left me weak and uncertain."

"I, too, have had an unusual night."

Quickly, I spoke of the midnight trek to the temple, the service there and the strange movements beneath the temple and their rumblings.

"I was there, Ari, among the people. I witnessed the rite of which you speak."

His abnormally pale face whitened still more.

"What did Theon mean when he talked about the personification of this new god, this Tezcatlipoca? Has this god manifested himself in some way? And what has Theon to do with it?"

I sighed. "I hoped you would know, Isaac. My command of language is so inferior to yours that I could follow only a few of the spoken words, while I assumed you could understand them all."

"Sometimes, Ari, it is inadequate to understand the words alone. There is the importance of meaning not voiced." Isaac grew paler as he continued. "There was much import behind the actual words which I could not understand. This Tezcalipoca, in his images, is a god of darkness, black in color, able to walk among men in the night time without being detected because he is the color of night. But what he does or wants did not sound clear when Theon spoke."

"I found myself shuddering almost as strongly as the ground beneath us when the priest mentioned this dark god", I replied in a quavering voice. "I especially did not like it when his name and my god name were spoken together."

I paced the room a few moments then returned to sit near Isaac on the padded bench.

"Will you try to learn about this god and about Theon's intentions?" I paused. "I hesitate to think about it because I am afraid it could turn out to be dangerous for you. I cannot predict how Theon will react if he gets wind of your investigation."

I paused and looked out the window toward the mountains which were the source of all the turmoil.

"Perhaps I am creating a tempest in my own mind over this, and yet there is an ominous question inside me that I can only attribute to the rare and threatening occurrences which have been happening in this place."

Suddenly a picture of the Olmec capital and the new temple flooded my mind's eye and as I watched blood began to flow down the temple stairs. It began as a trickle then quickly increased in volume and size until became a river of blood which poured over the steps and into the pool of sacrifice near their end and the water became as red as the blood pouring into it. So much blood! Many hearts had to be pulled pulsing from their bodies to create such an outpouring.

I cried out, frightened by what I saw, and my body slumped forward toward the floor. Vaguely, I was aware of Men-el's strong arms lifting me as one would a child and placing me on my sleeping couch and then everything but the blackness fled as the pain took over my mind.

Chapter 13

When I returned to full consciousness I immediately recalled what had transpired. I lay propped against many cushions with Isaac and Men-el seated close to me. Men-el cooled my face with a fan made from the same colored feathers as those in my cloak and headdress.

"I have come back from that place", I croaked. "My mind is clear."

I pushed myself up and stood on my feet. My legs felt a little weak, but my mind had recovered, and I recalled everything. I walked slowly from the room and stood on the balcony, my eyes searching the city below and before me for some sign that the people had grown fearful in the night. But there was none. As far as I could see, all of them went about their business in a normal manner.

Isaac joined me. "What do you seek, Ari? Do you expect to find the world changed?"

I turned toward him and laughed shortly. "Perhaps so, my friend."

Horror washed over me as I recalled the vision.

"There was blood pouring like a waterfall from the temple mount to the pool below. The cries of many people filled the air; some wept, but many others demanded more blood. I watched, helpless to stem the flow of blood, the rending of hearts from living bodies. And I filled with shame as I realized this was being done in my honor and in my name without my acquiescence."

"If your vision is truly prophetic we must lose no more time in this place."

He cleared his throat. "I fear that should we remain, we may yet get caught up in this religion Theon is determined to impress upon the native people. That must not be allowed to happen if there is any way to prevent it."

I thought on his words and even more on the underlying menace he felt from Theon and his cohorts.

Like a leopard held on a short chain my mind sought for a way to attack this new religion or, if it already had advanced too far, an effective means of escape.

"There must be a way I can get past Theon's guards and leave the temple. It is imperative that I see for myself the condition of our ships and our men. As much as I rely on my Egyptian friends, I must depend on my own eyes."

"I have been giving this very problem some thought." Isaac rubbed a hand over his bare head then continued thoughtfully. "Rem-Na is nearly as tall as you, although somewhat broader in the body. Clad in your garments and seated or sleeping in your apartment, it is just possible that he could pass as you for a while. At the same time, with your head covered by a cloth, you could pass for him. Except for Men-el and your own friends, very few have seen you up close, not even your personal guards, who watch you from a distance. Clearly, Theon does not want their presence to alarm you unduly."

"A few hours would suffice then you could return as your own person as if you had never left the temple."

He paused. "I think it would be wise, however, to choose a time when Theon will be occupied, as it is impossible to predict when he might decide to visit you here. I do not believe he remains as convinced as he previously was about the debauchery of your life. There have been small clues recently, no matter how careful you may be."

I waited several minutes after his words before I came up with what seemed a good idea. As I perused the thought, I grew increasingly confident in its wisdom.

"Then I shall plan a great celebration with much liquor and food and attempt to re-establish his faith in my hedonistic nature. Perhaps he will choose to believe that I am reconciled at last to his view of my destined life. At any rate, it is worth the attempt."

So it was that three days later as night began to fall and with a background of reddish glow from the fiery mountains, my apartment in the temple resounded with the sounds of musical instruments, the bellowing laughter of my Egyptian friends, and the gleeful cries of the women provided us by my guards.

Isaac and I joined heartily in the festivities and appeared to indulge ourselves with the greatest gusto. Senmut and I played at war games, feinting back and forth with our swords and fighting sticks, falling often in a simulation of drunken gaiety. Rem-Na occupied the women by singing love songs from his native Egypt, while attempting to caress several of them at a time.

One young woman in particular attracted my attention because she quite obviously attached herself to me, and did not drift toward any of the others. I could not recall seeing her before and her appearance was much too spectacular to be easily forgotten.

Her coloring seemed lighter than most of the women at my parties, almost pale in comparison. Her hair, dark as midnight, rather than straight and heavy, curled around her face in ringlets that seemed to carry on a life of their own as they coiled and bounced with a vigor I found astounding. Almost, she might have been from a whole different race than the rest of the girls.

"I am Tlazolt", she offered, "named after the goddess of love."

She knelt low before me, acknowledging my Quetzl persona, then she stood up with a motion like that of a dolphin ascending from the depths, her naked arms thrust before her as if to open a space in the air for her body to follow. She tossed her head, causing the ringlets to move in a sinuous, almost serpentine manner as she looked at me with a smile that tantalized as much as did the suggestive movements of her body.

"Your favor, my Lord."

Her eyes sparkled with mischief as she spoke so boldly to the one who was ostensibly her god. Words proceeded from her lips with a hissing or a lisping sound that seemed at odds with her appearance. I thought, looking at her and hearing her voice that she would prove an interesting conundrum to solve should any man choose to attempt it.

Part of that puzzle for me had to do with her clear ability to communicate with me in a language I understood. Yet, even as I listened, I knew somehow that her words differed from what my ears recognized. It seemed as if she spoke one word and I heard another.

I laughed, a harsh, loose laugh that I hoped would add to the impression of drunkenness I had been fostering in her and all the other guests at my party.

"Only a fool would be so bold as to withhold favor from so lovely a lady, Tlazolt. And I flatter myself on my ability to appreciate beauty."

I felt certain regret that she had failed to arrive while I

still pursued the kinds of delights her gestures suggested. At the same time, I was grateful to have at least most of my senses alert as I enjoyed this encounter with her. I did not know why, but I sensed the small hairs on the back of my neck rise, almost in protest, as she came close to me. I settled back on my bench and leaned my head against the uneven wall. Its texture aided me in my quest for a concentrated mind. As I relaxed I grew convinced that a dalliance with her might lead to more chaos than I could now imagine.

She replied, "I have brought you a gift from another god, named Tezcatlipoca. He has lived here many centuries, even millennia." She gestured to a young Olmec girl who came forth with a bundle of dried leaves in her hands. As the girl approached, I could hear the crackling of the leaves as she carried them. The girl pulled from her side pack a shallow bowl made of gold. Placing the leaves in it she lit them with a hidden fire. Very slowly as the leaves began to burn a trail of fragrant smoke rose and began to spread throughout the room.

Tlazolt took the brazier from the other girl's hands and slowly waved it beneath my face. The pungent vapor entered my nose and left me feeling dizzy and disoriented. Frightened by the effect it had on me I pushed the bowl away and leapt to my feet.

I cried out, "Remove this bowl! I did not request it."

Tlazolt gestured at the other girl who seemed to evaporate from the room as though she were a specter.

I stared at Tlazolt. Her expression changed from surprise to amusement as she observed my reaction. I could not be certain just how I might truly define my reaction. Initially, the smoke smelled strongly acrid and biting after which it seemed more tantalizing than objectionable. I sensed a strong temptation to have Tlazolt call the girl back so I could try it again. However, because I had committed my future to a bold course of action that I hoped would free us all from the tentacles Theon strove to wrap around us, I could not allow her temptations to influence me. I smiled at her, permitting my facial muscles to relax into what I believed to be the appearance of laxity and drunkenness.

Suddenly, I put my hand over my mouth and darted from the room as though seeking a spot where I might disgorge an overload of liquor and food. Men-el, who knew I had taken little of either, followed me with a puzzled expression on his face.

"What is wrong, Ari?" He dashed to my side as though to help me to a couch.

I made a few sounds that would carry beyond the privacy curtain into the other room where I hoped they would be interpreted as the sickness of overindulgence but I did not attempt speech. A mere gesture informed him that this was a part of the show I had been putting on.

Soon I returned to the party. I was pleased to notice that Tlazolt had departed, apparently having lost interest in me. I continued to join in the frivolities but I did not forget that piquant smoke from her brazier.

When the evening turned to late night and then moved near to dawn, I jovially sent the women off with several of the guards whose duty hours had finished for the day, while my friends and I wrapped ourselves in colorful blankets and scattered our bodies around the floor. In a simulation of the aftermath of a drunken orgy and to make identification more difficult for my watchers we avoided the beds and benches. My guards who came close to sleep by then settled down against the far walls of the courtyard with generous cups of wine laced with a mild soporific which would neither endanger them nor cause a suspiciously deep sleep to fall upon them.

Very quickly I dressed in Rem-Na's garments and made myself resemble him as nearly as possible while Isaac covered his own head and body with one of the brilliantly colored local blankets now piled on benches or casually tossed on the floor.

Rem-Na pulled one of the blankets around him and threw himself among the allegedly sleeping bodies of my other friends and fellow conspirators scattered on the floor while I followed Isaac out of the temple by passages I had not known existed.

My isolation from the rest of the Olmec world was ominously illustrated. As we passed through corridor after corridor beneath the temple my confusion grew. I did my best to remember the various twists and turns of the subterranean passages, but feared that I ended up with only the scarcest concept of the way.

When at last we reached the outside we were in a part of the city I had never seen before. Nothing could better illustrate the restrictions of my life than the severe limits placed on my travels around the city. It became increasingly obvious that the god and his subjects were never to have any real contact.

Chapter 14

The sky already began to lighten with the early streaks of dawn as we exited the old temple, its color looking not unlike the glow from the mountains. We walked down alley after alley and street after street past sleeping families and closed businesses. We moved silently across the boulevard of kings and passed the massive stone heads of former monarchs and deities that sat where they had been deposited many years ago. So majestic were they that it seemed clear that they, not I, must be the gods of this nation. The heads loomed many times larger than the figures carved in my image that inhabited the new temple and the pathways of the processional way.

Upon entering the sea in the vicinity of my ships I felt the last vestiges of confusion and sleepiness flee my body and mind. I felt clear, strong, young, as I ought, but had not done in months. The water flowing over my body washed me of much more than the perspiration that had covered me from head to foot in the close, airless room at the old temple.

The ships, when at last we grew close to them, bore a ghostly aspect in the pre-dawn light. They rode peacefully on the gentle waves, their outlines blurred by the delicate fog that persisted over placid waters. They looked much as I had long felt, fuzzy and immaterial, as though they and I had lost our connection with the corporeal world and were fading out of existence. I shook myself to rid my mind of those unhelpful memories and then had to laugh as drops of water from my flopping hair hit me in the face. I continued to swim with renewed vigor.

My heart leapt and I felt hot tears behind my lids as I saw the ships closely for the first time since we had arrived at this misbegotten land. It seemed to my mariner's eyes that they had been maintained well and kept clean in readiness for a quick departure from this place. Gratitude flooded me and I thanked whatever god had kept my men faithful and energetic throughout our time among these strangers. I hoped and prayed that their strength and commitment would continue until we embarked.

We swam past the supply ship to my flagship, Isaac keeping up with me as if he had undergone a miraculous rejuvenation since the day before, and we silently pulled ourselves aboard her just as the sun began to glide over the horizon. Already, seamen moved busily around the deck and it gratified me to see how elegantly our sails had been laid at rest and how clean was the smell of new paint on her hull.

Careful not to attract attention, Isaac and I crept below deck to check the oars and inventory our supplies. Everything seemed in order, the supplies which had been brought aboard piecemeal over the past weeks neatly stacked and stowed for sailing. Even my requested supply of chocolatl had arrived and got packed among the more traditional goods and artifacts brought aboard as remembrances of our unexpected sojourn in this new world.

At my bidding, Isaac sought the captain of our men-at-arms, a Syrian named Ben-herold. This Ben-herold, a warrior of great courage and fighting skills, was related to the king of Syria but had offended the royal family in some manner. Consequently, he deemed it expedient to find a new home and situation, at least until memories faded. Of course, like the rest of us, he had not anticipated our journey ending in so exotic and mysterious a land as this hot, tropical nation so full of overwhelming dichotomies.

Yet, despite all, he took it with good humor and a determination to make the best of what the gods had presented to him.

Meanwhile, I waited for them to join me on a section of the deck close to the prow. The sun began to show higher, brighter and hot. Now, safe from spying eyes along the shore, I rested and let the gentle movement of the ship soothe me. It seemed, from aboard the ship, that everything that had occurred since we arrived might have been a bad dream from which I awakened at last.

Isaac's return with Ben-herold shattered that small illusion.

"Lord Aribaal!" Ben-herold cried. "It is good to see you. I had despaired of ever doing so again."

He bowed low before me then grasped my hand in friendship.

"I am truly here, my friend. But not for long. As I believe you have been told, I live like a virtual a prisoner in the temple. It was only through subterfuge that I got away for even so short a time."

I stood up and paced back and forth a few moments.

"All appears in readiness. How long will it take you to muster the men who will sail with us? And how many will choose to remain here?"

"We can be ready to sail in a few hours' time. And most will go with us. Just a few have actually settled in here and wish to stay, mostly men with no families awaiting them at home and newly established ones here." He made a gesture of distaste, then added, "I suppose, though, they could have found a worse place to settle."

His words sounded fair enough, but I shuddered at the thought of what Theon planned for this little nation. A rebuttal came to my lips and I pulled the words back before they could be uttered. The time was not ripe to tell my men about the Baal worship and human sacrifice introduced by the mysterious priest. Once we had safely left his field of influence would be soon enough.

"Do you have a departure date in mind, Aribaal?"

"It will be soon, but I cannot say exactly when. We may not have hours when things begin to move. From this moment, as many of our loyal men as possible must be gathered either on board the ships or very nearby. Vigilance must be maintained, but in such a manner that it does not draw the attention of observers on the shore. I realize that this an almost impossible task, but I am constrained to ask it of you and our men. When the time is right, I will send a messenger and we will cast off as soon as we can board our crew and passengers. Anyone who tarries at that time will have to be left behind." I looked hard at Ben-herold. "Do you understand?"

"Completely." He nodded. "It will be necessary to keep the information from some of the men, those I know less well or suspect may have transferred their allegiance to the natives. But there are ways to get even them here, such as extra duty, change of roster. It can be done."

"Good. Good. Then so be it."

We made a few final arrangements and embraced briefly then Isaac and I left as we had come, swimming. It was fully day by then and very hot. Our bodies and loincloths dried almost immediately in the heavy air. A strong smell of hot sulphur pervaded the air and its presence could be felt on our damp flesh almost like fire.

It had to have come from the burning mountains on that strange wind that had come up suddenly and blew in the direction of the city. Heat haze and another pall, smoky and heavy, hung over the city so that everything distant could be seen only as through a translucent gauze curtain. Rem-Na's garments covering me felt heavy and stifling in the increasing warmth of the day and suddenly I was eager to be back in my quarters inside the temple.

The city projected a hive-like aspect in its frenetic activities. People moved around at a faster rate than normally they would in the intense heat of the day. I heard very little prattling conversation as we walked. There was a rare purposefulness abroad, as shopkeepers and workers went about their business. Even the children, who normally played noisy, often violent games, subdued their youthful enthusiasms. I felt tension in the atmosphere that was nearly palpable, a sense of something about to happen. I found myself and Isaac hurrying as were the natives of the city.

The old temple remained very quiet when we returned with the usual distant clatter and nearby swish of moving garments suspended as if time had ceased while we were away. There was no mad rushing about to find me, no indication that my absence had been noted. We wended our way back through the many corridors to my apartment. Except that the night torches had been extinguished, all was as it had been when we left. Slaves passed us as usual, eyes downcast, incurious, content to go about their normal morning tasks.

Rem-Na, when we entered my apartment, had already awakened and seated himself on my padded bench, with Men-el in attendance. Clothed in one of my cloaks of finest material, he grinned at me as I entered.

"This god life has its appeal, Ari. Men-el has cared

for me as though I were truly a royal." He laughed uproariously. "I could get to enjoy this a great deal, I think."

Feeling tired and irritable, I replied, "You say that, but little you know about the daily problems you would encounter. I do not believe your fascination with this life would be last very long, or your sense of the wonder and pleasure over such marvelous treatment. A few days of confinement and having your every movement observed, analyzed and reported to Theon would cure that quickly enough."

He sobered at my words. "You are correct. Such an existence would not appeal to me, after all, at least not as a permanent way of life." He grinned hugely again. "But it brought me pleasure for a few hours."

I smiled back at him. His cheerful nature proved compelling as always, and I could not remain in a temper in his presence.

I must have looked weary, for Rem-Na stood up, cast

aside my richly adorned cloak and started to leave my apartment.

"At least", he said, "should Theon send his spies to see if you really had a debauched night, one look at your haggard countenance ought to prove convincing. I think you need some sleep."

"I cannot argue with you about that", I said as a monstrous yawn split my face.

Men-el as ever aware of my need even before I stated it had already arrived at my side. He guided me toward my sleeping couch. Isaac, nodding, started to walk out with Rem-Na.

As tired as I was I had adequate vigor to notice Isaac's exhaustion which was obviously greater than mine.

"My dear friend", I pleaded, "please get some rest, as well. Your countenance looks so drawn and haggard it makes you appear aged far beyond your years."

He smiled and nodded at me as he walked out with

my young Egyptian friend, whose vibrant energy so greatly contrasted with both of ours at this time.

I lay back on my couch and pulled a light cloak over me. Just as sleep overtook me I heard whispered voices outside my door. One of the voices belonged to Men-el but the other was too low pitched for me to identify. Too tired to be interested in anyone's conversation or questions I turned my back to the wall and slept.

Chapter 15

I awoke dreaming that I stood aboard my flagship, and I could feel the deck roll gently beneath my feet as the men rushed around calling out directions and information to one another. Then a hand touched me gently and a voice spoke in my ear.

"My Lord Aribaal."

Men-el spoke, close by my ear, while other voices sounded more distant. The floor of my apartment rolled and swayed, responsible for my sensation of being on board a ship. Men-el's tone sounded hushed yet implied certain urgency.

"There are men here to take you to the great temple. Theon sent them. He said there is an emergency need for

Quetzlcoatl to be with his people."

As I attempted to rouse myself from the dulling effect of a long night of preparations and almost no sleep, I heard Helen's voice coming from just outside my door. She seemed to be asking audience.

"Men-el, I must find out why Helen needs me. Let her in."

He hesitated.

"Quickly", I cried out, as Helen continued to importune my guards.

As soon as Men-el left the room, Helen burst in, as if propelled by a massive shove.

"I had a fearful dream, Ari. In it, Theon in some way threatened Isaac's life."

I leaped from my bed and grasped Helen by the arm.

"How did he menace Isaac, Helen? And if it is only a dream, why are you so agitated?"

"I believe it is a warning."

I saw tears spring into her eyes as they grew round with fear. I reached out to embrace her.

"I will send Men-el to Isaac's apartment right now. He can reassure us as to our friend's well being."

She nodded against my shoulder, leaving a trail of dampness across my flesh. I shivered, whether from the morning chill hitting the tears or from something different and more sinister that I could not discern, but I nodded at Men-el to leave right away. He did, his rapid footsteps slapping along the corridor.

We waited tensely for his return, our arms entwined as to ward off any evil that attempted to attack us.

"All appears normal, Ari. Isaac sleeps, and other than his personal servant the apartment is empty."

Helen, hearing the words, said, "Perhaps it was just a bad dream after all, and not a warning." She ducked her head.

"I am a foolish woman."

"Whatever the dream meant, you are not foolish, Helen. I will have my friends keep him under their eyes, quietly, just in case your dream has a more ominous meaning than just to frighten you."

She nodded her agreement. "I shall return to my room now." She looked at me as though seeing me for the first time that night. "You need your sleep. You look ill."

I grinned at her. "Too much party, I think. In the future I will be more wary of overdoing it, I promise."

She gave me a searching look that contained a degree of skepticism and a touch of distaste.

"Yeess." She drew out the one word in a long hiss, as though questioning it even as she spoke. She looked again, hard. "Will you come to my apartment later?"

I smiled and nodded at her. "Look, Helen," I said as laughter began to bubble up in me. I had not realized how tense I had become during those few minutes together. "Even as we speak, the earth has returned to sleep."

It was true. The rolling of the floor that had tricked me into thinking I was at sea had calmed down. I heard Theon's couriers arrive to take me to the new temple, and a breathless quiet now descended on the city and the temple where I resided.

Whatever I might encounter when I reached Theon's lair, I knew I must not permit myself to be taken completely by surprise. There might be nothing dangerous at all, just a replication of the rituals I had grown familiar with in the past days and weeks. However, when I considered the ruses he had employed since I had known him, the degree of deception he used without any apparent regret, and the almost hypnotic control over the minds of the people, I dared not relax in his presence.

The changes I had brought about in my life endangered my ability to deceive the evil priest. As long as Theon believed that I remained in my liquor induced half stupor, his contempt provided me with a cloak of protection.

Precarious perhaps, but the only weapon I could see at that time. The bearers must have been instructed to make haste that morning. The city passed in a near blur as my chair bobbed and bounced in the hands of the strong men who carried it. More than once it tilted so far when going around a corner that I braced myself against a possible dumping on the street. I forced myself to let go and allow my body to follow the choppy movements as though I were asleep or nearly comatose from drink. I never imagined how difficult it would be for a sober man to emulate the unrestrained movements of a drunk.

At last, we arrived at the new temple where the steep climb and stone steps permitted the men to stabilize the chair's motion. I felt very grateful for that as I had come close to emptying my stomach from the erratic movements of the bearers.

I laughed soundlessly as I realized that, had I lost everything in my stomach, it could only serve to convince my captives of my apparent drunkenness. Losing, I could gain much. However, I did not have to survive that particular form of humiliation. By some mysterious means, my body settled down and I arrived at the sanctuary no more ruffled than usual.

As I gazed around the vast room, gloomy in the feeble light from a few torches along the walls, it seemed that the people gathered there had turned into statues scattered throughout the room while awaiting some sign from their creator. My arrival must have been the signal because immediately after the bearers lowered my chair loud music filled the cavernous space, followed by the arrival of two dancers, one male and one female.

The male tossed leaves onto a brazier and lit them, seemingly by the mere gesture of snapping his fingers. I stared aghast as the leaves emitted that same pungency that Tlazolt's leaves had done in my apartment. The two figures bent over the brazier.

So dark were they that I could not be certain if they were real or but illusions generated by my highly sensitized imagination. As they whirled and looped around the sanctuary, their very darkness in the sparsely lighted room made the whole tableau hallucinatory. I blinked my eyes several times, hoping to bring focus on the scene, but sharpness of vision eluded me.

The male figure, tall and slender, swayed and undulated like water forced through a small channel. Something about him made me think I should recognize him but I could not grasp why I thought so. He so blended into the darkness surrounding him that his features blurred into nothing but a smudge as of charcoal when a hand brushes across it, leaving vague shapes and a suggestion of motion.

The female moved sinuously, slowly, and her gestures looked familiar to me. Her feet remained nearly motionless while her body above them pulled together and stretched out like the lotus when the afternoon light begins to fail. Her hands shaped themselves into the appearance of serpents' heads and they moved with gestures changing from expansive to under tight control. All the while the rest of her followed them in twisting movements that emphasized the lush curves of her body.

From what little I could see the dancer could only be Tlazolt, the girl who had arrived so unexpectedly at my last and grandest party. However, her whole figure impressed me as different now, as if a slight shift in her essence had occurred. While I watched, a new persona materialized and overtook her, much larger, dark and muscular, making violent leaps and threatening gestures. This new personality merged with the slight form of the girl I recognized from my last party. For a few moments, there continued to be two distinct overlapped figures struggling for dominance before the larger one disappeared entirely and only Tlazolt remained.

As I puzzled over this, a tingle of apprehension

plunging through my body like the quick thrust of a sword. I noticed that both male and female appeared translucent in some mysterious way then gradually grew more ephemeral and faded like phantoms or illusions of my imagination. The male dancer began to shimmer in the air, as if he attempted to split into two separate beings. Almost immediately, there came a slight breathy sound and a totally black figure, dull obsidian, yet insubstantial, detached from the dancing man and disappeared into or through the roof of the sanctuary.

The dancing man paid no attention to the strange phenomenon, but continued to perform as though nothing unusual had taken place. He and the girl kept up their graceful movements a few minutes longer then as suddenly as it began, the music stopped and the dancers ran from the sanctuary, their feet barely brushing the floor.

I sat as one stunned by a heavy blow on the head. I asked myself what it was I had actually seen, but no answer came. I could but wonder if the burning leaves the dancers supplied exuded some strange, hypnotic vapor I could not recognize. I clutched the arms of my chair to anchor myself in reality, whatever that reality actually happened to be. As I waited to see what would occur next, the torches along the walls flared and the whole room grew brighter. No sign of either dancer remained and I could only wonder where they had gone.

Silence filled the sanctuary, so intense that it more nearly resembled loudness, a phenomenon I had not encountered before. Nothing moved, no sound of breathing could be heard and it felt as if life itself had been suspended. Then from behind the dark curtains that separated the sanctuary from the rest of the temple, Theon emerged. His body gleamed in the light of the torches as he dropped the feathered cloak from his shoulders, leaving only a short cloth as his covering. From the shadows around the sanctuary, music filled the room. A procession of feather clad priests joined the high priest in a song of praise offered to me. With great effort, I stayed still, while my heart pounded, whether from fear or anticipation I could not discern.

I pulled together the trailing thoughts of my mind, conscious that any untoward movement on my part could bring instant death. The enormous difficulty of acting like the sodden fool I had played for months proved depressing enough to convince almost anyone of my inability to understand the danger of my situation. How easily Theon could kill me on that altar of blood and afterward immortalize me with statues and ceremonies that would satisfy the priests and the people. When had he become so powerful and so dangerous?

It turned out that Theon had chosen to foster a further build up of tension, so he selected a varied group of animals to sacrifice, leaving the human captives to live a little longer. Some of the selected animals I had never seen before, strange creatures almost as large as the Nile crocodiles to which many Egyptians fell victim each year.

Exhausted by what I had witnessed that early morning and by having to carry on with my deception, it became easy for me to loll in my chair and pretend to sleep while I awaited my release from this new temple. Despite my attempts to sort out all that had occurred, I ended up in greater confusion than when the night began. The days and nights of enforced inactivity had taken a toll on me, a much greater one than I previously supposed.

At long last, Theon signaled that the ceremony had ended and my bearers toiled through the heavy heat of the early morning to return me to the old temple, which I now came to regard as a kind of sanctuary, however precarious it might be.

Chapter 16

Helen waited at my apartment when I returned. Her face resembled a mask of anxiety and as soon as she saw me she jumped up from the cushioned bench where she sat.

"Ari…" she began.

I interrupted her words with a quick kiss on her soft lips.

"Not now, Helen." I whispered. "In a few minutes we will find some private time. But now we must not show our feelings or speak our thoughts."

Her whole mien changed and she smiled a welcome, offering no further sign of anxiety. Once more, I stood amazed before her ability to shift to a whole directional change in the time it took to blink an eye.

She returned to her cushioned bench and sat quietly as I removed my clothing and Men-el cleansed me of the sweat my body had accumulated beneath the feathered cloak. I had hoped that as the dirt got removed from my physical body, the suspicions and apprehensions also might be washed from my mind. But it was not to be. If anything, once my body returned to its clean state, my mind filled with the viscous muck of fear and frustration.

It needed all my inner strength to avoid committing a violent act against my impassive guards. I knew that, could I restrain myself, they would move away from my door in a short time, as that was their habit and their instruction. The illusion must be maintained that they existed only to protect me from unwelcome intruders. No hint of constraint must come from their attitudes or they might well join the ranks of those animals to be sacrificed which Theon now engaged in collecting.

Holding Helen close to my heart I sent Men-el for

Isaac. I leaned over to whisper in Helen's ear.

"When Isaac arrives, we will hold a strategy meeting under the guise of a celebration. We must in no way show our true feelings or speak our plans loudly enough to be heard." I nuzzled her hair and despite myself, exalted in the clean, flowery scent it exuded. "What I learned last night emphasizes the degree of care we need to take if we expect to survive. I had hoped not to add to your fears, but we can trust no one but our most reliable friends and even they could be subjected to practices so deceiving that they might be unable to distinguish friend from foe."

She shivered in my arms but did not speak. Instead, she laughed lightly as though my words had been of flirtation rather than warning. I squeezed her to show my approval, and more. I wanted her to know that I not only accepted, but desired her as well. We rested as we had done several years before in Isaac's home at Byblos, and for a short while it seemed the years had never happened and we had just now come to know one another.

It seemed ironic that as our original contact had come at a time of deadly crisis, so did this renewal of our relationship and, indeed, the true beginning to our marriage. This new joining somehow managed to decrease my intense mourning for Nikkal. Not that I intended to forget her. I could not. But the time had come to accept what I could not change and thank whatever god had inspired Helen to stow aboard my ship.

Very soon, Men-el's arrival with Isaac in tow broke through the magical moment and we returned to the much less pleasing present. I instructed Men-el to send for food and drink. I left out the girls who usually accompanied us in our revels, making it clear in my request that this would be a special party, designed for my inner circle of companions alone.

I guessed that the guards and their officers might well believe that I planned to share Helen with my friends. While an unattractive and even repellant idea, it fit in with what these people had come to expect of me. It grieved me that my actions had forged so unsavory a reputation for their titular god.

Shame overtook me that I had caused many to become suspicious and even inwardly disrespectful of me, yet I also knew that their very contempt could help me succeed in my deception. The worst pain came because I so sullied Helen's name in this manner, but I could think of no other effective way to include her in our clandestine meeting.

As she moved from one after the other of my friends, feigning interest in each, she could safely convey my instructions and receive their words for me. The men knew their restrictions and, combined with the respect they had for her, would minimize the damage to her reputation. Helen understood completely her value in this situation. I knew she trusted me implicitly and would have no serious qualms about her part in the plan.

The guards, after taking visual note of what they interpreted as the nature of the gathering, moved outside where they could continue to watch over us without intruding on our party.

We entered into a kind of farce, imitating true revelers at a sybaritic party. The rise and fall of conversation and laughter, mostly erotic in character, filled the room with sounds which I felt certain could easily be heard by the guards. I knew that a few of my guards had some familiarity with our language, so I made sure that none veered into more serious conversation loudly enough for their voices to carry beyond the entrance.

It galled me to hear Helen laugh as she sat on Senmut's lap. I found myself wondering if she actually enjoyed it. There could be no denying that he made a handsome figure that any woman might want to know better. Then I recalled that during her years of slavery, Helen must have been forced to take part in orgies much as the one we now simulated.

I pondered on how much and in what way such a repetition as this affected her. Had she enjoyed it when she tempted the men she was assigned to entertain? I felt my gorge rise as I entertained a picture in my mind of Helen succumbing to the advances even of my friends. Senmut caressing her. Strange men I never knew holding her close and making love to her.

After I had brooded a short while on these ugly thoughts, it was all I could do to stuff down my anger. Filled with a sudden repugnance and convinced she wanted to be unfaithful I came close to bringing ruin to my whole plan. The images of her with other men appeared painted on my mind as by the hand of an accomplished artist. It was only after a powerful struggle with my emotions and against my newly acquired suspicions, however, that reason returned.

I could hear Helen's voice, pitched low and seductive, as she spoke of supplies, schedules and which of our men could safely be told what. Shame flooded me. In my near paroxysm of insane jealousy, I could have destroyed every one of us. I did not understand the source of so great a flood of destructive emotion. It was unlike me. I felt as if some evil thing had assailed me and twisted my vision until I saw through other, suspicious eyes what did not actually exist. I shuddered as I realized how near the brink of destruction I had carried my friends and my faithful wife.

I leaned back on my cushions, breathing spasmodically through a heavy and inexplicable pressure on my chest. After a few moments, I felt the pressure lift and my breathing returned to normal. Sweat broke out on my brow and I felt as if I had been engaged in heavy labor.

Helen, pausing in mid laugh with Isaac now, looked at me with concern. She rose from the bench where she had sat close to my Hebrew friend.

"Are you well, Ari?" she asked. "You are sweating."

I nodded silently, unable as yet to trust my voice.

She left Isaac and came to where I rested.

"Your color has fled, my husband. How can I help you?'

After a few moments, I replied, "You have already helped me just by your presence. I am well enough, Helen."

I pulled her down beside me and whispered, "I believe some malignant but unseen presence has joined us here. We must put an end to this gathering." To the others, I said, "We all are tired, my friends. It is time you all returned to your own apartments."

Unwilling to speak more, I turned away from them as though falling into a drunken sleep. I lay across the bench with my legs dangling over the edge, not very comfortably, and pretended to sleep.

My friends, who knew quite well I had not drunk enough to explain my actions, called out noisily to each other as they took their departure. Only Helen remained. Even the unseen threat looked to have departed.

Helen sat beside me and ministered to me, wiping the sweat from my face with a cloth she had a maid dampen for her. Through the slits I forced my eyes into, I saw the maid make a kind of face at her as if the two women had joined together in sanity against the madness of my incontinent behavior.

While I did not enjoy being mocked, however mildly, by one of my servants, at the same time it gratified me to recognize that the woman accepted my performance as real. That information would almost certainly be conveyed to Theon very soon.

I remained on my couch until the maid had completed her ritualistic withdrawal from my presence, bowing and backing away in the most humble manner. As soon as she exited, I grabbed Helen and pulled her down beside me.

"I do not know what happened here, but whatever it was has shown me the folly of waiting much longer to depart these tormented shores."

Even as I spoke, there came a deep rumble from beneath our feet as the land did slow, dramatic undulations, producing the sensation of much greater movement than the eye saw. Perhaps the progress of the floor had been set in action from far beneath the earth where some living creature might be preparing to swallow the temple and all of us within.

I grasped Helen tightly as if it were possible for me to hold her firmly enough to save her should the earth open under us. We clung together like children while the floor continued its sinuous movement that reminded me again, however incongruously, of Tlazolt's serpentine dance gestures. Then as suddenly as it had begun, the action ended. The floor settled down, leaving only a few misaligned tiles as mementos of its extraordinary activities.

Helen's eyes, brilliant green as always when she grew afraid, had widened until I could see white almost all the way around the color. I felt her tremble in my grasp then quiet as she realized that the worst seemed over for now.

"What is happening, Ari?" she whispered, fear bringing a hoarseness to her voice.

"I wish I had answers. All I know is that it is very like the earthquakes found among the isles of the Aegean. But in this case, I have heard that, instead of an island, this is all part of a huge land mass so extensive that no one has seen the whole of it. It appears that it rivals in size Etruria itself."

A shuddering movement overcame me, causing me to pause.

"I have come to believe that this place is under a curse placed on it by some malignant spirit, perhaps called up by Theon, possibly of earlier origin."

I dared not express to Helen the fullness of my fear and uncertainty. It would gain me nothing and might increase her trepidations to a dangerous level. While I knew I could not handle Theon and his evil cohorts by myself, I also knew that telling my friends the whole story as I saw it might frighten them and make them unable to act against the evil priest. In the end, after all my soul searching, I decided that Isaac alone could deal with my prognostications, whether accurate or not.

If I sent for Isaac right away, I knew it would add to Helen's fears, so I decided to wait the few hours until the temple denizens awoke and began their daily rituals. The delay proved nearly impossible for me.

I spread out across my bed with Helen pressed against me as though to seek protection from whatever evil forces were at work. I could only wish that her confidence in me were valid. But I knew better. Surely, she could feel the trembling that vibrated deep within my body. But she showed no sign. I stayed as still as I could, forcing myself to remain quiet as she finally slept.

Chapter 17

When at last I deemed it reasonable to call upon Isaac, I sent Men-el to fetch him. Helen had repaired to her own apartment to prepare for the day so I was alone with whatever guards, servants and overseers had been assigned to me.

My Hebrew friend arrived a few minutes later, looking only very slightly rested. I despaired of his health if I could not free us from that place soon. Each day, he appeared to age more until I could readily believe he might fade away so totally as to disappear.

Grumpily, Isaac complained, "I just nicely fell asleep when I was disturbed by your servant. Is there an emergency or do you have something against rest?"

As he opened his mouth to continue his little tirade, he got a look at my face and his final words were cut off before they could escape his lips.

"My sleep has been troubled and I wanted your company, old friend."

I knew my expression made at least a partial lie of the words.

"We can go out to my balcony and catch a breeze."

I moved in that direction.

Immediately, one of the servants assigned to me dashed out of the next room, ready to accompany us and serve me. I could only wonder whom she served, really. I knew some of my servants had been placed with me to spy on me and my friends, but I did not know if this was one of those. I waved her away.

"Men-el will accompany us", I told her.

She seemed reluctant to leave, but for what reason I did not know. I stepped out onto the balcony and shrugged my shoulders. Perhaps, I thought, I now see spies where there are none. However, I decided on caution as opposed to letting my captors make all the decisions.

The balcony showed certain signs of the earth's agitation. Part of the balustrade had crumbled, leaving a small gap. However, the floor stayed firm beneath my feet and the rest of the railing also seemed intact. I signaled Isaac to join me.

There was a wide stone bench suitable for two to sit where I sometimes rested in the cool of the late afternoon. I sat and invited Isaac to join me. Men-el took up station by the door, vigilant as always. His senses, fine tuned after many years as my protector, seemed almost visible as he listened and watched.

I told Isaac about the presence I had felt in my apartment.

"I experienced a similar presence in the new temple last night," I added. "Theon had dancers who burned a handful of strange leaves which brought forth a kind of smoke I had never encountered before."

I probed my memory for the sensation.

"There was a kind of sweetness to it, mixed with a headiness that made me feel quite dizzy, perched insecure on a high and precarious height. Tlazolt, the girl who showed up at our previous party and danced for me, last night danced at the temple for Theon. As she passed close to my chair, she changed her dance style so that she might almost have been Nikkal performing for me. Many of her movements and gestures appeared almost identical to some of Nikkal's. Once I nearly reached out to pull her to me before my good sense returned and I withheld my interest and amazement. Of course, she looked and moved nothing like Nikkal, except for those few twirls and dips that seemed to imitate my wonderful wife. Immediately, I feigned extreme drunkenness and fell back against my seat which ended her seductive performance."

"A male accompanied her, a stranger, clad in black so deep that it gave forth no light at all and frequently made him look as though he were but an insubstantial shadow and not a man at all."

I paused to pull my thoughts and memories together. I deemed them so outrageous that I had trouble finding a way to capture and hold onto them.

"I cannot say if the peculiar smoke was responsible or if I experienced rare visions from my mind or some unknown god, but at times it appeared that the male performer had an insubstantial spirit joined to him which moved in and out of his body as he cavorted about the platform. And I also seemed to see another female being with Tlazolt, much larger and darker than she, who moved with threatening gestures, and who blended with Tlazolt and ultimately became one with her."

"After more capering, the two intrusive beings left, the male seemingly through the roof of the temple and the female fading away like a puff of smoke or a fog before the rising sun. Then Tlazolt and the dark man gamboled across the stage a little longer before running from the room and disappearing into the inner precincts of the temple."

I watched Isaac's face as I related my experiences at the new temple. It expressed horror and some fear as I spoke.

Then, as one who girds his loins before a battle, he shifted his body to a more upright position and said, "It appears that Theon has gotten himself involved with spirits that may be beyond his ability to control. I know of nothing we can do to help him with this situation, except to call on God, who made us all, and throw ourselves on his mercy."

He stood up abruptly and turned to look at me.

"And we must be ready to leave."

Encouraged by his increased vitality, I said, "We will intensify our preparations from this moment."

As we spoke, Theon burst in upon our conversation.

Once again, I felt resentment against his assumption that he had the right to interrupt me at any time for any reason. On this occasion he wore a troubled expression. Both fear and confusion passed over his face as if in competition with each other.

"You are needed at the new temple, Ari."

To accompany his words a new series of movements came from the ground beneath our temple. Outside, I heard something fall and crash, followed by fearful cries from voices in the outer courtyard. I rushed to the balcony and looked down. A large figure of a god unknown to me but which I had seen daily since my arrival had been tossed by the earth's motion like one formed of unset clay. The head fell to the ground and rolled a fair distance from the torso which had broken in two nearly exact sections.

The cries, almost immediately silenced, came from the horribly crushed body of one of my watcher guards. Immediately, a group of his companions rushed to pull the injured man from beneath the statue, but their efforts were in vain, as the man's body had been mutilated beyond redemption.

I turned away, sickened by the sight and by the ruthlessness of whatever lay beneath the visible world and had such a lust for blood.

Blood. Never had I heard of so much blood hunger anywhere else. Did this thirst for blood always reside in this place or had it been carried here by Theon and passed on to the priests and the population by his teachings? If it had always been here, I wondered how it manifested before Theon. Had tribal wars been carried on with so much ferocity that the spilling of blood became the major goal of their military rather than conquest or the protection of their own people?

I shook myself to clear my mind. At this point, there was little reason for such speculation. It was my job to get my people safely away from these cruel shores, this land inhabited by many fierce and predatory creatures inhabiting equally the ground, the underground and the air.

I suspected this land would forever remain a paradox to me, even as my understanding of their language improved. How they could enjoy such creative and mathematical skills and yet saturate themselves with so great a taste for blood escaped me entirely.

Slowly, feeling like an exhausted old man, I rejoined Theon in the reception room. He remained as I had left him. Not for him to rush to the aid of a stricken minion. He had reached such a pinnacle that any contact, however minimal, with common men seemed beyond his ability to inaugurate.

That realization made me pause and look hard at the priest. Why then did he come himself to my apartment instead of having me summoned to him? Recently, it had been his practice to send messengers to call me to the new temple while he remained remote, inaccessible.

His flesh had gray undertones that caused the sagging

facial features to turn almost green. New and deep wrinkles formed around his eyes and mouth and deeper yet in his jowls. He was not a well man. I could not discern what form his illness might have taken, but he looked used up. His hands nearly claws, the eyes sunken into their sockets and lips stretched into near non-existence, he bore the air of a man near death.

I did not know what to say to him. Instead, as the building shook again, a small interruption unworthy of much attention, I walked toward him.

"What do you want to do in the new temple, Theon? Why am I needed?"

He looked shocked at my question. Never before had I questioned his instructions.

His lips moved as if he sought to find words, but it took several seconds for anything to come forth.

"It is your place, as the god of these people."

He nearly stammered as he spoke then recovered and,

in his usual haughty manner added, "Your chair will be ready in a few minutes."

Despite myself and my many doubts, I could only admire his ability to gather together his failing inner forces and leap over any objections I might have the temerity to offer.

I grinned at him.

"Of course I will be ready when it arrives." I turned away and called Men-el. "Theon needs me in the new temple. Will you help me get ready?"

I watched as Theon bristled at my tone with Men-el. In his mind, Men-el would forever bear the mark of a slave, despite his having been freed, and he clearly resented my speaking to my former slave as to a friend and confidant.

Men-el, aware of Theon's reaction, grinned at me as he said, "Yes, Ari, it would be my good pleasure."

He grinned again and headed for the large chest that held my wonderful feathered cloak and headdress.

Theon jerked his shoulders in a gesture of mixed anger and disdain, and fled the room, the rustle of his lavishly embroidered cloak seeming to hang in the air behind him.

As he left, he threw back to me, "Be sure you are ready, Aribaal. You have caused me more than sufficient embarrassment. Please do not add to this list of indiscretions."

I grinned at Men-el and presented myself for garbing. A small and useless victory, I thought, but one which pleased me all the same.

"Ari, I am concerned that you permitted Theon to see how you have changed. Is that not too dangerous?"

I considered his words before replying. "I can see how that could be true. However, before I leave I will drink some wine and throw out even more to give the semblance of drinking a lot before leaving. That way when I arrive at the temple, I can appear drunk and drugged."

I spoke solemnly so that he would not think I took this too lightly.

"I think I do not underestimate him, my friend."

"Never forget that he is an unusually clever man, Ari, and that he also has exceptional powers we do not understand."

Brought down from my feeling of exaltation, of having impressed Theon in some way and by Men-el's gravity, I replied, "I will not forget. While at times I think it is all a deception, at others I am convinced he has help from demons we know not of." I paused. "I promise to be careful around him. This morning's indiscretion will not be repeated."

Men-el sighed in relief and continued to dress me for an audience. My nervousness and anticipation increased as he placed each item on my body.

Shortly, I returned to the reception room where Isaac waited, forgotten by both me and Theon. He rested against the far wall on the other side of the large room and farthest from the balcony where I returned to see what progress had been made clearing debris from the sudden movement of the earth.

The dead guard had been removed and the others had been joined by a work crew who now busied themselves with the removal of the pieces of statue. The head currently rested in the hands of two workmen, its face turned toward my balcony. Was it my imagination, I asked, or did the stone face bear a malignant expression as it gazed upon me? I shook myself and decided it had been a trick of the light.

I returned to my receiving room and Isaac.

As I rejoined my friend, I could hear Men-el moving about in my bedroom, packing away the unused articles of my ceremonial garments and accouterments. His nearness gave me the confidence to speak somewhat freely with Isaac.

"I must leave as soon as the guards arrive to escort me," I said. "The unfortunate death of one of them has delayed them long enough to give us a few minutes of private conversation."

"Not totally private, I am sure, but much freer than most times." He grinned. "I expect Men-el will hold off any invasion of maids or other servants expecting to wait on you."

He turned serious. "This unanticipated meeting with Theon has spiked my concern for your safety, Ari. I doubt he would have you killed, but I cannot be certain of that. I do recall him saying that, should you die, he could have a gold statue made of you that could serve to satisfy your worshipers."

He rose and paced the room a few times. "I sense that things are coming to a critical point very soon and you will be forced into action. Be vigilant, my friend. The time is near."

As he spoke, I felt a shiver pass along my spine and the feathers on my cloak seemed to quiver with a kind of tension I had not felt from them previously. It made me wonder if it might be possible for them to retain some of the life force of the birds who had been sacrificed to make my wonderful garment.

"I intend to be ready."

"Alertness hidden beneath the semblance of drunkenness will stand you in good stead today, my friend." Though I had never been threatened by anyone from the city, he added, "Be careful even as you travel in your chair. It would be easy for one of those poison sticks to penetrate your flesh before the guards could ever suspect anything."

Isaac paced the floor again, his agitation seeming to increase. "You must maintain your vigilance at all times from now on. With added threats from those dancers and whoever has joined them, you cannot afford to let down your guard even for a moment."

I nodded my agreement then took a sip of the potent liquor provided me at all times. As for the rest, I poured it out on the ground outside my balcony. The odor of liquor, spilled or otherwise, was no stranger to my apartment.

Just then a line of guards arrived to escort my chair to the temple. Ostensibly for my protection, against whom or what I did not know, they were well armed with knives and the long tubelike weapons for blowing the little sticks dipped in poisonous saps. These had powerful ability to drop an enemy quickly and permanently while also causing much pain.

I nodded at Isaac and Men-el, who had joined us in the reception room. I stepped forward to settle into the chair held for me by my bearers. As I started to nod at them to begin the trek to the new temple there was a slight flurry on the balcony.

Pu Ko appeared, looking so flustered that it was instantly clear that what he wanted to say he considered worth his life to convey to me whatever the cost. He approached and threw himself on his knees before my chair.

I nodded dismissal at my guards and chair bearers who melted into the passageway outside my apartment.

"Rise, my friend. I would hear you".

His whole body appeared to tremble as he gained his feet.

"My Lord. I come to you for help of the greatest magnitude."

He lifted his eyes to my face, and spoke in a voice that seemed eager to choke all the air from him.

"The high priest Theon claims that you have commanded him to present you with the blood of many captives and some prominent members of our leadership. He claims you wish our king to join them in sacrifice and he has already taken him captive and placed him in a large cell filled with those awaiting death."

I felt the temple shiver beneath me, a brief but fierce shudder as if all the forces of fire and earthquake had joined together.

I needed to cry out that there was nothing I could do to relieve either him or the land from such an edict. My voice froze inside me as if a huge wad of something had been forced in there against the words that strove to be released.

I stared at him a moment then found my voice saying "I will look into this. Perhaps it is not as serious as it appears."

A tiny glow of hope appeared in his eyes and he bowed before me and thanked me even as tears flowed and he turned to leave. I watched him stagger away as if all his strength was used up to supply the courage for him to approach me without any real hope.

I watched Ku Po leave, a somewhat revived man and I grieved that his faith had been placed in so feeble and ineffective a vessel as his supposed god.

I nodded and the bearers returned.

After a parting smile of encouragement from me, sloppy from the implied overindulgence in liquor and other drugs, we set off for the temple.

The slight red glow I had seen inside the old temple increased to an intensity that surprised me. Outside, it made the impression that the whole world had turned red. Even the trees that normally showed brilliant green foliage, now acquired an overlaid aura of radiant red-orange light.

Despite Isaac's trepidations, the journey to the new temple through the hot red air proved uneventful. Even the weight of the atmosphere all around me and the continual minor undulations of the land beneath my chair seemed to offer no immediate threat. No assassin leapt from the crowd to assault me or my bearers. All was as still as possible in a city under siege by fire and earthquake.

Chapter 18

After Theon's nearly hysterical assertion of a great need for my presence in the new temple, it sounded unusually quiet when I arrived. Of course the Baal priest arrived before me as he always intended, but the expected bustle or near panic I anticipated did not materialize.

Theon moved close to me and whispered, "Remain at peace, Aribaal, no matter what you see and hear. I will direct you if you are needed."

I felt a growl beginning to form deep in my throat. I chose not to reply to him. Anything I said could cause him to become increasingly suspicious, especially since my words would not be friendly. I permitted myself to sprawl a bit more as if I were hung over or still slightly drunken. With the liquor I deliberately spilled on myself it should be no problem to convince anyone of my wayward habits.

Neither Tlazolt nor her dark dancing companion identified as the personification of the evil god Tezcatlipoca could be seen. As discreetly as possible, I glanced around to find them. But no. They had not arrived. However, I had a strong conviction they soon would.

I propped myself in a corner of my chair, trying to restrain my growing impatience and edgy sense of anticipation as Theon and his associates droned through their usual words intended to praise me and all other gods in the vicinity. They went on and on interminably and finally sacrificed a few small animals.

Despite Theon's panicky sounding words in the old temple even the town folk showed up only in scant numbers. Those who did arrive appeared bored whenever I permitted them to settle on anyone. I began to feel foolish, as if I had sought fear as a companion and found it. Inwardly, I admonished myself for my response.

I still sensed a foreboding, a peril that loomed over me and over the whole temple. I remained persuaded that Tlazolt hovered not far away with her dark dancer. The impression of doom ought not to surprising, given the fire and quakes the land had been experiencing for some days already. Yet I felt there was something more. It stretched my ability to play the unconcerned drunken fool, to resist a desire to look above my head into the rafters of the roof, as if some threat overhung me there, ready to pounce on me at any moment.

Nothing did, however, and the rites continued to their usual end. Despite the disappointment of anti-climax, I had never before been as relieved as when finally I got carried out of that temple. The chair crew wended their way back down the steps and past the well. I resisted the urge to let my glance fall upon the murky water. I could not bear to spy any bodies that may have risen from the depths to float bloated and decrepit on the surface of the well.

Confused by the ordinariness of the temple rites after the panicky words of Theon, I could only speculate about the reasons both for the priest's show of fear and for the lack of expected drama. Something had changed and I wanted to know what. Swaying in my chair as the bearers threaded their way through the streets I fought to continue the pantomime of drunkenness even as my mind wrestled with the meaning of the change.

So eager had I become to seek the information I needed that I nearly leaped from my chair to dash through the throngs toward my temple apartment. I managed to restrain myself until I arrived. Even then there followed the ritual removal of my ceremonial accouterments. I grew so edgy after the temple experience that my skin felt invaded by legions of insects moving over my body. It required all of my self-control not to fidget during the rites.

My Egyptian friends awaited me at my apartment. Senmut said, "Na-Amen, we need to talk where we cannot be heard."

He glanced around my receiving room, his eyes seeming to go everywhere, searching for watchers and unwanted listeners.

"Where is Men-el?" I asked. "He usually greets me and keeps notice of anyone suspiciously interested."

"Strange rumors abound in the city. Some say the end of the world is imminent. They blame it on the rivers of fire and on the earthquakes. These rumormongers make the residents of the whole city nervous and fearful. Men-el has gone to learn what he can."

Senmut waited a moment then added, his eyes still busily seeking possible listeners, "He is the best able among us to pick up bits of news. No one feels threatened by him. He offered his apologies and promised to return soon."

I nodded, despite the turmoil of my mind. I felt evil brewing ever since I watched Tlazolt and the dark one cavorting in the temple. What form this evil might take evaded me, and my jittery discomfort continued to grow as my mind still wrestled with might be happening. One thing I knew for certain. Tlazolt and her dark companion had not come to bring peace and confidence to me, my crews, or any of the population.

I stepped onto my veranda and looked around. I could see much of the town. Things appeared quite normal to me with the residents going about their usual business as best they could despite an atmosphere of intermittently heavy smoke and air which had turned red in color, its noxious fumes irritating to noses and throats. I could only hope that the air had not become so poisonous as to kill any of the people.

My warrior friends joined me on my veranda, now strengthened by repairs made by my bodyguard, the only ones other than my personal friends and servers permitted to enter my private precincts.

"Look past the city to the south", Rem-na said.

"Does the air not show more fire than before?"

I followed his gesture and it did seem that the flow of fire from the mountain had altered both in length and in breadth. It appeared to crawl toward the city like a feral cat on its stomach with claws outstretched while it crept toward its prey. Even as I watched, little rivulets broke free from the body of moving fire and created new directions for their courses.

Worried about what could happen if the river of fire kept coming toward us, I said, "I wonder what Isaac makes of this."

I looked around the room. Isaac was conspicuously absent. I would have expected him to be there with the Egyptians when I returned from the temple.

"Does anyone know where Isaac is?" I asked. "It is not like him to be away at a time of crisis when we must make plans for an immediate withdrawal of ourselves and our fleet. I do not like the look of all this."

Before anyone could reply, Men-el returned. He seemed distressed.

"In the city they are saying that the gods have abandoned them. A coughing sickness has come upon many and they blame it on the heavy air. It is as if the air solidifies even as it enters the throat."

He looked at me. "There is talk that Theon has a solution he intends to offer them today, before he begins the rites. He will most assuredly send for you to join him, in your robes and plainly to be seen by all who gather there."

His face twisted with concern.

"I get a nasty feeling about this, Ari. Lately, every time I see Theon, I sense a black presence around him and possibly in him that I interpret as an incarnation of evil."

He shuddered.

"Wherever you go and whatever you do today, you must be armed. If you cannot conceal a sword on your person, at least carry a dagger to protect yourself and any other who may need you."

His words brought a thrill of fear which passed through me like the brief reaction to hitting an elbow on something hard. But this new sensation did not hold briefly but rather seemed to increase in effect as it passed throughout my body. I felt impaled on some alien spear which held me immobile while inwardly I twisted and turned to escape its vicious grip. With much effort, I finally rent myself from the cruel embrace.

Fear seldom captured me, even before Theon sacrificed me to the god of Byblos. I seemed born with a built in buffer against fear, one which rejected it utterly whenever it attempted to take control of my life. Even when I fought the leopard in Egypt, faced the Libyans and their paid assassins as captain of Egypt's paltry western army and challenged the great ocean between Carthage and this new world, I enjoyed a sense of adventure that proved far stronger than the trepidations caused by imminent danger.

"I have never needed a weapon before, Men-el. Could you be reading more into this than actually exists?"

I managed to speak in a calm voice despite my inner agreement with his ideas.

His eyes, rounded like those of someone who sees doom waiting on the horizon, denied my question.

"I do not speak frivolously, Ari. There is something powerful and ugly in this city and it is trying to overcome you and all of us, all that you stand for."

He stopped and took a deep breath. This calmed him.

"Even though I may never need it, I promise I will carry a weapon as long as a hint of threat remains."

He relaxed more.

"Now", I said, "will you please go to Isaac's apartment and learn why he has not joined us? This is not like him and I worry that his health may have begun to deteriorate again."

He nodded at me then turned and left quickly, as if

driven by some emotion beyond his understanding.

I remained waiting for him on my veranda. My eyes seemed glued to the destructive scene such a short distance from the city. The fire river moved slowly but inexorably toward us. Even though most people I could see appeared to be about their normal business, the city exuded an atmosphere of barely controlled fear and anticipation.

My wait was brief, but it was not Isaac who accompanied Men-el, but Helen. As they entered, she pulled away from Men-el and dashed to me, weeping, tears pouring unchecked down her face, her eyes rounded with fear like those of a horse confronted by a leopard.

"Theon has taken Isaac to the new temple, Aribaal. I suspect he means him harm."

"What? What? He cannot." I sputtered, confounded.

"Why would Theon wish to harm Isaac? Isaac has never threatened him in any way."

"I do not know the reason but you can afford to waste

no time. Theon wants you there as Quetzlcoatl, and there is some plan he has in mind." She grasped my hand. "Do not delay, if you value your friend."

Even as she spoke, I hurried to call for my feather cloak and headdress. Men-el, as he began to garb me, told me that the chair waited. I gestured to close off the curtains between my private apartment and the corridors where my guards stood.

I pulled Helen into my arms as I attempted to quiet my spirit. I could feel my pounding heart against hers and the strong beating of my heart seemed to blend with hers and for the first time in our marriage, our hearts truly joined as one. I held her several minutes before I pulled away, once more caught up in Isaac's plight.

Forcing myself to postpone for the moment my newly discovered recognition of our potential life together, I said, "Tell me what you know, Helen. If I go rushing there without knowledge, not only will I risk losing Isaac, but it would almost certainly endanger all our friends and you, as well."

I paused to take a deep breath.

"Certainly, it would scandalize the people to see their god acting in so strange a manner."

She replied, "I awoke early this morning, uncomfortable with the feel of the movement beneath our temple."

She paused and shivered.

"It felt as if some giant hand was shaking the ground back and forth as a cook does the seeds she is roasting in the oil. I went searching for anyone who could tell me what was happening. The guards at my door were incoherent with fear and since I have great difficulty understanding their conversation at any time, it appeared that getting anything from them would prove virtually impossible. My fear had to be subdued before theirs. It would not do for their 'White Goddess' to show signs of panic. "

She hesitated once again, her body trembling as if she were ill. She collected herself and spoke further.

"I saw Isaac. He was being encouraged toward a palanquin outside the main portal as if he were both a captive and an honored guest. His guards appeared confused as to how to treat him. He glanced up and saw me but offered no sign. So much despair came over his face that I could hardly bear to look at him. His expression thrust terror into my heart as if driven there by an arrow."

Before I could respond, a sudden jolt shook the floor beneath us and a large stone vase rocked on its base near the door to my balcony. I grasped Helen's arm and pulled her outside to investigate and show us where escape stood.

I heard cries from my frightened servants and even the carriers of my chair of state. Some fled toward the gates as if there were demons in pursuit. Their screams as they ran told me that much of the weeping seemed for their families in the city between us and the fiercest movements.

From my place of prominence I could see that in the city many people ran around, frantically calling to each other. There did not appear to be serious damage anywhere, but that fact did little to reassure me. Just because nothing drastic had happened as yet, that did not guarantee that nothing would. Helen clung to me for support. I led her back into the room since the movement of the floor had ceased again.

"Finish your story, Helen. There is so little time."

"I am very sorry, Ari, to be so frightened. Everything that has occurred this day has held implications I cannot fathom." She swallowed then continued. "Isaac was dressed in a very simple robe and seemed confused by what was happening, which suggested to me that he was wakened from his sleep by the temple guards. They hustled him into the palanquin and set off quickly in the direction of the new temple."

She sighed. "That is all I know."

My heart began to beat faster and faster as she related her story. Why would Theon want Isaac? What possible service could my friend afford him? I felt reluctant to learn the answer.

I sent Helen back to her apartment and gestured Men-el to hurry my robing.

Then, as my mind and heart began settle, I told Men-el to dismiss the guards for a few minutes while I pondered what was happening and what I should do. My fear grew almost palpable when I considered the possible ramifications of rash action on my part. Such a reaction could prove disastrous both to me and to my friends.

I sat on my seat at the edge of the balcony and watched the distant smoke rise from the angry mountains. I felt the heat from its rivers that moment by moment seemed to flow closer to the city.

After a brief time, I knew that somehow I must locate Isaac and speak with him. It had to be done discreetly so not to arouse any more suspicion than

unavoidable. I called Men-el.

"Quickly! Go find Senmut and Rem-Na. and

bring them to me."

He swiveled on his heels and dashed past the

astounded guards. I smiled at my protectors and

assured them that Men-el had not gone mad.

Chapter 19

I waited for Men-el to return with Senmut and Rem-Na, not patiently, but striding from wall to balcony and back.

My heart flinched each time the faintest sound came from outside my curtains. They all arrived at almost the same moment, my Egyptian friends fully clothed and armed.

Senmut cried, "What has happened, Na-Amen? First we were awakened by the earth's movement causing the crash of falling masonry then Men-el comes rushing to get us."

He looked around as if in expectation of demons about to ooze through the very walls and devour us all. I glanced around, as well, almost as edgy as he. Given the strange things I had witnessed in the last few days, I could believe almost anything, especially the presence of evil spirits in this place.

"Much is happening and I do not have the time to tell you all of it, nor do I know all." I took a deep breath and went on. "Theon has taken Isaac to the new temple and I am worried about his plans. He also sent for me, which indicates that some important ceremony is arranged."

I looked closely at my two very loyal friends. "I intended to remove my feathered cloak and just not wear the headdress. Yet that would itself make for problems. Therefore, I ask you, Rem-Na, to dress once more in my Quetzalcoatl garb and take my place on the palanquin."

I clapped him on the back.

"We can meet again in the temple robing room before the rite. That is where I sometimes rest to prepare myself for whatever surprises Theon has planned on for that particular occasion."

Rem-Na looked frightened and said, "But they will

know I am not you. And Theon. What will he do when he sees me?"

"We will have to deal with all that when it arises. I promise you I will find a way to protect you even as I am protecting Isaac."

"Of course you will, Na-Amen. I would never doubt that."

He walked to the ritual side of the huge audience room and removed his garments in preparation to don mine.

Men-el helped me off with the feathered cape and placed it on Rem-Na. Rem-Na laughed as the feathers fell upon his shoulders.

"Before I garbed myself with it the last time I had no idea this cloak was so weighty, Na-Amen. Is it not strange that the very same feathers that lift birds into the heavens could press a man so solidly onto the earth?"

"Perhaps", I said, as I put on clothing of an ordinary citizen of good family, "each thing has its intended use and does not adjust well to being forced into another role."

"Maybe so, my friend."

Senmut, who had left with Men-el to check the area of my home temple, arrived at that moment and paused in the doorway, a confused expression on his face.

"I certainly will do whatever you say, but what is happening? Why is Rem-Na dressed as you and you as he? Will you enlighten me?"

"There is no time. Suffice it to know that we must leave as soon as possible and that Theon has stolen Isaac and transported him to the new temple. I am desperately worried about him."

I paused long enough to catch my breath. I continued to address Senmut.

"It is up to you to protect Helen. If Theon has the confidence to abduct Isaac right from under my nose and remove him to the new temple without so much as a word to me, what would stop him from taking Helen?"

I paused briefly to permit the full import of my words to penetrate then I continued, "Have her pack what she can, concentrating on her most valuable items. Be certain that nobody, not even her personal servant, gets wind of it. When she has done this, it is incumbent upon you to remove her to my ship to wait for the rest of us there."

"It shall be done, and may the gods favor you in your endeavors."

"Once she is safely aboard, you must send the foreman to round up as many of our men as you are certain you can trust. Make sure they get aboard and ready to sail on a moment's notice. Then you have to rush to the new temple to meet Rem-Na and me in the robing room. There is no time to waste."

"All shall be done as you ask." Senmut raised a hand in salute to me.

I smiled in response, confident that nothing save his untimely death would prevent him from the completion of this mission.

He walked briskly from my apartment, his lightweight cloak flying out behind him. I laughed joyfully, happy in the knowledge that at last there was something I could do, that no longer must I sit on an elevated throne like some useless bit of stone transformed into the likeness of a true man and questionable god.

I felt freed from some strange spell cast upon me by Theon through the power given him by whatever dark malignant god who allied with him to destroy not only me but anyone who displeases him for any reason.

I waited until my sedan chair left with Rem-Na ensconced and clad in my ceremonial finery, then called my lifelong friend to me.

"Men-el. Go now to the new temple and assure yourself that Isaac still lives and in good health. You can find me in the robing room."

As my chair bobbed its way out of the old temple,

none of the carriers appeared to notice a change in weight or appearance of the god. I realized that there was much to be grateful for, in that the solemnity of bearing a god around the city carried with it so much responsibility and mystery that the men laboring beneath the burden permitted themselves no curiosity. Never had I noticed any one of them looking at me as we traveled the area around the old and the new temples or inside the city. It was as if they feared to look upon my face.

As to any alteration in weight or size, there was little difference between us. Of my friends Rem-Na was the most like me in size and shape. Also, the fact that I had sent Men-el with him was in itself a confirming factor. Men-el was to meet me in the temple as soon as he could remove himself from the audience room.

When I had given the entire entourage a few moments to precede me I followed them from the old temple, very discreetly so not to attract any undesirable attention.

Once more I managed to get through the corridors Isaac introduced me to without attracting unwanted attention.

The thought of Isaac in Theon's hands sent a shudder of fear through me as I contemplated the possible plans the priest might have for him. In the past it never occurred to me that my friend could be in danger from the Baal priest. But much had changed since we had arrived in this merciless part of the world. Nothing was as it had been. It felt as if all innocence had died and been replaced by vicious hatred whose source I did not know.

The streets were filled with people milling around as if afraid to stop moving lest something terrible catch them as they rested. Many cheered as my palanquin passed, some followed behind it while others merely stood and stared. No merchants had opened their businesses as yet, perhaps because they could no longer trust the earth to remain stable beneath their feet. Those few faces I dared look upon closely as I sidled through the throngs looked drawn and their eyes pleading as they cried out to the one who was seated in Quetzlcoatl's place. It grieved me mightily that in no way could I alleviate their fears.

Despite the early morning hour even the air seemed filled with noxious life, as the distant smoke and the nearby dust from the movement of the earth came together to form a heavy haze over the valley between the two temples. More and more people gathered to follow or precede the palanquin and it was a fairly simple matter for me to blend in with them, my head covered to disguise my hair color, my body slightly bent so to appear closer to the height of the native people. Inwardly, I thanked the gods for the change in my skin color after Theon sacrificed me to the Byblos Baal. At least I did not have to cope with that problem.

Except for my midnight foray with Isaac to the ships this was my first time among the people of this nation and they made me feel like a giant compared to them. I experienced a strange gratitude for the earthquake and the smoke which kept the population so preoccupied they failed to note the differences between us.

I mounted the stairs behind the chair carrying Rem-Na, those roughly cut steps leading to the temple itself. When the chair moved toward the great central door into the temple courtyard I eased toward the eastern wing of the huge building where I suspected Theon would have taken Isaac. The crowd grew so vast that it was difficult to move laterally across the stairs as I climbed but I managed it by pushing aside those in my immediate area as I walked.

A young boy appeared on the step above me and as I watched, a citizen shoved him aside and the child nearly tumbled his way down the steps, a death sentence had he fallen. I grabbed at him and caught him by the bottom of his ragged garment. Setting him on his feet I gave him a small salute and gestured him to the part of the stairway that hugged the wall. He stared wild eyed at me then turned and scampered up the steps. Quickly, he disappeared into the crowd at the top.

So intent were all the citizens that but for an occasional growl or remark no one took exception to my rudeness or noticed my differences.

I paused briefly before the entry to the east wing. Guards had been stationed on either side of the doorway just as they were outside my apartment in the old temple. I looked about for a means to pass them without being noticed but none presented itself. I felt completely desperate by then, afraid for what may have befallen my friend. I struggled to control my dread and frustration.

Once I reached the top of the stairs, I walked a short way toward the west side of the temple. Looking around for some sign of hope my eyes fell on the small child I had just encountered. His face looked as pinched and desperate as any I had ever seen anywhere. I gestured him to me as I hesitated close to the middle of the top step. He ran to me, eager to do me a service, anticipating whatever reward would meet him.

In my broken Olmec, I pointed out the guards who stood listlessly outside the east door, boredom stamped on their faces as they guarded an entrance that had never yet been challenged. Obviously, they anticipated no trouble, no intrusion.

I said to the boy, "I will give you this coin", holding out one of a small enough denomination not to get him overly suspicious, "if you distract the guards for just a moment."

A mischievous look on his face, he nodded his agreement. I decided that small boys were much the same wherever you found them, eager to bedevil those they saw as officialdom. The child ran to the guards and began chattering loudly and pointing downstairs. He tugged fiercely at the garment of one of the men, tugging him toward the stairway.

Both guards lowered their terrifying dart throwing

weapons with their deadly poisoned tips and stepped away from the door then leaned over to check the people ascending and descending the stairs. As the guards moved away from the door with their attention riveted on my young co-conspirator, I slipped past them to the inside. I pressed the coin into the boy's outthrust hand as I passed him, moving carelessly, indicating to any casual observer my right to be where I was.

I thought I knew where I could locate Isaac. A recently constructed part of that wing had been designated for those who had been set aside to be sacrificed. The area accommodated all anticipated sacrifices, both animal and human, and consisted of a number of separate rooms of differing sizes.

Quickly, I ran along the corridor, keeping close to the wall at first, pausing at each pillar to check for observers. When no one showed any interest in me I began to walk openly. It appeared that no officials feared a grand escape from these holding pens and rooms.

People came and went in both directions and I heard a murmur of voices that seemed to come from the direction I headed. The strange configuration of the corridor made it impossible to be certain where sounds originated. Farther along, the din of animal cries blended with human sounds, all of which seemed both amplified and diffused by the rough stonework of the unadorned walls in this part of the temple.

I paused to look into several rooms opening off the hallway, but none of them held Isaac. Most held youths, both male and female, awaiting their call to the altar. Very few of the doomed young people even looked up as I opened the viewing slot in the door. I felt convinced by their appearance that they had been drugged as I had been at Byblos when Theon plotted to sacrifice me to the Baal.

At intervals I kept hearing an echo like padded footsteps somewhere in the corridor but I could not determine its source. The passageway had so many twists and turns that I must be traveling in circles like a vast spiral leading up to the main sanctuary of the temple.

I remembered the dark shape which Theon called Tezcalipoca who had danced with Tlazolt in the darkness of the night temple. Sweat broke out on my forehead when I thought of that pair of dancers and the menace that hung about them like a miasma. If my mysterious follower were one of them, I could not be sure I could cope with him or her while rescuing Isaac. I certainly did not wish to encounter them together.

Sweat formed tiny rivulets that trickled down both sides of my face as I opened door after door to discover no sign of my friend. It was not until I reached the last doorway before the entrance to the great hall of the temple that I saw him.

Isaac sat slumped on a bench of dark wood, naked except for a loincloth, his sinewy arms and chest exposed to the view of anyone going by. I drew my breath in sharply. I had not realized how thin and unwell looking he had become, as though the life force within him had begun to recede like the tide in the bay below us. He sat alone in the room and I saw no guards anywhere near him. Why, I wondered, did he not just stand up and leave?

"Isaac", I whispered loudly then entered the small room. "What happened? Why are you come to this place?"

He turned toward me listlessly then stood to his feet when he saw who it was that called him.

"Ari! Why are you here?"

"I have come for you, of course. Why else?" I crossed to him and took his arm in my hand. When had it grown so flaccid, so ropy? "Surely you could not believe I would abandon you."

"You must leave this place now", he cried out in a hoarse voice. "There is no time to waste."

A small voice near my legs said, "Is this why you wanted to fool the guards, sir?"

I swiveled. The child who had helped me had now joined my friend and me in the cell.

"What are you doing here? Did someone tell you to spy on me?"

I contemplated using my dagger on him and ridding us of a potential threat.

"No. No, Lord." The boy ran to me and grasped me around my legs. "I just wanted to stay with you, to go where you are going."

I half laughed in relief as I gently pushed him away.

"I do not believe that would be wisdom, my boy. Anywhere that I am may become quite dangerous indeed very soon. You will do well to run as far and as fast as possible in any other direction."

"I want to stay with you."

The child planted his feet firmly on the rough rock of the room floor as if determined to plant himself and allow nothing to uproot him.

I laughed. "Then keep yourself a safe distance from me, just in case." I turned back to Isaac. "Pull yourself together, old friend. It is time to leave."

Isaac, startled by the arrival of the boy, at first looked flabbergasted and unable to understand what was happening.

Then, shaking himself like a wet dog, he cried again, "You must leave, Ari, while still you can. There is no safety for you here, at least unless you come here as Quetzlcoatl." His eyes filled with tears. "Go. Now. Get back to your temple and resume your duty. There is no other hope of saving your wife and friends." He stopped to catch an uncertain breath. "It is too late for me. Go!"

He sat back on the bench, his head between his hands the very epitome of dejection. He looked up again.

"I tried to hang on to the hope that one day I could return to my own people and receive relief from my sins at a priest's hands. But now, I never will have the chance. Instead, I must die as sacrifice to a bloodthirsty pagan god, with no hope of ever embracing Abraham's bosom. I have no priest to lay my sins on the back of the scapegoat. Instead of my substitute fleeing into the jungle with my sins I am condemned to carry them on my own back until the knife finishes the cycle and then to live with them for all eternity."

Isaac's eyes widened in terror as he considered the words he himself had uttered. I knew not how to comfort my friend. The only solution I could see was to remove him from this prison and from this country and return him to his own land.

He trembled violently for a few moments before calm settled on him like an invisible cloak.

"I am reconciled, Ari, but you must leave right now." His finger pointed toward the door. "Go now while yet you live."

Chapter 20

Had I need of further encouragement, from behind me Theon's voice said, "He speaks the truth, Aribaal. If you would save yourself you must return to the old temple and prepare properly for your appearance as Quetzlcoatl. I cannot promise anything otherwise. As Quetzlcoatl you have position and safety. As Aribaal you are in grave danger."

"From what enemy am I in danger? From you, my self-proclaimed father?"

"The people of the country have concluded that it was the arrival of the foreigners who came in the ships that caused the mountains to cast forth fire. They believe that these strangers have been keeping you captive and through witchcraft prevented you from working your magic on the hills to pacify them. They say the ships are conveyers of evil spirits from the nether lands."

He smiled as if to comfort me.

"These agitators continue to foment unrest among the people. They spread rumors that the ships arrived with you as captive and there will be attempts to leave again soon. The king has instructed the guards to redouble their vigilance."

The Baal priest paused, a peculiar light in his eyes that showed reddish in color as he spoke those words of condemnation. Clearly he would do all he could to keep me prisoner. Triumph showed on his countenance, so secure was he in his vision of the future for my people and for the native people.

Aghast, but unwilling to show it, I said, "What of Ku Po? Does he also encourage these dissenters?"

I did not wait for his reply.

"If the priests are under your influence, as I believe them to be, you can dissuade them from such a false belief. Then they in turn can influence the people."

"It is not so simple, Ari. You know that these are a fierce people, quite willing to kill first and question after. While it is true that they see me as their chief priest, this does not mean that my every word is accepted as absolute."

"That gives me some hope for the people", I replied.

Theon recognized my sarcasm but said only, "There is much you do not understand, Aribaal. Do not meddle into matters outside of your province."

His words now quickened excitement in me. Seemingly, Theon still thought of me as the degenerate wastrel I had presented to him. Or perhaps he was simply so full of his own greatness that he could see nothing beyond himself. Either way, I decided to use this to help my friend.

Theon replied to my query. "As to Ku Po, his influence with the king has diminished recently. TuTopiltzin consults him rarely now."

In a slightly whiny voice, I said, "But what have the priests got against Isaac? He has never been any threat to these people. In truth, he has entered into their culture as deeply as possible in the time he has been here." I grasped Isaac's thin arm again. "He is nearly wasted by age and illness. Why would they fear him?"

I watched as the young boy moved closer to Isaac and sat down on the floor near the older man's feet. I heard a few whispered words but I could not hear clearly enough to interpret them and neither did I adequately understand the language.

"Exactly, my dear Aribaal. I do not think they do," Theon continued.

He stopped for a few moments as if seeking the right words. "It is because he cannot hope to live much longer that I have chosen him to be the sacrifice necessary to appease whatever gods control the earthquakes and the fire from the mountains."

Stupefied by his words, I felt my breath catch in my throat and no words made their way from my mouth. I stared at Theon.

He said, "I was certain you would understand, Aribaal. We have a whole new world here, so far from our home, and it is ready for us to civilize. We can educate these native people, teach them new skills such as shipbuilding and sailing, encourage them to find other natives as trading partners. It is as if the gods located us in this place to direct them now and for our descendants to continue doing so in years to come."

There was such fervor in his words that he almost convinced me. As his passionate, crazy words flowed over me, it required all my strength to hold back my reaction. I knew I must make him believe I concurred with him. I let my face fall into an expression of awe.

"Could this be the answer to my life-long question, Theon? Could this be the end of my quest?"

I glanced at Isaac from the corner of my eye. No longer apathetic, he listened with attention tinged with disbelief. Even so, he did not speak, for which I was grateful.

Theon replied, "I am convinced of it, Ari. You are my son and together we can be the architects of a whole new society. A civilization we can shape to our own standards. It will be a glorious world we will create. Then we can both truly live among the gods and not need any subterfuge."

As I listened to Theon I became convinced that he had grown completely mad. His bloodlust had overcome anything honest and valuable that previously may have been part of who he was. His need to own and control this whole race now became the dominant factor in his life. Any hope I had of persuading him against human sacrifice fled as I watched his face darken then turn scarlet with passion.

As he continued to rant, I felt the dark god Tezcatlipoca hover over him and sometimes even float within his essence. My heart grew numb with the fear that I might not be able to save Isaac from this madman and whatever new and powerful forces he could now summon.

My mind utterly rejected the possibility he might actually be my father as he claimed. I had never accepted the idea as viable for many reasons, not the least of which was the lack of any sense of rightness. I could believe that for some reason I could not fathom, Abishima of Byblos had not sired me. That premise offered some support from the physical differences between me and the rest of my family. But just the thought that this lunatic might have impregnated my mother caused my stomach to reject all its food almost on his feet.

His minions dashed in from the outside corridor and directed servants to remove all sign of my physical upheaval. The Baal priest looked with disgust at me and at my spoor. Even as I stood there in my discomfort, perched on the edge of fear and distress, I felt grateful that the incident now served to send him and his accomplices away. He waved his priests and acolytes ahead of him toward the temple sanctuary. He stood and stared at me a few moments, as if there were more to follow, but in the end nothing did.

Abruptly, Theon turned and started out of the room where Isaac sat once again wrapped up in his own sorrows.

He said over his shoulder at me, "I will leave you now, Aribaal. It would be to your advantage to resume your position as Quetzlcoatl. Should they lose the physical god they worship, the people willingly would substitute your image in stone or gold. Do not deceive yourself that your current life must endure for their religion to continue."

He left and signaled his guards and acolytes waiting in the corridor to go ahead of him. I watched as they marched away, already forming a line of priests and acolytes arranged by rank and position. My heart overflowed with distress and desperation. The heat of tears hovered behind my lids and I concentrated my strength on holding them back.

How could I save Isaac? In any ordinary situation,

Isaac would be the first person whose counsel I would seek. But in this situation he was of no use.

Senmut and Rem-Na were totally involved in affecting our escape plans. There was none to help me. If I were to save Isaac, I was entirely on my own.

Despair fell upon me like a black cloak thrown over my head and shoulders. Everything I knew, everything I had ever done to counteract dangerous situations, fled before it like leaves before a gale.

I might never have been the captain of Pharaoh's army or the Commandant under Dido of the Carthaginian forces. I might never have ventured into places where no sailor had ever journeyed before. I felt as weak and helpless as Theon believed I was.

How could someone as worthless as I save myself and my wife, let alone a whole group of sailors, soldiers and friends? I promised her I would take her back to our children. What kind of fool was I to make such impossible claims? And how could I communicate all this to them? I could only hope that somehow my Egyptian friends could slip through both the people and the natural catastrophes all around them and make it safely back home.

I put my head in my hands, unable to look at, let alone accept, what must transpire.

A small voice spoke near my knee. I could barely make out a few of the words, as they were in the local language of which I understood so little.

"I cannot understand your words, child. What are you saying?"

Unexpectedly, Isaac spoke.

"He is saying that he will get a robe for me and a staff and we can walk out of here with the worshipers who mill around all day. He said I can be his grandfather who came to seek healing for his lameness."

Stunned first of all that Isaac had managed to pull himself out of his doldrums and secondly that he could communicate so readily with the child, all I could do at first was stare stupidly at both of them. Then as if a great light had come to banish the darkness I knew it would work. About Isaac's familiarity with this difficult language, I would ask questions later. Now was the time for action.

I said, "I have an instruction for the child but you must convey it to him as I cannot."

Isaac replied," It will be as you ask."

He sat on the bench and pulled the child near. I could hear him speaking but the words meant nothing to me. Briefly, I explained what I needed the boy to do.

With a quick grin, Isaac instructed the boy.

The child threw me a grin which spoke much about him. Despite being told I was his god, he indicated no fear of me. In fact, he made it clear that he saw us as co-conspirators, intent on upsetting our enemy's plans.

He might need some spooling in later, but now his cheekiness showed as an asset. He nodded at me and turned toward Isaac as if to a close relative.

With mixed feelings I turned him over to my Hebrew friend.

Chapter 21

I hung back a few steps as Isaac, with the boy in the lead, walked slowly and bent over as if in great pain to reach the top of the ceremonial staircase. The guards indicated no interest in the old man leaning on a staff and led by a boy. When I got near them, Isaac signaled me.

"I have decided to call the child Joseph because he is a visionary who has been sent to rescue us from this place." He paused then sent me an impish grin. "Besides, you could never learn his real name well enough to speak it properly."

"Joseph it is," I replied, happy to cater to his decision.

I knew it was a Hebrew name but had no idea of its significance.

Isaac sat down on the second step, his hands clasped around the stick as he leaned on it for support. I stood just below him holding the boy's hand as a grandfather might. It was my hope that anyone seeing us would take us for a family group come to worship at the temple. I kept my head and face out of sight, my hair covered loosely with a rough shawl.

"Joseph", I said.

The lad looked at me sharply, his pointed face alert and listening.

"You will go to the harbor. Have you seen the ships we came in?"

He wore a puzzled expression. Isaac leaned toward him and spoke in a voice too low for anyone to hear.

The boy responded with an understanding nod.

I leaned toward him again. "The largest one, with a horse's head on the front is the one I want you to get to by some means."

The boy seemed confused. Isaac spoke with him again and I learned that he had never seen a horse and did not understand what it was. I looked at Isaac, who thought a moment then spoke to him again, once speaking my real name. This time Joseph grinned.

"What did you tell him?"

"I described the horse head then told him to get near and call out, 'Friend of Aribaal.' That would have to get someone's attention."

"Can the child swim?" I asked doubtfully.

Isaac talked to him a little more then replied, "He says so. Apparently he has lived around the water his whole life and swimming has been part of his entertainment from early days."

"I hope you have the correct information. I would hate the boy to drown in his eagerness to impress us."

"Hardly 'us', Ari. You. He wants your approval. Mine is irrelevant."

I nodded my understanding.

"Tell him he is to get on board my flagship somehow, hopefully with help from the sailors left on her and report to

Ben-Herold, the Syrian. He is to say, 'Isaac in greatest peril and will join you tonight before the temple meeting. Helen and others follow right behind. Be ready for cast off at a moment's notice.' Remain there until you hear from me or from this man – Isaac –who will tell you more. "

I stopped and stared at the boy.

"Can he remember that?"

Isaac and Joseph conferred a few minutes while I tapped my foot impatiently. The time had arrived when I must change places with Rem-Na once again and appear in the sanctuary as Quetzlcoatl.

After what seemed a very long time, Isaac nodded.

"He is ready."

"Are you certain he will recognize Ben-Herold and be able to repeat what you have told him?"

I tried to keep skepticism from my voice and my face, but I felt extremely uncomfortable leaving the fate of Helen, my whole contingent of friends and myself resting on the narrow, bony shoulders of this urchin.

"I know he will." Isaac spoke with such conviction that I dared not question him further.

"So go with Joseph into the city then make your way back to the old temple. There you will join Helen and assist her to the ship. Both of you must wait there until you hear from me. It may take many hours, but wait. Then send Joseph back to find me in the temple. Tell him he must not, for any reason, approach me but wait for me to address him." I paused. "In fact, it would be to our advantage for him to stay out of sight but still able to see me, and any attempt I make to signal him."

Isaac nodded in response.

I stared at my old friend. Even as I watched it seemed I could see the mantle of age and infirmity slip from his shoulders like an old worn out cloak, dirty and full of insect holes. I could almost feel his eagerness to stand straight and march down the staircase like a soldier. I knew, however, he would restrain that impulse until it made good sense to release it.

"May the gods be with you, Isaac, and guard you from all danger."

I placed my hand on my friend's shoulder.

"May the God of Gods, the Almighty, be with you, Ari, and may he send his angels to direct and save you."

Isaac offered the blessing for me.

He and Joseph went off together, Isaac leaning once more on the staff in his right hand. Now, however, that same staff appeared to slow him down. I sensed that inside he had become a coiled spring just waiting to be set free and would more readily dash down those gray stone stairs, past the pool of infamy, than lean on the now unnecessary piece of denuded branch that only pretended to hold him.

I watched until the crowd on the stairs swelled in number and expanded across the whole stairway, until my friend and his youthful guide disappeared from sight in the mass of people. None appeared to notice that while the greater number on the stairway headed up, my lone friend with his escort went down.

Voices, some murmuring and others speaking loudly, coalesced into a cacophony of sound. I shuddered. Theon had been right. The population of the city had come together in some sort of agreement, unspoken perhaps, that action must be taken against the forces of nature that now had control of them.

Left to their own judgments, I do not know how they would have chosen to fight for their property and their rights. I suspected they would have fled to the north, away from the center of the earthquake. Some might have gone inland and fought their way south and west to the interior.

However, Theon and his associates had convinced them that what they must do is sacrifice as many lives as the priests demanded. Only this way, they had been promised, could they end this time of terror. Nothing else would work.

As I stared at the throngs on the staircase, I thought I caught a glimpse of Senmut among them. At first I was certain I must be mistaken. Then I saw him again, slithering in and out among those ascending.

I stepped from my place of sanctuary for a few moments, hoping he would see me before I had to move back again. He did. My friend, canny as he was, showed no sign of having seen me but managed to maneuver himself to my side when he topped the last step.

"Na-Amen, I feared I would be too late."

He took my hand in his and would have kissed it as an obeisance had I not jerked it away before he could complete the gesture.

"Has something gone amiss with Helen? Does Theon know about our plans?"

Before he could pull his thoughts together to reply, I shot a barrage of questions at him.

"No. No." he replied. "All seems as usual.

However, at her insistence I personally escorted her to your flagship. Ben-Herold welcomed her."

"Then why are you here?"

"Yes.", he said. "Rem-Na managed to get word to us that Theon plans a huge ceremony in which you must take part. The priest does not know about the switch with Rem-Na but our friend fears that his unmasking could take place any moment. Right now Rem-Na waits for you in the small robing room off the central sanctuary. He says you know where it is."

He drew from his belt a short sword and a dagger.

"Please keep these with you just in case you need them. They belong to Rem-Na who wanted to arm you. I cannot imagine that anyone would attack you in the temple itself, but what of the corridors? They are long, convoluted and very dark. It would be a small challenge to find a place to lie in wait." He paused. "Should I accompany you tonight? It would be safer."

I nodded to acknowledge the danger.

"I will join Rem-Na there as quickly as I can. You, however, must return to the old temple and invent some means to deflect the curiosity of Helen's servants. They must be persuaded that the god has sent for her. Send her ceremonial garments to me in the temple. That act should satisfy the most curious among them."

He agreed. Bowing slightly, he turned sharply and again walked the stairs. This time he descended. He did not look back. When I lost sight of Senmut, I turned my attention to my own transit past guards and overexcited citizens. By means of a complex series of corridors I finally made my way to the small room beside the vast sanctuary.

Rem-Na waited. His face showed white from the fear that overtook him as he anticipated my arrival. As soon as he laid eyes on me he altered the expression to one more in keeping with the brave warrior I had always known. It made me wonder what he would see on my countenance should he come upon me unexpectedly when I strongly encountered the pressure of my responsibilities towards him, Senmut, Isaac, Helen and all of our crew. I suspected my face would indicate at least as much fear as his did right then.

"My friend", I said. "It does my heart good to find you so stolidly at your self-imposed duty. How could I ever repay you for your courage and devotion?"

His face flushed with pleasure, leaving it a brownish hue colored over with the pink of gratification. At that moment in the flush of embarrassment, he looked again like the young boy he had been when first we met at Nyto's academy in Egypt. I grinned at him then glanced about for my feathered cloak and other accouterments. I found them neatly arranged on a bench against a wall.

With Rem-Na's help, I donned the cloak and the feathered headdress of Quetzlcoatl. I watched as he caressed the feathers he laid across my shoulders. My old friend knew this garment well, having worn it as my surrogate twice. I wished I could ask him to do it again so I could dash to the ship early and take charge of our departure. But it was not to be. As soon as Rem-Na saw me clothed in them again his face grew concerned.

"Na-Amen", he said. "When you go into the temple, you must be extremely watchful. There are forces in there this evening that would do you harm. Perhaps do harm to all of us."

"I will be on the alert. We are too close to our goal to lose it now."

I gave Rem-Na a quick embrace and sent him to his next exploit, to guard Helen.

The men who bore my chair into the temple had never been instructed to guard me in any way. Also, I could not discern the loyalties of those men who actually had been assigned to guard me as I traveled among the accumulated mass of seekers who already filled the temple. With all the milling around it would be a simple matter for an assassin to come near enough to my chair as I passed. A quick slice of a knife across my throat, a poisoned dart from a small blower, a nick from a poison-dipped spear and my life would be ended quickly and my hopes destroyed.

Such thoughts began to torment me even when I dismissed Rem-Na to join the ships in the harbor. I wished desperately to keep him with me, to enjoy the comfort of having so good a friend at my back. But I knew it could not happen. Any such alteration of my schedule would immediately call attention to the unusual character of my involvement in the ceremonies on this night.

After I sent Rem-Na off to his duties I waited for my chair to return for me. Theon would surely send it. It was to his advantage, whatever his plans, to have me in his sight during this night's festivities. Sometimes it seemed to me that my whole life had been spent finding ways to accede to his demands and predictions. I hoped I could, after these last days passed, rid myself of the mad priest.

Chapter 22

In what I knew to be a short time, but which felt more like an eternity, my chair arrived. Slowly, so as to give the illusion of uncertain footing and of drunkenness clouding my head, I plunked myself on the seat. I leaned back in a somewhat precarious position with every intention of remaining that way until the bearers set the chair down inside the sanctuary. Unpleasant it might be to fear that every step taken by my bearers could toss me out of the chair and onto the floor, but nowhere near as much as it would to be caught out in the travesty of a god in which I now indulged.

I had never witnessed such crowds in the temple before, not even on the night Tlazolt danced with her dark spirit. It appeared that every bit of space had been filled with frightened, restless people who awaited miracles from the god. Even had it been as cold as the Italian mountains in winter, I should have been atremble and sweating on my throne chair. I realized that just one false step could lead to my assassination by any one of the crowd in the great hall.

As my glance roamed around the huge room it fell on Ku Po with whom I had not spoken for some days. The king's chief counselor stared at me as though studying me with great intensity. That caused me some concern. Even as I worried about seeing him, I sensed that something troubled the counselor as well.

I felt torn between a desire to acknowledge his presence and the fear that such a move might betray me. He stood beside the throne which remained empty. He wore a cap-like headdress composed of cut off multicolored feathers woven to fit as a helmet. This feather helmet had been further adorned with a molded bird's head, its beak sharp and feral, its gaily colored feathers interspersed with and emphasized by shiny black plumes that appeared to threaten the multicolored ones they encircled.

I thought how like this land that juxtaposition appeared, the beauty of intense color against the blackness of the jungle and the spirits which inhabited it. I permitted my eyes to move around the assembly and whenever they happened to light on Ku Po I caught him staring. He seemed to be trying to understand something about me.

I attempted to sort out from his demeanor whether or not he believed my charade or if instead he saw through me. In my attempts to live two separate lives on a day-by-day basis how much, I asked myself, did I actually reveal to the man during our clumsy conversations? I shrugged and the feathers of my cloak lifted and floated as if in a breeze, surrounding me in an aura of many colors.

I forced my eyes and thoughts away from him. I did not make the mistake of believing him a fool. He displayed a considerable gift of diplomacy which I saw him use a number of times, and recognized even when I understood little of the facts of the case. A sense of intelligent power enveloped him and inspired confidence in his observers despite the few occasions I had seen him appear to waver in the presence of the dark spirits that he neither recognized nor understood. At such times, he appeared more like a diplomatic neophyte than the sophisticated man I knew him to be.

Finally deciding to acknowledge him, I permitted a small nod the next time I caught his gaze on me. I tried not to look too alert but permitted an indication that I knew where I was and possibly why. If he wished to help me at all I hoped he had caught the silent message. If there should be a serious conflict between me and Theon I dared chance that Ku Po would find little reason to support the Baal priest, who had come here as an intruder and attempted to change their whole world.

My bearers now carried me to the throne chair beside Ku Po, usually reserved for the king.

He leaned toward me and whispered, "Strange rumors have been flying through the palace. His majesty Tu Topiltzin asked me to come tonight in his stead, O great Lord. I am here to assure that your subjects do not fail to recognize who and what you are."

I nodded my head at his words. I did not understand exactly what they implied in this situation but I felt grateful to have the ku present. I turned slightly away from him and watched the activities in the great room.

The temple musicians, who had been playing quietly in the background, now picked up the tempo and volume of their performance and sounds began to vibrate along the stone walls. Dancers appeared from the sidelines and began to move across the platform with short choppy steps. The girl performers wore long, colorful skirts and brightly patterned shawls that floated around them. The males wore only loincloths which remained solidly fixed in place despite their athletic antics on the dance floor. The worshippers in the great audience hall began to sway in rhythm with the temple dancers, hopping as well as they could in the crowded space and with the debris from the shaking of the earth still covering much of the floor. Even from my chair I could see that many people, still moving with the dancers, continued to look above and around the great hall stiffly poised to tune if necessary.

The singing and dancing continued for a considerable time then Theon strode out from the right rear of the altar, clad now in a jaguar skin with the fur formed into a hood covering his head. He looked taller than usual, perhaps because of the cat headdress. He moved with unusual grace as if he challenged the dancers in their own milieu.

He swirled around in front of the altar a couple of times then turned toward me. In two long strides he approached my chair.

"Ari", he whispered. "I am gratified that you chose my way."

A small smile quivered on his lips.

Before I could reply he added, "I will see to it that your friend does not suffer when his moment of sacrifice arrives."

I half opened my mouth to reply then realized that Theon had not yet learned of Isaac's escape with the boy and my Egyptian friend. Joy rose in my heart. So far my friend was safe.

"In the meantime, enjoy the rituals, my son. I believe you will find them most entertaining."

I began to relax, ignoring the tremors that had resumed their activity. At first, the movement appeared to make the temple floor dance in an almost friendly manner. The faces of most citizens relaxed their strained expressions, but a number of people continued to stare upward toward the roof of the temple, showing unease despite the temporary quiescence of the floor.

Then suddenly, with a great lurch, the floor and walls

began to move hard and fast, first side to side followed by up and down turbulence which reminded me of the sea during the massive storm that threatened to kill us on the sea. Large parts of the roof structure and walls began to crumble and large blocks of walls fell on the bodies of those caught too close to the failing walls.

Screams vibrated from all sides and areas of the temple. The bodies of the dancers, including those still waiting for Tlazolt, stumbled and fell. The cries of many people failing to keep their feet in the great room of the temple overcame all sounds from the musicians as if the people's voices now provided music for the dancers who continued to drop to the floor with each menace from the earthquake.

Then as suddenly as it began the shaking and tilting of the floor stilled, leaving the temple in chaos and the fallen trampled more by feet than by masonry.

My chair and Ku Po's seemed impervious to the

agitation of the structure of the temple. Citizens continued to flee. Friends and families of the injured helped each other to stumble through the doors and begin their stumbling trek down the great staircase, one or two half carrying an injured one. Bloody and frightened, many residents continued their escape, all the while looking about them as if to watch for any further attack by the elements.

I looked around the huge sanctuary for growing signs of tragedy and could not avoid the bodies remaining on the floor. Several temple workers, seemingly unable to alter their routines despite the drama of the earthquake, began to pull bodies out of the middle and sides of the floor, clearing a large space in the middle, and more near the doors to the inner precincts of the great building. It looked as if Theon refused to accept the evening plans as either fulfilled or needing to be abandoned. He strode among those dancers still on their feet and uninjured, demanding in broad gestures that the performance continue.

After Theon's confident words and my knowledge of Isaac's escape I felt assured that all my friends had reached the safety of the ships. That certainty comforted me and made it possible for me to continue my masquerade. A few more minutes and I would leave to join them. In the meantime, I must maintain my calm and restore my aura of certainty and awareness, as if totally cognizant of the source of the quakes. Only then could I show myself as Quetzalcoatl for those citizens who chose to stay in the temple after the destruction that left so many dead or injured.

That conviction enabled me to release much of the tension in my back and shoulders and rest against the padded throne. Whatever Theon had arranged for this night's entertainment I would not abandon or permit to sidetrack me from the course I had set. Shortly, with only a small dose of good fortune, I would join my family and we would be on our way home.

Theon sang a song in the native language then swung

away toward the much diminished chorus. He laid a hand on each singer and followed the gesture with a new song. That done, he left in the same direction he had arrived. He seemed oblivious to the injured and the destruction of the temple, so wrapped up was he in his hopes and plans that already crumbled around and beneath him as a terminated project might be.

Right after Theon left the sanctuary I sensed a slight movement in the curtains behind and to the right of my throne. Casually, as if by inadvertence, I permitted my head to turn in that direction. The boy Joseph had returned from escorting Isaac to the ship. He looked eager to convey some message to me but I could not think of a way it could be accomplished. I had no choice but to remain in the chair and give every outward sign of indifference toward what went on around me.

I looked directly at Joseph in an attempt to let him know I had got at least part of his message. Isaac got safely away. What I could do about any other question was another thing entirely. As if in direct reply to my inner question, Ku Po stood up abruptly and left the sanctuary. One of Theon's minions stepped forward and spoke briefly. All I could garner from his words was that a brief cessation of the ceremony would now take place but for what reason I did not understand.

The bearers assisted me to my palanquin and made their stately way from the huge space room and returned me to the robing room we had departed to enter the sanctuary.

Ku Po waited there near the child Joseph. His presence made me uneasy. I did not know him well enough to predict how he might receive what I planned if he found out about it.

The ku said a few words in the careful way he always spoke to me.

"My Lord", he said. "There has been a delay in the ceremonies to await the arrival of the dancer Tlazolt and her accompanist." He shook his head in a marveling way. "It is well that the king did not come. He would not be pleased at such an interruption."

Just then a dull grumbling roar passed through the temple and the floor beneath our feet began a slow, stately undulation. Somewhere in the near distance I heard the crash of falling masonry and could only wonder what had fallen and what else would do so. I looked at Ku Po and saw that he was as frightened as I. His face twisted as if to battle the fear that overtook him.

Incoherent cries flew at me from every corner of the slowly disintegrating sanctuary. Even as the movement ceased, walls and parts of the roof continued to drop to the floor, often hitting a citizen as it fell. Spurting and flowing blood began to take on the aspect of a small freshet from the mountain, but red instead of clear.

I forced panic from my heart and my face as I confronted Ku Po.

"Why do we wait for the girl, Ku Po? There are many other dancers in the temple already and some of them easily rival her in skill."

His announcement distressed me more than I wished to acknowledge. Did it have anything to do with my friends, with my wife? I felt impotent remaining in the temple while there was a strong possibility that my people were once again endangered.

"The dancer", he continued, "journeyed toward the mountains to worship the goddess of fire and earthquake. It transpired that the insecurity of the ground and the many separate streams of liquid fire from the mountain made it nearly impossible to pass. In fact", he went on, "the runner she sent ahead us told us that there is actual danger to the girl and her entire entourage and they had to turn back. We have no assurance they will arrive at all."

While I did not wish her ill I felt relieved that she might be delayed long enough for me to remove my retinue and myself from this terrifying land. Without understanding much about why, I felt certain that she represented danger to me and mine.

Even as the ku and I talked together I could feel the earth move once again. This was followed by more falling masonry and accompanied by the cries of terrified men and women who struggled against the movement and the large pieces of rock that nearly covered the massive floor.

The room we were in seemed to lurch like someone suddenly released from restraints. Small offertory objects began to drop from shallow niches along the previously unaffected walls near where I waited on my throne. As the little figures started to crumble so also paint began to fall from large pictures covering walls of the room, leaving incomplete and scrubbed looking pictures of my purported exploits. I watched colors drop onto the floor so I sensed what would happen to me should I be so foolish as to remain a moment longer than necessary.

I said to the ku, "It is time you left. I am convinced that this whole segment of the roof will collapse very soon.

Ku Po answered strangely. "You are not a god, are you? You are just a man elevated by the priest as a god by his proclamation. Is that not correct?"

His words hit me with a blow akin to having a great weight dropped on me from above. My knees buckled and I waited with tightly held breath for him to call the guards. Beneath my feathered cloak my hand slid along the edge of Rem-Na's blade, brought me by Senmut.

If necessary, I would slice Ku Po from breastbone to lower belly in an attempt to protect my wife and friends. Even as the thought came to me I regretted that it actually could become unavoidable. I felt a kind of kinship with Ku Po, whom I admired as a man of singular integrity. Nevertheless, I would kill him in a moment if I had to do so.

"It never was my intention to deceive your people, Ku Po. Theon, ever my nemesis, took advantage of an illness that attacked me as we arrived here. By the time my fever subsided I had already been acclaimed a god and my wife a goddess."

I let my head drop to indicate my shame at my part in the deception.

"Ever since then I have been trying to find a way I can leave with my friends and my wife without destroying the faith of your people."

Ku Po did not respond immediately but watched my face closely as if to find there the answers he needed.

"I believe you. From the beginning I had my doubts but did not dare indicate them in any way. I still do not know how much the king may have been deceived by your priest." He stopped and looked at me a few moments. "He is still very young, you know, with little experience at diplomacy." He paused. "It is my job to help him through his training in kingship." He sighed. "It is not always easy to teach someone so young and sure of his power.

He remained silent a while and when he spoke it was with strength and certainty. He became again the strong leader I saw when I first landed on these shores.

"I will do all I can to assist you. How do you intend to go about leaving, with the whole city up and moving around at this late hour?"

"I have a plan, a good plan that actually may be aided on this night by the earthquake and the flying fire." I stopped and looked carefully at Ku Po. "Do you intend to betray me?"

Gazing into the blackness of his eyes I tried to fathom their depths, their truth. As deep and as dark as they were I thought I could see some light far back in them where his essence must reside. Even as I watched I saw that light move outward toward the blackness of his eye color. Where the color had been opaque and heavy like a curtain between us it now seemed to brighten and the black changed to a warm brown. I could not know if his eyes actually altered color or if it were an illusion only I could discern, but from that moment I knew I could trust him.

"Ku Po, you must take your family and leave the city tonight before it collapses and there is no place to run."

His countenance dropped. "My family is gone. The last great shaking hit our neighborhood especially strongly. I was with the king but my family was at home. My sons had their tutor and my daughter stayed with my wife in her room." He paused to clear his throat.

Uncomfortable now, I suspected I knew where his words would go.

"The entire house came down during a huge tremor that appears to have lifted it up and thrown it back down as one might a piece of pottery during a tantrum. No one and nothing came out alive. We sifted through the leavings but found only death."

He lifted his head slowly and his eyes, now tragic, looked squarely into mine.

"I have been in mourning ever since and would not have come here tonight had not the king asked me especially. By now he has fled either to the north or the west. When he is safe he will send a runner to find me and lead me to the location of his new court."

"Where will you go tonight to escape the devastation?"

"I will join those who head north away from the rivers of fire. I have already packed up some of my easily carried valuables and can leave as soon as the city's destruction looms imminent."

He paused to swallow something that clogged his throat then continued.

"The king has instructed me to save myself. He demanded that I not try to save the inhabitants of the city and put my own life in danger. I will change my clothes and blend in with the mob so not to tempt thieves and other offal that join in such exiles as this to rob those who flee."

"It may be you can join me on my ship for the first part of my journey. We plan to head north, hugging the coast as long as possible before we turn back into the great ocean. We can leave you off near a settlement where you there is refuge."

He smiled for the first time in the midst of all this chaos.

"I have never been closer to a ship than watching yours from the shore. I have never been on top of the water or propelled by it in any way. I frightens me, but appeals as well. I think I would like that."

He rubbed his hands together as if washing them of the past. "Time is slipping away from us. Let us put your plan into action."

Just as we began to discuss implementing the plan one of the guards entered, looking flustered. He bowed low before me with a slightly bemused look as he caught us talking together as acquaintances.

Ku Po also bowed before me and touched my hand in submission. In that moment I could have lost all, including my life. A brief word from the ku could have brought destruction on me as rapid as from the earthquake and the fire.

Instead, a deep and reverent bow from the ku stabilized my quivering body and I felt more confident than I ever had done.

Bowing with his eyes downcast so not to look in my face, the guard spoke.

"Oh, Lord, the priest Theon sent me to return you to the sanctuary. He says it is time for the ceremony to proceed."

Shock rushed through me like an uncontrolled spring flood. I had allowed all thought of Theon and his ceremonies to fade into the background. Had I gone insane, I wondered.

I stood up and permitted the servants who also entered to groom me and straighten my headdress for my appearance as

Quetzalcoatl.

Meeting my eyes, Ku Po bowed and said, "Great one, go in peace and minister to your subjects."

Still stunned from recognition of my folly, I stood and walked carefully to the palanquin that had now arrived with its bearers. I longed to ask the guard how much destruction had taken place from the shaking of the city, but I dared not. The god should not need to seek such knowledge from a mere mortal. I shrugged. Possibly, I would learn soon enough.

As we neared the sanctuary a maelstrom of movement and sound reached me. It made me fidget because I did not know why so much noise and confusion now reigned there. I did not even dare ask about it. All I could do was wait, while the guards lowered my chair to receive me then do my best to figure it out. My heart pounded rapidly and I felt sweat break out on my face and run down my back. My limited understanding of the language and my deliberate ignorance of the customs left me incapable of understanding the rituals in any depth.

We entered the voluminous space of the sanctuary. Bits of masonry and small clouds of dust continued to fall from the roof, mingled with grasses that dropped from the rafters. Despite the chaotic atmosphere inside the temple most of the people remained, perhaps hoping that my presence would bring them deliverance.

When my bearers carried me past them I could hear murmured prayers as the people reached out to me, begging for mercy. Uncharacteristically for me, I tried to listen to their pleas. I wished I could tell them to run for their lives because I expected the city to die any minute. But I could not. In my heart I measured their lives against those of my people and decided that the ones I had promised protection came before the ones who lately desired assurances from me. However, I knew I would do what I could to help these innocent ones even if I possessed no power to alleviate their dangerous situation.

In my helplessness I watched as Ku Po re-entered and stood beside the king's empty chair. He caught my eye and smiled slightly as if he were offering me comfort, which he may have been doing.

Before I could smile back the music began, great swirling sounds punctuated by drums whose reverberations called to the earthquake noise, air to earth, as the floor once more began its mad vibrations. Then, from the far left side of the platform, as if she did not notice as a large section of an inner wall fell to the stone floor, came the figure of Tlazolt. Her whirling movements echoed the outlandish rhythms of combined music and the cries of terrified people.

Once again she looked to emulate some of Nikkal's favorite moves as she danced alone for a short while. The girl's precarious voyage in the path of the volcano appeared to affect her not at all. Suddenly, a tall, deeply black figure joined her and the two stepped and leapt as one around the stage, once more appearing to enter each other's essence then separate as before.

The tempo of the music twisted and increased until it became a violent crescendo. Then it stopped as suddenly as it had begun. Tlazolt ceased her mad dance. Her partner disappeared even as I watched him, but I could not see where he went. Frustration struck me when I attempted to observe him as he disappeared before my straining eyes. It mattered nothing how hard I looked. He could not be seen. I finally had no choice but to surrender to the clear impossibility of following the dark dancer with my eyes. He proved far too elusive for my vision.

From the passage whence I entered trumpets now began to cry out their blaring notes. Like a deer before a bowman I remained transfixed. Confusion gained the upper hand.

Behind the trumpets came a palanquin of jewel encrusted gold, dazzling to the eyes after the blackness of

Tlazolt's performance. Seated on the chair, her figure clothed in pure white to show off the glorious red-gold of her hair, her pale complexion almost transparent in the gloom of the darkened temple, Helen entered into the sanctuary. As the white goddess of their prophetic religion she could not have been more perfect. Even her pale garments, covered with jewels, floating around her as the chair swayed attested to her ethereal being.

Ku Po, ever the diplomat, rose from his chair beside the throne and gestured to Helen's bearers. They obeyed his unspoken demand and Helen seemed to float from the palanquin to the chair he had vacated beside the throne. So beautiful and elegant that the sight of her made me wish with my entire being to turn the flow of time backward that I might make amends. I wished I could offer her a rightful place in my life. But alas, it may be too late. I could see no way to escape the violent death Theon planned for me and likely for Helen.

The many months since Nikkal's death when I stubbornly chose to ignore Helen, punish her for surviving when Nikkal did not, now brought me sorrow I could scarcely contain. I waited too long before accepting its reality.

The ku moved to stand behind her as if in testimony to the import of her presence. From my seat on the other side of the throne, I could only watch her with the pain of despair in my heart. I wanted to weep. Had all my plans come to naught? Had Helen become hostage to keep me in line?

If not, did she realize that she had placed herself in a most precarious position by coming here to the temple at this time of unrest and collective terror? Could she not feel the ground beneath her tremble in preparation for the massive movement I believed would occur very soon?

She whispered something and the ku leaned down to hear her words. Ku Po then walked over to me and spoke in my ear.

"She suggests that the two of you leave your chairs simultaneously and hand-in-hand present yourselves to the gathering as if this were a customary occurrence. I think it to be expedient that you do this and that the two of you promenade a few minutes in front of the altar."

He sighed. "If it works it will moderate much of the power of Theon's plans." He added, "Then together you must be carried from this part of the temple in your chairs. When you reach your apartments you will find clothing for both of you that will help you blend in with our people. You must head for the ships immediately after changing."

I noticed the child Joseph in his hiding place. He had pulled away from the wall where he had waited for my next move.

His eyes rounded with combined fear and excitement. Even in the midst of all the confusion around us, I recognized that this day was certainly different for the boy. Never before could he have so much as hoped for anything like what had overtaken him here in the temple. I sensed fear in him that we would all leave him and abandon him to whatever fate awaited the city's inhabitants.

Chapter 23

Helen and I did our stately half dance in front of the people, who appeared thunderstruck by her beauty and our presence among them. Never before had one of their gods done such a thing. So effected were they that not a sound, not even an indrawn breath could be heard.

When it seemed expedient I escorted my wife from the main sanctuary. I looked back over my shoulder and saw Theon watching us, helpless to interfere. It would not be to his benefit to stop us or give even the slightest appearance of shock or dismay.

As soon as our chairs reached the robing room, I signaled our weary bearers to let us down then dismissed them, telling them I would send someone to the bearers' room when I needed them. Their exhaustion clearly superseded any desire to know my reasons for their lengthy rest and the change in plans.

As we stepped from the palanquins I was accosted immediately by Joseph who had run behind us, cleverly keeping just out of sight of our bearers. He jabbered away in his language with its peculiar sounds. Too exhausted even to try to understand him, I shrugged in frustration.

He spoke again. His small body tensed with his attempt to communicate with me. I could only watch him with eyes that saw too little and a mind that could not process his words.

Then Helen spoke.

"He said that Isaac urges you to hurry. He fears that Theon may have grown suspicious, especially as your friends have left their apartments in the old temple and he knows not where they have gone. He is sending a guard of soldiers to seek them in all the rooms of the temple there and in this one, as well."

His eyes rounded with combined fear and excitement. Even in the midst of all the mess around us, I recognized that this day was certainly different for the boy. Never before could he have so much as hoped for anything like what had overtaken him here in the temple. I also sensed fear in him that we would all leave him and abandon him to whatever fate awaited the city's inhabitants.

Helen, who now busily engaged in changing her attire, spoke to Joseph. While I myself could understand very little, I realized that Helen had used her time well and learned much of the language.

"I assured Joseph that he could come with us. He appears to be alone in the world. I can learn more later but for now that is about all I got from him. He will accompany us to the old temple and stay with us there until we can leave."

I signaled my agreement. I could not in conscience leave the boy behind. With the city under siege from the forces of nature and the urgency of the city's inhabitants he would almost certainly be killed. I smiled at him and that small gesture seemed to fill him with the pleasure of recognition, of acceptance. He rushed over to help me remove my cloak and headdress. He displayed great eagerness to assist me off with the ceremonial robes and on with those of a local merchant.

Helen's new wardrobe consisted of an embroidered skirt and a loosely woven top. Because her glorious hair had to be hidden it would be tightly covered by a many colored shawl that she pulled close under her chin to show me. No one seeing her hair would fail to recognize her. For the rest, her new skirt and tunic looked like those worn by the women who sold items in the marketplace. Up close, she would deceive the townspeople well enough if she kept her head down and walked like a much older person.

I nodded at Helen, who nodded back. Then I bowed my head once more at Joseph, a signal that we were ready. I might not have the knowledge of his language to instruct him with words but my years of military experience served me well in the area of unspoken instructions. The boy apparently understood and took a position beside and slightly in front of me with Helen tucked in behind me so I could protect her should the need arise.

No one attempted to stop us as we began the slow descent of the stairs. The ground beneath the temple continued to move sporadically from time to time as we walked down, down, down, always closer to the well where the dead held sway. At the lower platform where the flung bodies entered the dark waters, I permitted my eyes to shift in that direction. My usual attitude when I passed that place was to ignore it and refuse to acknowledge the existence of the well of death. On this occasion I forced myself to look there, determined as I was to overcome my fear and disgust.

Bodies continued to float up toward me with each tremor of the land, seeming to remind me that they had lived as I now did. Then they dropped deeper into the water like divers eager to touch bottom. As each body began its progress toward the lower reaches of the well another surfaced to replace it. Dismayed but determined not to show fear, I looked more closely as body after body, some freshly killed and others with only a little flesh clinging to the skeletal remains came and went.

I shivered and prepared to turn away when a newly dead body seemed to push its way ahead of the others, demanding my attention. I blinked. Was it possible? I asked myself. Surely, not. The corpse turned my way a little bit and I saw the face clearly. It was the countenance of King Tu Topiltzin. I stared at it unbelieving. As the body shifted slightly, I could see a massive wound on the back of the head as if a great rock or wall had crushed it from above. How could such a thing be? Ku Po told me the king had escaped into the interior and sent him messages almost daily. If that were so, how could his lifeless body show up in the well of the dead?

As I watched, the king's body slowly turned head down in the water and began its decent into the nether world. While I understood almost nothing, I did realize that much was happening in that city and that my ignorance could cost me my life. Perhaps I only imagined it was Tu Topiltzin's face I saw.

I asked Helen, "Do you trust Ku Po? Can I trust him?"

She gave me a hard, questing look as if aware that my inquiry bore greater import than a casual conversational device.

"I have always considered him a man of integrity. Do you doubt that?"

"I no longer know who can be trusted. People seem to come and go even within their own skins and some even appear to blend into one another."

I cut my words off abruptly. We had reached the

street leading to the secret entrance into the temple.

Joseph had been dawdling along examining this section of the city which was new to him. Now he caught up with us.

I half-whispered, my words meant for him as well as for Helen.

"We must be alert now for guards or temple staff who would recognize us or even question two strangers in the vicinity of the inner temple. All our hopes and plans depend on getting back unseen and hopefully unmissed."

Helen nodded without speaking, her eyes frightened. This side of the building was in shadow, faintly illuminated by the light from the increasingly present river of fire. The molten river had advanced toward the city since I left my home in the night hours. The powerful odors of heat and liquid metals had increased while we were away and seemed to surround and envelope us.

I located the door, almost hidden in the wall of great

stones. It moved sluggishly as I struggled to open it and it resisted. The earthquake had shifted it just enough to strain my strength. Joseph joined me and together we put our backs to the door. As small as he was he possessed considerable strength. Even as we worked together I shuddered at the thought of what would happen to the boy had we not met and had he not joined us in our venture. At last, the door opened enough for us to squeeze through. All we had to do was find our way through the maze of lower corridors to our apartments, while not allowing Joseph to be seen and captured by the remaining guards.

I could only hope that my experiences of the day thus far had not robbed me of my memory map of the corridors which Isaac had planted in my mind. But I need not have worried. Instinct took over where my detailed memory failed.

When we finally reached our access to the corridor near my apartment, I felt wrung out like a cloth squeezed and then left damp and lifeless. Helen and I removed our disguises before we entered the hallway near the apartment. I was left with only a loincloth to cover me but Helen had layered her garments over a thin white dress which now clung wetly to her flesh. Joseph, of course, wore no disguise and looked as he always did. We left our escape clothing inside the door to the stairs that led to the labyrinthine passages below. They remained ready for us to use when we left the temple for the last time on our way to the ship

Helen headed for her apartment while I entered mine. The rooms seemed basically unchanged although several walls had partially crumbled and left places where there was nothing between the gap and the roof. A few statuettes and trinkets had disappeared, quite likely broken during a heavy tremor. No debris spread itself around on the floor or elsewhere, a testimony to the faithfulness of the temple servants even in so precarious a time.

The floor still moved sluggishly and frequently as if it

had become natural for the ground beneath us to move and shift like water. Almost, it felt as if I had already boarded my ship and the sensation produced a kind of dissociation from my life here in the temple while not yet connected to my quest for a new one. I might have continued to muse on this thought for some time longer had not Joseph called my attention to new sounds in the corridor outside.

While I could not interpret his actual words, the sense of them was clear. Someone or some ones now headed toward my apartment. I signaled Joseph to conceal himself behind some hangings that still remained on the wall despite the quaking of the city. He disappeared.

Suddenly, Theon entered.

"Aribaal," he said in a demanding voice. "Why did you leave the temple? How did you leave? Your palanquin bearers told me you dismissed them. Why?"

All that came forth in a gush from his mouth.

"And where is your wife? Did she return here with

you?"

In a quiet voice which I hoped might both calm and deceive him, I replied, "We both came. On foot. Helen is in her apartment right now, changing her clothes."

I sighed in feigned exasperation.

"I believed it had grown too dangerous to be borne through the streets right then. People were desperately afraid and were likely to strike out at anyone, especially someone being carried while the very streets threatened to collapse beneath the city dwellers feet. I thought the old temple would be safer for her."

Theon settled down a little.

"Perhaps that was wisdom. You are correct in thinking that unrest has begun to reign in the city. People run around like ants whose hill has been stirred with a stick. I will consider your alternative ideas as I return to the new temple."

He stopped briefly then continued, "I expect you to

return as soon as you can get dressed. Your official robes and headdress are still in the temple where you left them. It did not please me that you left without informing me. All the musicians and dancers await your return. It is time for the sacrifice."

I felt the blood drain from my face. I wanted to ask him about the sacrifice. Had Isaac been recaptured? Did Theon have someone else in mind? I had no answers and dared not question the priest.

He turned in that half-dance he had acquired recently and left, his robe swirling around his legs. I knew he would never consider walking through the city. It was certain that his chair awaited him, probably with armed guards to protect him and awe the citizens as he passed. I doubted that he would encounter any danger. Was he not Pe Gyo, the worker of wonders? None would dare lay hands on him.

Relieved and happy, I watched as he left, escorted by a number of fierce looking warriors with painted faces and very dangerous weapons. Even if some of the citizens might question his powers to themselves they would never challenge him or his escort. The incident involving Theon's arrival in my apartment, however, provided a push to move me and my wife to hurry to the seafront.

With Joseph as companion we set out together in the disguises we wore when we fled the new temple. We walked quickly, at times nearly running as we moved toward the waterfront past destroyed houses and dodged the rubble that had accumulated on all sides. Dismayed, I feared that our desperate journey through the city became impossible to complete. If we were not betrayed, the danger would not lessen when we stumbled and staggered over and around streets that had transformed into traps for injured and weary feet.

I wore Rem-Na's dagger and his short sword, hoping I would have no need of them. Our way led us through the marketplace to reach the ships. Those places with their nearly destroyed businesses and panicked residents threatened us with exposure far more than I wished. Even covering our hair and faces might not prove adequate. I needed to depend upon the busyness of the merchants who stayed back a little too long and now needed to gather what they and their servants could carry and head north as quickly as possible.

Helen walked hunched over like an elderly woman. It must have been excruciating for her to scramble around the rubble and keep away from those building materials which continued to break off and fall around us, while also keeping her head down and her back bent. But, wonderful woman that she was, she managed somehow.

We were but a short way from the water when I heard a man call out, "Hey. Are you one of the men who arrived with our god? Where are you going?"

I ignored him, hoping he would be discouraged and go away if I did not reply. However, he chose not to cooperate but rather came closer to see me better. I ducked my head even lower, to hide myself from his gaze. He moved closer. As he attempted to look into my face I shrugged away, my many-colored cloak falling from my head to my shoulders. He looked at me and a shocked expression came to his face.

He fell to his knees on the rubble, ignoring the pain he must have felt when his legs contacted the sharp pieces of masonry.

"Quetzlcoatl!" he cried out in a wondering voice. "Have you come to save us?"

He started to stand as if to call others to see me. Panicked, I acted out of instinct rather than reason. In one swift move, I pulled the dagger from my waist rope and quickly slit his throat. As his life poured out, he made one gurgling sound then died.

I felt tears gather in my eyes. I had killed this man who wanted only safety and a blessing from me. Yet even as

I took his life I knew that he must go if my friends and Helen were to remain alive. I pulled my cloak back over my head, wiped the knife on some fronds growing beside the street and gestured Helen and Joseph on. They moved more quickly now, not so careful to avoid the rubble. Joseph cast one last glance at the dead man then ran to us. Helen put a hand on his shoulder and held him close to her as they struggled side by side to reach the harbor.

Behind us I could hear a commotion and I guessed that the man I murdered had been found. I said a silent prayer to all the known gods for the hope of an afterlife. I did not know if I truly believed in an afterlife or not, but I thought it likely that he did. I did not worry a great deal about pursuit by those who discovered the man. They had enough to cope with in their attempts to flee the fires.

Even so, my heart hammered like a fist pounding on a heavy door. For a moment I feared I might die. It was not the people I feared. But I did not wish to enter into combat with any god, especially one who appeared and disappeared

seemingly at will.

Chapter 24

We now drew near the sea. I smelled its salty freshness at moments when the smoke cleared slightly and the metallic odor of the river of fire blew away from me. Even that slight hint of sea increased my desire to push harder and faster. I glanced behind me. Both Helen and Joseph had increased the tempo of their flight to match mine. This close to the water there were fewer buildings and those that did exist stood lower and clung to the land in a way the higher construction in the city could not.

Joseph ran to catch up with me. Pointing, he cried, "Ships."

He ducked around me and began to run toward the shore.

"Joseph, come back", I yelled.

I realized I had not spoken in his language, but it was enough to catch his attention. He turned and I waved him back to me.

"You can't just run to the ships, Joseph. We do not know what has happened since we last had contact with our men."

He looked confused and I nodded to Helen to translate for me.

As she spoke to him in his language I fought a battle within myself. I wanted as much as the boy did to run to the shore and get aboard my ship. Reason won the battle and I hung back from the water and slightly behind a small outbuilding as I observed the shoreline near our ships.

I watched many people struggle to walk along the water's edge, laden with as many of their possessions as they could carry. I guessed that these newly homeless ones would cling to the beaches as long as possible before setting out into the great forests inland to pursue their way north. Mothers carried infants while larger children walked as closely as they could to their families. Clearly, this was no time to wander away from each other. Their brightly colored garments acted like banners of encouragement to each other and as symbols of their refusal to submit to the powerful forces of nature. Some even sang while they bent under their loads, their voices suppressed, but clear and very beautiful.

Near our ships a group of warriors stood in a casual looking group. Despite their relaxed postures, their weapons stayed close at hand. I did not know if they remained there to protect the refugees in transit, to protect us and our ships or even to prevent us leaving.

I called Helen to me.

"I need information", I said. "See if Joseph can get close enough to learn what those men are doing. If they are a threat I must know that."

She gestured Joseph to her and they had a somewhat protracted conversation. Obviously, Helen was struggling with her ability to communicate with the boy. At last, he grinned and called out. "Yes."

While I was reluctant to send him into possible danger, I knew his peril to be much less than ours if we tried to approached the ships without first doing a careful reconnaissance of the shore and the streets nearby.

Without looking back, Joseph meandered toward the beach. His casual posture illustrated even to my eyes a child with a desire to join anyone who might welcome him. He joined up with a small group of families coming upon the strip of shore nearest our small fleet. I could watch him talk to the family nearest him then he slowed down and approached the warriors who stood there, holding their poisoned spears in a relaxed manner, yet alert and able to move in the blink of an eye.

He spoke with them a few minutes, singling out one especially fierce looking man with the most colorful body paint of them all. They spoke and laughed together then the guard waved a hand along the beach. It seemed clear he was explaining something to the boy. Joseph nodded. He made a brief reply, laughed again then gestured toward the group he had joined. He turned and hurried toward them as though he were a family member afraid to be separated from the rest.

Helen now sat on the ground, her garments gathered tightly around her as if to protect her. Leaning against one wall of the building, she kept her head down while various people passed by, oblivious to her plight. To my eyes she looked to have dropped from exhaustion. Her posture defined her as an old woman too weak to go further.

Joseph arrived, slightly out of breath and full of excitement.

I led him to Helen and he squatted beside her. I joined them as they talked. After a long time Helen translated for me.

"They were sent there to keep the ships safe and at the same time to prevent anyone from joining those on board.

They show no hostility toward us and our people, just caution. They did not say why they are cautious."

Helen ceased speaking for a few moments then said, "Ari, I am concerned about that one who talked with Joseph. There is something about him that makes me uncomfortable and I do not know what it is."

I looked toward the warrior to see if I could discern any threat from him other than the unusually heavy body paint which he wore like armor. Suddenly he turned our way and I felt him staring at me even from so great a distance and with so many people between us.

The hair on the back of my neck rose as I watched him. I shifted away from Helen and moved a slight distance from the small building where she rested. I felt for my dagger and adjusted my body just enough to give my hands access to Rem-Na's short sword Senmut had pressed on me. I felt a rush of energy and power like that before a battle, when my body prepares itself for a life and death struggle.

I shook myself to rid myself of the terror that assaulted me so suddenly. I had fought men much larger and surely better trained than he. I successfully led Pharaoh's army against a joining together of his two most dangerous enemies and fought the cunning leopard with no more than a dagger and my bare hands.

In this case, however, I sensed an alliance of a different sort. I had to consider that the whole group of soldiers might attack me in unison and I knew I could not fight them all at once. The hairs on my neck continued to stand up in response to a warning I could not interpret. Was this some god or gods trying to communicate necessary information to me?

As I waited for a response to my inner prayers I noticed that the colorful warrior had shifted his position and emerged from the group. He headed toward where I stood, where Helen and Joseph sat. If I gestured them to flee would it initiate a confrontation with those wiry men and their long shooters of poison? If I did nothing would I condemn them to a terrible death from the poisoned arrows?

I continued to watch the painted man as he moved ever closer to where we rested. He did not walk fast, but leisurely, as if he had all the time in the world and as if the ground beneath his feet had ceased to move in its slow rolling motion. So unaffected by the unstable earth did he appear that he might be strolling in the air above the ground.

I made a hand gesture to Helen in the hope she would see and understand. Very deliberately she rose, still as if bent with age, and began a walk of the aged toward the refugees headed north. Joseph accompanied her, a bemused look on his face. I could see her lean toward him and seem to whisper though I heard nothing she said.

When I turned back, the warrior had already covered much of the ground between us. I surmised it must be an effect of the strangely colored sunshine, but as he approached, he seemed to shimmer in the harsh red daylight.

I recalled the late night dance Tlazolt and the stranger had executed in the temple when their essences appeared to move at will from one to the other. The warrior demonstrated a similar experience although no one else seemed to notice even as this transfer of essences showed so clear to my eyes. Whose essence? Why? Could no one else see this phenomenon?

My knees began to shake as I saw him come closer, the other person with him constantly slipping in and out of his body. I did not know who this spectral intruder could be but I suspected it was Tezcatlipoca. I had learned that the Tezcatlipoca Theon told me about was the brother of Quetzalcoatl in the spirit world, who in his evil heart hated his brother and had tried many times to kill him.

If so, had he now come to destroy me? Did he resent my masquerade as Quetzalcoatl? Had he transferred his hatred to me as his brother's changeling? If he came to kill me, what chance did I have against a spirit being who could change his appearance any time he wished and move in and out of another's body at will? Better than anyone else, I knew my impotence against those who ruled the nether world. Theon might be able to pass me off as an immortal to the gullible people of the nation but I knew the truth.

My role as the god was nothing but a travesty and Tezcatlipoca more than anyone else would know that. In my fear and dismay, I had no option but to await his arrival and do what I must at that time.

When the painted one got near enough that I could discern some of the images on his body, I saw across his chest the image of me both as the god and as myself. There were also pictures of Helen and the friends who had landed on these shores with me and behind them all was the outline of a ship.

My blood seemed to freeze in me as I considered the meaning of these images. Apprehension turned to anxiety and anxiety to panic as I realized their interpretation. The evil brother intended to consume all of us. In some mysterious way he planned to enter us and absorb us into himself and destroy us like so many dry leaves put to the fire.

I could not let this happen. For the first time I totally realized that I had brought this on all of us when I permitted Theon to join our excursion. I squared my shoulders to confront my enemy and attempt to do what must be done. As I inwardly prayed to all the gods I had known in my life I sensed an upheaval in the warrior's body. I was as if the earthquake which kept the ground moving so frequently beneath our feet had entered the painted body. In some incomprehensible way, I saw that body lose much of its power like an emptying bladder of nearly invisible air, leaving us on a more nearly equal footing.

The nameless one shook as one waking from a deep sleep. In a swift gesture he flung down his arrow throwing weapon and pulled a dagger from the waist of his garment. I saw or thought I saw a strange transparent bubble form around my opponent and me. It might have been made from a very sheer fabric more suitable to a dancer than a fighter. None standing near seemed to notice.

Helen and Joseph continued their ponderously slow progress toward the stream of refugees. I could see them through whatever substance surrounded the warrior and me. I wondered if I looked as insubstantial to those outside our bubble as they did to me. If I could not conquer this multi-colored warrior I would never see Helen again. That thought brought me sorrow I could not have imagined a few months ago. How foolish, I thought, to have treated this wonderful wife of mine in such an uncaring way. Would that I survive, I thought, and have the opportunity to make it up to her.

The other men who were part of the group of guardians continued their conversations as if they had not yet missed their companion. As I turned toward this ephemeral being whose countenance expressed a taunting challenge though he never spoke a word, it seemed that he and I had entered a strange world populated by only the two of us. And yet I could see and hear everything that went on in the outer world I had previously inhabited.

After what impressed me as a very long time he came toward me, not showing the dagger he appeared to hold behind his back. Before he reached me he did a slow twist that turned him around completely, exposing the oddly shaped knife he carried. It hung in the air behind him as if resting on an invisible shelf.

Seeing that magical weapon caused a fine sweat to break out on my brow. Not only did it hang there in the air with no visible support but at its end it had a small vicious hook that looked quite capable of rending apart flesh when it was pulled from a wound. Truly, this was not an individual with a heart of compassion.

His eyes glittered as he watched me react to his weapon. My first response was to jerk away from him as from a poison spitting animal. He did not follow my gesture but held steady and waited to see what I would do next. I had no doubt I had met an opponent stronger and far crueler than I.

He wasted no time. With the speed of an Egyptian cobra, he swiped at me with his vicious knife. In that miniscule fraction of a moment, I was certain I would die. With no time left at all, I attempted to accept what must be. And then it was finished. In some mysterious manner unknown to me, my body bolted from the thrusting weapon and I pivoted away with a twirling motion too fast for my mind to comprehend. Beyond my understanding, Rem-Na's dagger appeared to drag itself and my hand toward the man's chest. I was no match for the warrior's strength and skill, but somehow my hand thrust the knife into his body with a force I could not believe. It must be that some other entity guided my hand and imbued me with strength I needed to end this insane conflict.

To me, we appeared frozen in time, no longer able to

touch each other or anyone beyond the bubble. My attention wavered and I could see Helen, walking slowly after the group of refugees, still bent over to emulate extreme age and infirmity. Just in front of her trotted Joseph, occasionally glancing back to reassure him of her continuing presence.

Movement caught my eyes. This came from inside the bubble though the warrior did not change position. Instead, the painted scenes on his body began to move of their own accord. They shifted position and rotated around his torso as though moved by a disembodied hand beneath them on the skin.

Suddenly, in the center of his chest where the dagger entered appeared the image of a mountain from which rivers of fire emerged, pouring their flames over the visible parts of his body. The warrior cried out in pain as the fire continued to slide along the contours of his body. From inside the man's wound poured a mass of disgusting looking creatures, part animal and part human, and all totally evil. There were vicious insects, some reptilian and still others completely unrecognizable.

He jerked and twisted, flopped, resembling a fish caught and left out of the water to die on the alien soil. His uncontrolled movement continued for some time as I watched, powerless to move, to help him or to put him out of his misery. Then he twitched a few times and lay still. In the final moments of his agony, something dark and viscous fled from him into the ether and disappeared screaming. The warrior lay dead before my eyes. The bubble disappeared and I pulled free.

I swiveled and dashed to catch my wife and Joseph. Grabbing Helen, I dragged her with me toward the water. The rest of the warriors stood at water's edge as they had done previously and watched us with curiosity but made no move to intervene. Joseph caught up with me, his feet flying as if he might take to the air like a bird. I began to feel dizzy and my arms weak and I did not know why.

I plunged into the water and began to swim toward my flagship. The debility in my arms increased and they felt as heavy as if I bore a mass of stones in them. Floundering, I grew aware of Joseph beside me. He swam with all his youthful energy and tugged at me at the same time.

"Helen", I managed to sputter out. "Where is Helen?"

A small boat appeared beside me, Senmut in its prow, and in its reaches I could see Helen huddled on the bottom with just her head showing over the edge. Her eyes, wide and frightened, filled with tears as she watched me struggle against a force I did not understand. I could see Senmut as he moved the little boat with a tool that looked made from the shell of a huge tropical nut.

It clearly caused him to work as if moving a great load beside the small craft. Any hope of joining my friend and Helen aboard the tiny vessel fled as I realized it would be Helen or me on the boat. I nodded at Senmut to encourage him in his efforts.

"My friend", I gasped with gravely diminished breath.

He turned his head and nodded toward the flagship riding ready a short distance away. I realized that he wanted me to know he had taken on the responsibility for Helen's safety and encouraged me toward the ship. I attempted a return nod but could not be sure it came across as such.

Understanding or not, my friend continued his rowing with the makeshift oar. I found myself floundering. I did not understand why I had such trouble swimming. I had always been more than competent in the water. Was I not a Phoenician, bred for the water? Why now did my skills elude me?

I remained still a few moments to regain my faltering breath. It was then that I saw the blood release from my arm just below the shoulder. It came from a jagged hole that had opened the door of my body and permitted a massive flow of blood. Even in a brief glance I knew that the painted warrior had made contact with his vicious knife and that my life forces had now been exposed to the sea.

I turned onto my back and rested a moment. There seemed little point in struggling. It was impossible to make headway even in so calm a sea. As I lay back and permitted my body to float loose on the water, I stared at the sky overhead, with its stripes and clouds of brilliant hues. Red in all its manifestations from the hottest yellow-red to the cooler violet-red fought for dominance, exemplified by a hot red sun. Everywhere I let my eyes rove I saw nothing but red. It seemed that the whole world had turned red while I fought for my life.

I tried once more to swim, but my strength had fled completely and left me but a piece of jetsam bobbing on the water like a powerless leaf fallen from a tree. The sky above seemed to open and in the opening I saw Carthage. I saw Elissa and Accroupi. From a corner of my eye Byblos appeared. At Etruria, my cousin Ribbida and my children stood in a circle of light and I reached out to them but they did not notice.

A hand grasped mine. I turned my head and saw Men-el and Isaac together reaching to pull me with them. Both were swimming with my exhausted body held between them by their hands. I feared that in their own tiredness they might drown trying to save me and I struggled a little to get away from their hands that felt strong as iron. My struggles were brief as I drifted away from them, the sun and the vision of my family.

Chapter 25

I awoke suddenly as if someone threw cold water in my face. I struggled to sit up. I coughed twice then realized how weak my arms, my back had grown. My body refused to obey me but remained lying back against the cushions that held me partly upright. My world seemed to rock back and forth like a mother's arms. I did not know where I rested or why.

Suddenly, as in a flash of bright light, memory returned and I asked, "Are we sailing?"

Helen's voice replied. "No. We are still in the

harbor."

She leaned over me and her face became a mask of horror.

"Somehow, Theon has stolen Isaac. He cannot be found anywhere aboard the ships. All of them have been searched to no avail."

I attempted to get up and go find my friend who had given so much for me, but my strength failed.

"Where are Rem-Na and Senmut?"

"Just outside your cabin, hoping to see you. Are you strong enough?"

"I have no choice. Send them in."

My friends entered hesitantly.

"Come. Come, my friends. I am well enough. I do not even know what happened. You must tell me."

Senmut, with much of his old fire showing in his eyes, replied.

"That warrior with the strangely painted body caught

your shoulder with his jagged knife to which he had added some sort of poison. It was not enough to kill you but it made you very sick. Fever, swelling of the arm assailed you, Ari, and you were lost in your mind for several hours. We did not know if you would live."

"How much time?"

"Only a day. After you slept your senses returned. It was during that time that Isaac went missing once again and the earthquake quieted."

At this point, Rem-Na broke in.

"We think Theon has carried him off to the new temple. He came here full of anger, screaming that you had snatched us from his grasp. While he demanded that all of us must join him in the new temple, it was Isaac he especially wanted."

He paused and waited a few moments before he went on.

"He seemed to believe you owed him Isaac as

sacrifice. He ranted a long time before he calmed down." He thought a while. "The oddest part of it is that Theon left the ship without Isaac. I watched him leave to assure myself he really was gone. I could not discern Isaac among his retinue. I do not know what happened. One minute Isaac was seated outside your cabin and the next he was not. He had simply disappeared. We looked everywhere, including our sister ships. But he could not be located."

I relaxed my body and let my mind wander at will. I remembered the flight of Tezcatlipoca's spirit from the fading body of the painted warrior. In its blackness no features could be distinguished. It appeared a flat black substance, vaguely human in shape, waving in the air. It might have been a banner of sorts, except I knew it was not. I had never seen such a thing before and my very blood felt cold as I watched. When the warrior's corpse finally collapsed just the skeleton remained. It was as if the whole man had been devoured by that foul spirit, leaving only the bones as a reminder he had ever lived.

I shook myself like a dog to force my body to move. As I recalled the terrible fate of the warrior I realized that Isaac might be the demon's next victim. Maybe Theon offered a lesser threat that I had supposed. The greatest one might be Tezcatlipoca, the eater of souls.

I finally succeeded in leaving my bed. My friends rushed to assist me but I waved them away. For a short while my legs were reluctant to bear my weight, but I stood stubborn as they stiffened beneath me. I took deep breaths to pump my body full of air, that amazing sea air that never failed to revitalize me.

I began to walk, my first steps faltering, and with each step I felt my body respond to the challenge, to my will. I could feel the breath of life flow through me as an inner wind and I gained strength with each stride. By the time I reached the ship's rail, I knew I could face any enemy Theon or anyone else sent against me, whatever the odds.

"I am ready", I said. "We must hurry. Too much time has been lost already and we do not know what has happened to Isaac in Theon's hands."

Men-el, who had remained in a corner of my cabin as guide and nurse, pulled up to his significant height and said, "There are four of us and the boy. These are better odds than we have enjoyed many times before."

I could only smile at his brave words. He, as well as I, realized we were up against a formidable force. The temple personnel remained under Theon's direct command. As well, the guards assigned by the king and full of confidence, unaware of his horrifying death, carried their lethal dart shooters and remained alert at all times.

Nor could we ignore the near certainty that the whole city sat on the verge of destruction. Even from where I stood I could easily see the vast increase in russet smoke that covered the city. The air became full of strange flakes of still hot ash that seemed to come directly from the overflowing mountain to the south. All that, combined with the intermittent quivering of the ground that still made ripples in the land, alerted us to the existence of many unfathomable perils.

Certainly Men-el recognized the dangers. He was not foolish, neither was he ignorant. He had been my closest companion and playmate my whole life, despite the fact that he had been my slave. Almost two years older than I, he had been told by my mother shortly after my birth that he would bear the responsibility for my safety. From the moment of that commission he never wavered from it. He fought by my side through many struggles, including my duel with the leopard in Egypt.

"There is no army I would as confidently keep by my side." I said. "We will swim to shore, each of us independent of the other except Joseph, who will remain with Men-el. They will protect each other and join us when we access the temple and help protect the rest of us."

I stripped to my loincloth and watched as the others did likewise. I worried a little about carrying weapons under such precarious circumstances, but could think of no other options. My knife and short sword I strapped around my legs so to reach them in an instant.

"When we reach the temple we can borrow cloaks from the storage areas. These will adequately cover our weapons for the time needed. We must make our way to the holding room for the sacrifice where we will find Isaac."

At this point, I stopped, and looked at all my friends grouped around me.

"It will be the task of Men-el and Joseph to rescue Isaac from his prison and guide him from the temple to the ship."

I looked sharply at both of them.

"This is your assignment. You both have special gifts and experience that makes you the best qualified for this assignment. You, Joseph, have already proven yourself a crafty and brave conspirator and Men-el is strong, determined and intelligent. He will not be deterred from his duty. You have Isaac's life and ours in your hands. Never lose sight of that."

Joseph's dark-skinned face with its slightly slanted eyes immediately began to glow under my praise.

"I will try to be worthy of your faith in me."

While I could not totally decipher his words, I recognized enough of them to understand their content. Men-el gestured to the boy and both slipped quietly from the ship and began to swim toward the beach. I watched them a few moments then turned them over to whichever god had responsibility for their protection.

I nodded at Senmut and he followed them into the sea. I watched his direction for a few moments then gestured Rem-Na the other way. Then I went to the helm to talk to Ben-Herold.

I caught him up on the assignments I gave the others

then I said, "If any sailors or their families that should be with us are not yet here, send a messenger to find them. If they choose not to join us have the messenger leave them in peace and rejoin the ship. I would not coerce any of our men to leave if they are content here."

"Why would they be?" asked Ben-Herold. "This world is not a good place to live. When you cannot trust the gods of this land to care even for the mountains and the rivers, it is wise to leave. The world we left behind is far more hospitable than this one."

I laughed. His words revealed his displeasure at being coerced to stay in this place. I anticipated no problem persuading him to leave.

We talked some more about our plans. Ben-Herold had his role well in hand and would be ready to cast off the moment the last of our people boarded.

"As I understand your instruction, should you be prevented from joining any of the ships.it becomes my greatest duty to get Lady Helen back to your family."

I nodded.

"Her deliverance is your greatest priority. All of my friends are very important, but none as much as my wife."

He nodded.

I trusted him greatly but just to solidify his commitment, I told him that my family would reward him generously should the alternative plan become necessary. He protested my need to promise him a reward, but I also noticed an expression of pleasure in his eyes. I did not doubt his fidelity.

I left him and went into the main cabin where Helen waited. She had removed the clothing she wore as the crone and resumed a garment from her own wardrobe.

She nodded her maid from the cabin and rose to greet me. Once again her beauty stunned me. Even the smudges beneath her eyes, testimony to the exhaustion and stress she felt, only enhanced rather than diminished her loveliness.

My heart pounded. The sight of her stirred all kinds of emotions in me. I felt an actual pain to know I had to leave her once more and might never see her again. I held her tightly and longed for just an hour before I left. But I had less than minutes, time for one quick embrace only.

Reluctantly, I let her go.

"You do whatever Ben-Herold tells you, Helen. He has my complete trust and will not fail to keep you safe."

She looked at me with eyes that glittered with unshed tears.

She smiled and nodded. I left.

Chapter 26

Ben-Herold saw me off with assurances that he
could handle his end of the job. The water had warmed
considerably since I swam toward the ship earlier. That
made me nervous as I could not understand what was
happening. Why would the sea water in the harbor turn
so warm? Would it keep getting hotter until it was
impossible to swim in it?

The city, as it emerged through the miasma of smoke
and poisonous stinks, showed as nearly empty. Most
residents had already left, fleeing north or west, leaving only
those too weak or too frightened to enter into such a perilous
flight. Many were infirm and incapable of keeping up with

the crowds. The elderly and very young clung to the crumbling remains of their homes even as more pieces plummeted from walls and rooftops. I could only grieve for those unfortunates. It grew evident that all would perish. I wished I were truly the god they thought me. Then I would have the power to reverse this catastrophe. Amazingly, the temple seemed relatively undamaged. Much of the roof had fallen onto the stairs and, I learned, some floors within the temple itself. The guards held their posts, but in an edgy manner, constantly looking overhead as if to catch the walls should they fall. In their concentration on the crumbling architecture they had little interest left for intruders. Perhaps they could not even imagine anyone wishing to infringe on the temple in such a perilous situation. They were clearly uncertain how long even they dared remain.

Evidently, word of the king's death had not reached them. I suspected such news would bring them to flee immediately and scramble to save themselves in the uncertain atmosphere of the city.

The floor suddenly lurched to my right and I nearly fell, keeping my feet only by using all my strength and determination. I glanced around. No one appeared to see me struggle against the frequent movements beneath me. Even so, I felt watched. After so powerful a jolt the remaining citizens began to run around, crying out in fear. None among them took any interest in me.

I shuddered like the city itself. Pulling my shoulders tightly together as if to form a barrier against an arrow or sword thrust, I continued on my harrowing path through the growing heaps of rubble, at last reaching the stairway.

Incredibly, the staircase remained intact and I moved to the first upward step and began the climb toward the sanctuary. I was alone on the stairs with nobody to share the flight with me. Despite what my senses perceived, an impression of scrutinizing eyes now covered me from top to bottom and I forced my mind away from such terrifying thoughts the sensation conjured up in me. There could be no doubt that I was totally exposed there, the perfect target for an assassin's arrow or spear.

I located the cell where Isaac had been imprisoned. When I passed the open door I noticed a drooping figure on the bench where previously Isaac had slumped. He neither moved nor looked up when I approached him. He kept his head in his hands as if he were blind and deaf.

"Come. I will lead you out from this prison."

His only reply was a tired shake of his head. No word escaped his mouth. He put his head down again and tried to ignore me completely.

Horrified at his seemingly total disinterest, I knew I could not allow this poor man to be sacrificed by Theon if I could prevent it. I grasped him by the shoulder, pulled and pushed him out the door. He tried to escape from me but his strength could not match mine. I shoved him ahead of me down the corridor until we reached the stairs.

I took him to the top of the stairs and gave him a gentle push to get him started. He turned and looked at me, confusion on his face. Then he started down. Hesitant at first, he gained momentum as he descended and quickly gained the ground. He glanced back at me once then disappeared among the refugees still filling the byways.

Once he had disappeared, I went back to the animal pens. I unfastened the several barriers and, dragging and pushing the weakened creatures, got them started toward whatever safety they could find. I watched as a pair of feral cats, long and beautifully colored, stopped their flight for life and began to fight each other. Weakened as they were, their strong antipathy to each other overcame their lack of strength. I left them to settle things as they must.

I shook myself free of the terrible doubts that had kept me captive for all the years since that fateful day of sacrifice at Byblos. Then I went to find Theon.

Chapter 27

Silence, broken by small unidentifiable sounds, vaulted through the corridors of the temple. Once or twice I heard the shuffling of feet on what sounded like crushed rock or maybe plaster. When I reached the robing room, for some inexplicable reason I turned in there. Laid out on a broad bench the feathered cloak of Quetzalcoatl awaited the arrival of the supposed man-god. I stood very still and stared at it for several minutes. Why had it been readied for me at this inopportune time and who did it? Even as the question formed in my mind, I knew I must wear the cloak and the headdress one more time.

The feathers seemed to wrap themselves around me as I donned it. They might almost have been living, softer and more comforting than ever before. Once properly on my body, the cape rested lighter than heretofore, almost as if the feathers had decided on their own to lift their weight from my shoulders. When I reached to position the headdress, always a challenge even to Men-el whose capable hands usually placed it there, it felt truly made for me alone. I did not understand what happened but I knew I must still follow whatever god chose to guide me.

Clad in the persona of Quetzalcoatl, I left the robing room and headed for the sanctuary just a short distance further on and on the same level as the holding rooms. As I neared the massive room I heard mumbling voices, pitched too low for me to decipher even if I knew the language. From the sound before me several people had gathered there and suddenly I was assailed with doubt.

Why had I come here? Why put on the robes of the god? Whom did I wish to impress in this temple so desecrated by vicious spirits and ruined by nature? What hope had I of doing any good? Did my coming here at this time put my family and friends in even greater peril? Should

I have fled to the ships and left Theon and the inhabitants of the city to the mercies of their own gods?

The questions in my mind generated a peculiar response. The quake, which had been mostly quiet for a few brief hours, again began to shift the temple from side to side as if trying to shake it loose from the mountain. Light from outside increased and grew redder. So glowing it became that the whole world outside looked to have burst into flame.

I arrived at the entry to the sanctuary. From the interior there came the sound of musical instruments being played while voices sang accolades to the gods who resided in this place. Theon, clad in vestments embroidered with many scenes and figures, stood quiet and expectant. I experienced a sudden presentiment that he waited for me.

Suddenly, he glanced my way and recognized me there. He threw up his arms to stop the musicians.

"My Lord, you are here." He came close and bowed deeply before me. "I began to worry that you might not come. But of course you did. It is ever your way to comply when summoned by those who need you."

I stared at him aghast. I had sought the power that guided me. Was Theon, after all, the source of that power? My knees shook and my legs protested having to hold me up.

Suddenly, the very cloak that had felt so comforting and light in the robing room grew heavy and threatened to crush me beneath its increased weight. Fighting what I knew must be an attack from some malign spirit, I straightened my legs and pushed hard against the stone of the floor almost as if I expected to rise from the room and fly out through the broken roof.

"What do you want from me, Theon?"

"This terrible disaster must be stopped, Lord. When I called it into being I had no wish that it cause such destruction."

The priest almost sobbed in his despair.

He called it into existence? How could that be?

Where would he obtain such power?

"Theon", I cried. "Look at me. I am not truly Quetzlcoatl, the god of this land. You know me. You have always known me, even in the times you so determinedly sought to take my life. I am as always Aribaal, whom you claim as son."

He ignored me as if I had not spoken.

"It is your dark brother who has brought this about, Lord. He…."

Theon's words broke off in a great sob. He looked around in panic.

"Come with me. The dancers and musicians wait. The acolytes have prepared the sanctuary."

"Prepared it for what?"

My confusion grew tremendously as I watched my enemy dash ahead of me into the resonant space. The sound of the music intensified until it vibrated throughout the room and, I thought, the temple as well.. When I entered I could see the small group of unarmed guards and temple denizens who had gathered. Most of them appeared frightened, whether of the quake, the fire or Theon I could not determine. Perhaps their terror had been generated by all of them working together.

A woman danced on the platform, her body moving in gestures that once more vaguely reminded me of my lost Nikkal. In that massively overheated room I felt my anger and resentment rise. I could only interpret the dance as a mockery of Nikkal's. The dancer was Tlazolt.

Despite all the noise they made, there were relatively few people present and these were obviously so frightened that I sensed no threat in them. Only three instrumentalists provided the music I had heard and two terrified girls the vocals. It was a travesty of the grandiose assemblies before the coming of the destruction.

I looked around for Isaac. If it were so that he had been brought here by Theon then where was he? I hesitated, torn between going after my friend and dealing with Theon and his remaining people there in the sanctuary.

I had not searched the holding cells for Isaac this time, hopeful as I was that in some way, he remained safely aboard ship. Tlazolt continued to dance, agitation replacing grace in her movements. In her frenzy, she used a small, vicious knife to make bloody cuts along her arms. Then she waved her arms to spatter her blood in the sanctuary. Theon stood motionless in the middle of the large room, his head thrown back, his eyes staring at the roof.

Had they all gone mad? The priest, the dancer, the music makers all acted as if they had no idea where they were or why. Everything seemed suspended in time, waiting for something to happen.

I knew I must take charge of these people. I suspected their very lives depended on that. Who else could herd them from the temple and start them on the way to safety?

I strode into the middle of the room and called out, "Who challenges Quetzlcoatl?"

"I do", replied a familiar voice from the doorway.

Herding a stumbling Isaac before him like an animal to the slaughter Rem-Na marched into the sanctuary. He walked as he had done those many months ago in Egypt, his head high and his back very straight.

"I challenge not Quetzlcoatl but the stateless man who has stolen his godhead from him."

When my longtime friend entered, my heart lurched so painfully that I thought I might die on the spot. Rem-Na, the friend I had trusted with my life more times that I could count. How often had we watched each other's back in battle, whether against an army or, here in this new world, against vicious spirits? Rem-Na whom I chose to represent me when I needed to meet with Ben-Herold and my other friends to plan our escape? I could not believe what I saw and heard. Who had so bewitched him? How had it been accomplished?

At his entrance the music died, so suddenly that I almost sensed the notes still hanging in the air, ready to fall like suspended decorations onto the stone floor. It felt much like my life inside the bubble when I faced the multi-colored warrior, except that this was a greater sphere of anticipation as if the whole world held its breath to see what would happen next.

"Rem-Na, my friend, why do you choose to challenge me? Who has influenced you in this way? How have I failed to prove my love for you? When have I treated you shabbily?"

He barked a short laugh.

"Have you ever really considered me, Na-Amen? Senmut you respect because he is of the house of Pharaoh. You would risk everything for Isaac because of his friendship with Accroupi. Even to your slave, Men-el, you show great respect."

Rem-Na slowed down his speech to a more normal speed and intensity. He looked about him in a confused manner. Tlazolt came to stand by him. Her newly arrived presence clearly bolstered his confidence and his voice resumed its powerful tones.

"Do you recall the times in Egypt when the whole school population was given weeks of freedom to visit their families? Senmut would run off to the royal court, Isaac joined you and your Egyptian family while I spent my time on the river, trying to reach the homes of some relatives who clearly did not treasure their opportunity to have me visit them."

He stopped and smiled a rictus of a grin. To my eyes it seemed that his long narrow face turned into a bare skull as I watched. Then it reverted to the face I knew.

He continued his aggrieved reminiscence.

"The idea came to me when you dressed me in your feathered cloak and sent me to this temple to free you from your public meeting." His angry eyes met mine and appeared to glow red from the fires outside the huge building. "It felt so wonderful to be carried through the streets while the citizens bowed before me and worshipped me. The feathered garments could not have been intended for anyone but me.

And…" he paused, "there was

Tlazolt". "Tlazolt?"

"From the start, she was mine. You had lost your Nikkal, but I had been given Tlazolt." He gestured toward the dancer. "Together we can rule this new world. I will harness Theon's powers and we will establish a new civilization in this place whose influence will overpower the whole world. Soon we can return to our old homes and bring them under our sovereignty."

My friend disappeared behind a mask of lust as his powers seemed to expand before my eyes. My hand lay on the short sword I had stuck into my waistband beneath the feathers. Could I destroy this friend who had been so overwhelmed by an evil spirit that he had no strength to fight what was happening to him? Even as I watched him I could see passing back and forth on his enraged face the black veil that signified the presence of Tezcatlipoca, and I knew I would not kill him.

I leapt toward Rem-Na, my sword held facing backward in my hand. Rem-Na, still grinning from the infused thoughts from the sorceress Tlazolt, stretched to his full height. When he did that, his head turned toward me, bent slightly to one side, exposing his features. I watched him carefully as he turned his head to a spot between Tlazolt and me. With the butt of his own weapon, I took advantage of his lack of attention and clubbed him just above his ear. The blow dropped him to the floor, instantly unconscious. I feared I had hit him too hard. As he fell I saw a long sinuous black thing exit his body and slither like a snake to the roof and outside.

Tlazolt shrieked and flung herself on me in a rage.

Her long fingernails raked my face and I felt blood flow from the wounds. The unexpected attack left me weak and shaking. It was not her physical strength that paralyzed me but the hatred that emanated from her body.

She cried out again and once more threw herself at me. But this time I acquired some degree of preparedness. I struck her with the base of my hand, catching her just at the curve of her chin, which caused her to fall beside Rem-Na with her arm flung across his chest.

I stared at the two of them, lying together like lovers and I felt tears begin to pour from my eyes. Had I lost my friend forever? Had I, in my quest to find my own real background, neglected my friend's greater need? I resolved that, should I regain his trust, I would never overlook him again.

I became aware of movement behind me and I pivoted on my left foot to face whatever had come to my back. Theon, apparently unaware of the scene before him which so devastated me, tugged at my feathered shoulder and tried to pull me toward the altar.

"Good", he said. "We are all here so the sacrifice can begin."

He nodded toward Isaac who had not spoken. Once more, my friend wore the dejected look he had the first time I found him imprisoned in this temple.

Theon finally noticed the bodies on the floor. "What are they doing there?" he asked in a plaintive voice. "Call the guards to remove them. They are no longer necessary." He waved a dismissing hand in their direction then he moved away, toward the altar. Only one acolyte and two confused looking guards remained. All others had fled when the earth moved the last time.

"It is over, Theon," I said. "There will be no sacrifice. The gods have decided on their own sacrifices."

"And who are they?" He spoke as he took steps toward me again. He stopped very close to me and I could smell the scent of strong incense on him. It reminded me of when he sacrificed me in Baal's temple and I gagged at the sickly sweet perfumed oil. I showed him my back while pointing toward the door leading to the stairway, the much touted stairway to the sun.

"Look outside and around the temple area as well. The streets and alleyways are filled with the dead, the dying and those refugees who waited too long, still hopeful of deliverance."

I nodded toward the door leading to the stairs and city below. A nauseating smell came from the open entry. It spoke of death, corruption, hot flesh and illness. Beneath all other odors I could discern the metallic signature I associated with the river of fire.

He drew himself to his full height. His face, always thin and sharp boned enough to appear nearly skeletal, pulled in on itself even more as he put his nose in the air and looked at me with contempt.

"These cannot be called sacrifices, Aribaal. They just got in the way."

"In whose way, priest?" I grabbed him by the band of his cloak and twisted the fabric a little, tightening it around that neck I had so often desired to twist like a chicken's.

I held him thus until he coughed, lacking air, and I had to loosen him and permit him to take in breath. He threw me an angry look then moved again toward the altar. Over his shoulder he admonished me.

"Aribaal, you have not yet grown into true manhood. You have lived here many months and, despite your attempts to avoid all knowledge, you must have surmised that the land is crowded with deities striving for dominance."

He continued to walk slowly as he talked. "I do not understand how you managed to deceive me, but here you stand, ready to challenge my greatness."

He stopped then pointed dramatically at his chest.

"Me. You dare to challenge me!"

He swiveled and pointed a bony finger at me.

Off to my left I sensed movement. Looking that way, I noticed that one of the guards had picked up his arrow shooter and began to lift it to kill or to threaten me.

Without hesitation, I called out, "Put down your weapon. I am Quetzlcoatl. You can do me no harm."

The bemused guard with Theon on the one hand urging him to kill me and me on the other commanding him to disarm, after looking from one to the other of us, dropped his shooter and fell on his face before me.

"You may rise."

I gestured the guard to his feet. As he rose I told him to check on the man and the woman who lay injured. Looking to neither side he hurried to the space near the corridor door where both Rem-Na and Tlazolt had fallen.

"Lord", he called to me. "The woman is gone. Do you want me to find her?"

I gestured with my hand. "No. Let her go. Just tend to the man."

Watching Theon return to the altar and resume his preparations while I kept a wary eye on Rem-Na made me dizzy. I became aware that the dizzy sensation had been with me for some minutes but I paid it no attention. To my right I could see Theon attempt to drag Isaac toward the altar.

"There will be no spilling of Isaac's blood", I roared in a voice that reverberated throughout the sanctuary. "Release him now or you will die in his stead."

I pulled the short sword from my waist cloth. With weapon in hand I dashed across the space between me and the altar of death.

Just as I was about to leap on the platform and force Theon to release my friend a figure appeared between me and my prey. Even though he wore the figure of a painted warrior, I recognized Tezcatlipoca. His dark essence hovered around him like a near visible aura so that I could not mistake him.

The pictures on his painted body shifted and moved every few moments. One design depicted the city flattening beneath a roiling cloud of fire that seemed to come from the heavens. Beyond, he bore an illustration of our ships tossing and bowing on a harbor that looked to be near to boiling as it emitted great swirls of steam into the air. I could see bodies being tossed or leaping from the ships as my people attempted to escape the water that killed.

I screamed, "No!" and attacked the demon. From the corner of my eye I saw Isaac jerk his arm away from my nemesis and his viciously curved knife.

Freed, he sped toward the corridor door. As he reached it Rem-Na came to his feet. It was clear he was hurting, but his strength did not appear to be badly dissipated. He moved to grasp Isaac as he ran. I saw Isaac draw up and stop as Rem-Na spoke to him.

I could not hear his words and neither did I have the

leisure to observe his actions. I made a quick prayer to whoever might be listening and ran straight toward my false adversary with my short sword held pointed at the center of the demon's skin painting. When I reached where he had stood he disappeared as though he were naught but smoke. I stumbled as I tried to stop my headlong rush and nearly fell, catching my legs under me at the last second.

I sensed his return as a disturbance of the air behind me. I turned, my arm slashing at the place where I suspected he had landed. I felt the blade bite into flesh and blood gushed hot on me and poured down my arm as though I, not he, had been cut. When I regained my feet I looked at my enemy and saw that he had, once again, become only a painted man. The deceiving spirit had left him to die alone.

I bent at the waist, my breath pounding inside me. I struggled to slow it down a little so I could reorient myself. Looking up, I found Rem-Na standing before me, his face an agonized mask.

"What have I done, Na-Amen?" he cried out as we confronted each other across a short space.

It proved a boon that I had exhausted my energy so completely. It kept Rem-Na alive. Had my strength permitted, I should have run him through with all the cold precision I had learned in Egypt. My wound from the fight with the first painted warrior had left me short of blood and weak with exhaustion. Yet, to save Isaac and the rest of my friends I would have found the strength to run him through. Now that I had reached near collapse, Rem-Na had betrayed me. I pulled my arm back to make a final thrust at him when I felt it prevented by a strong hand on my wrist.

"Hold your sword, Ari." Isaac joined me and his voice reflected new power. "Rem-Na is not your enemy. Your true enemy is he who conjured up these evil spirits and set them among us to confound and destroy."

I relaxed my sword arm just enough to indicate I was listening but still held it at the ready. In that atmosphere of lies, deception and betrayal I dared not relinquish it entirely.

I had forgotten Theon, who now decided to vie for my attention.

"Ari", he called. "The temple is falling. Bring Isaac to me and his sacrifice will stop the earthquakes. If you hesitate all will be lost."

I twisted my body to see all parts of the sanctuary. Isaac held his position beside me and waited for my next move. Rem-Na, his face still doleful and frightened, stood as one turned to stone and did neither move nor speak.

Confused and exhausted, I stumbled. Only Rem-Na's quick movements kept me on my feet. He grabbed me and stood me up as one would hold up a baby learning to walk.

"What can I do?" He pleaded with me. His eyes focused on me, felt like knives through my head.

My breath continued to rend my inner parts as it forced its way past my lips. My air passages felt scraped dry as by a large rough faced rock deep into my body's interior.

Certain now that I would not survive to lead my people home, I said, "Take Isaac to the flagship. Make sure everyone is safely aboard then wait for me. If the tide becomes full and I have not arrived, leave."

I bent over my painful belly.

"Isaac will point the way as he did coming here." "No! I cannot just leave you here."

Rem-Na's face showed even more pain than before.

"If I do not arrive to sail, there will be nothing left to do for I will be dead. Believe that no other alternative is possible."

He hesitated and began to speak. I cut him off.

"If you truly wish to reinstate my faith in your friendship, Rem-Na, you will not steal my remaining strength through argument."

He opened his mouth then closed it again with a click of his teeth.

Nodding, he replied, "It will be as you say."

He saluted me as he done when I served as his captain in Egypt and I knew he would not fail me. In one quick step he grasped me to his heart then turned quickly and moved to Isaac's side. Without further words, he gestured

Isaac to accompany him and strode with long steps toward the door to the outside. Isaac kept step with him and in moments both had left the sanctuary and begun the descent of the stairs.

Chapter 28

Confusion assaulted me from all sides as horror overtook me. In the chaos of the temple, nothing was as it seemed. I should have anticipated that.

Theon, still waiting near the altar, leaped into action like a horse that has felt a thorn. He ran at me, hesitated then dashed toward the door. He turned back and shrieked at me.

"You cannot do this. You are ruining everything. Call Isaac back here, Ari, before it is too late."

Wearily, I replied. "It always was too late, Theon. What you want is so evil that it could not be permitted to continue."

I stopped talking and leaned forward against pain.

Blood oozed from my shoulder and I could not distinguish my blood source from that of the defeated painted warrior. My whole body now was bathed in blood.

Theon continued to scream at me. I no longer could

distinguish his words. I only knew they were pejorative, angry, evil and frustrated.

I turned as quickly as I could and headed for the door myself, hope now in my breast. With Rem-Na safely off with Isaac and the rest waiting for me, I just might make it to the ship alive and reasonably able.

As if responding to a cue Tlazolt appeared on the platform, her body leaping and jerking to a music I could not hear. She never looked at me but continued to dance as if she alone were present. The hairs on the back of my neck testified otherwise, however.

I swiveled as fast as I could, to find yet another warrior at my back. Painted, too, his body illustrated a fire covered harbor with refugees on the shore falling victim to quakes and destruction, their bodies falling black and dead at the edge of the sea.

Theon continued to scream but his demands had changed. Now he called the warrior to his service by demanding that he deliver me to the priest.

Even as I moved to escape the first thrust from the warrior's dagger, I could see a dark malignancy hover about him, never quite visible but always clearly present.

I called out, "Whatever god has been protecting me, I plead with you to give me the strength and ability to conquer this demon and save my friends. I do not know you but you know me."

I threw off my feathered cloak. My headdress had already fallen from my head. Now I stood as naked as did my enemy, with only a loincloth to cover me.

Having called upon the unknown one, I entered the battle. I realized that I had neither the strength nor the wiliness to win over the demon but I had no alternative except to try.

Facing my opponent, I held my dagger tight against my abdomen as I waited to learn his tactic. He grinned at me as he recognized my limitations. He danced around me, forcing me to move more than I wished. His blade flicked out here and there, leaving tiny cuts on my arms and my bared shoulders. They were just deep enough to draw blood but not to do serious damage. The blood loss he expected would weaken me further and offer him an even greater advantage.

He was right. With each slicing of my flesh, I could feel power leaving me. As it became clearer that I could not possibly survive meeting him on his own terms, I determined to alter the terms. I ran hard at him, making him struggle to maintain his balance, at the same time pushing him hard into one of the pillars.

I heard his head hit the stone of the pillar just as a new, more vicious assault came from the earth beneath us. The whole temple shook violently from side to side as the leopard of Egypt had done to force me off his back. As my foe struggled to regain his feet a large chunk of carved rock fell from the pillar, landing on the warrior's exposed head.

The stone held a carving of one of the gods but I was too busy staying alive to notice which.

A wound opened on my opponent's head and from it came that same black substance that had infested the other warrior. He breathed his last in a great sigh just as the whole pillar began to crumble.

I ran for the door, barely escaping in time as I heard a loud crash from with inside the sanctuary. I heard Theon's voice cry out in protest but had no inclination to go back to look for him. Moving as fast as my wounds and weakened muscles would permit I hurried down the steps into a city I would never have recognized if I had just returned from a journey?

Fires had broken out all around the area, flames leaping from abandoned homes, now turned to useless rubble. Dead and dying filled the streets like so much clutter, unworthy of attention. Looking back I noticed that the temple appeared to lean toward the west as if it were bowing to something I could not see. I expected it must fall, but it held steady despite its peculiar position.

Each street I passed seemed littered with crumbled masonry and ash from the south. The heat grew more intense and my skin felt as if it were held over a low flame that might break into a massive one any moment. As I ran I raced against fire from the mountain as well. The heat beneath my slivered flesh reminded me of Byblos and the horror of

Theon's original attempt to destroy me with that same element. Wrapped in fear and tempted to surrender to pain and discouragement, I found a last modicum of strength in my aching legs. The quaking ground beneath me seemed to dance to some macabre rhythm of its own.

My whole body was wet. Sweat mixed with blood trickled slowly down from my shoulder wound even to my legs. My feet, now cut from running over the shards of masonry, added to the bloody trail I left behind me.

Just when I was certain I could go no further, I saw

the ships, still afloat on the rising tide. On the desk of my flagship, I saw my crew running around, getting all their equipment together, readied to be buoyed up to launch. I began to weep from the joy of their presence.

Suddenly, someone saw me and called out. The rest came running to the railing. As I watched two figures launched themselves from the ship. They were followed by another, small one. The three swam fast toward me. I jumped into the water which, by now, had grown as warm as an Egyptian bath. Even so, the sea washing over my wounds even with the salt stinging them proved energizing and I began to make progress toward my friends.

Senmut, the largest and strongest, reached me first. He encompassed me in one arm and began to tow me along beside him. With his strong arm to hold me up I began to succumb to the pain and weakness I held in abeyance until then.

Rem-Na and Joseph arrived side by side and Rem-Na

took my other arm and pulled me along with him. Joseph, like a playful dolphin, continually darted in and out making sure I could still make progress. Then we arrived at the ship.

On board, Helen met me, carrying bandages and clothing.

"Lay him on the pillows I placed on deck."

She spoke in her most commanding voice, the one I imagined she would have used had she remained in her father's regal palace.

Without a word to me she began to clean my wounds and I felt a number of tears blend with the seawater she used to wash me. She cleansed the cuts, covered them with a vile smelling paste then bound them with clean cloths.

As I drifted off into semi-sleep, I heard the orders and movements involved in casting off into the sea. I vacillated between sleep and wakefulness for several minutes. I did not know how many. At first, I did not care.

When I felt the first true sea breeze, I struggled to my

feet to look behind. I saw the leaning pillar of the temple come crashing down. For a moment, I thought I glimpsed Theon running away from it as it fell, but decided that it had been an illusion born of my experiences and my vivid imagination.

Fire suddenly erupted from the inner courtyard of the temple and all I could think was that the priest must at the end have attempted a fire sacrifice in the hope that his Baal might hear and save him. I, on the contrary, hoped he did not.

I now had to admit to myself that I would never know if Theon had fathered me or not. My mother would not tell, as it could only humiliate and embarrass her to have anyone learn that the rituals of Ashtoreth may have brought about my birth. My Phoenician father would never accept either her or me if he believed that. Of course, as to me, it must help him that I am officially dead and no longer a threat to his position in any way.

But my mother, as far as I could know this far from Byblos, continued to function as high priestess, although she may have withdrawn by now. It always was her prerogative to do so. However, I think she liked the status it gave her in the community.

The ship began to pull away from the city and I continued to watch it burn. Even as we distanced ourselves from it I could see more and more destruction happen. The rail to either side of me suddenly became crowded with observers and the air murmured with their comments.

I felt someone move close to me and turned from my scrutiny of the city to find it was Ku Po.

"My friend" he said. "You are badly injured."

He put out a hand and gently touched the tear in my shoulder where the jagged knife had cut and snagged. I did not know what that mess of salve had been made of, but whatever it was it had marvelous healing properties. My major wound already had begun the recovery process.

KuPo looked very different. He had permitted his hair to grow and now wore it clubbed back from his face and tied with something that looked like dried vines. He wore only the loincloth of the warrior with a gaily colored blanket across his shoulders. This was a new ku, one who no longer hid behind the pomps and ceremonies of politics. His broad face and slightly tilted black eyes afforded him an aura of physical power unleashed where before all his strength appeared related to his position as advisor to the king.

"Why have you decided to join us? I thought you would have traveled far to the north by now. Many refugees have, I believe."

He smiled, showing his teeth with gold and jewels drilled into them.

"When I found out who it was that killed my king I decided that court life did not suit me well at all." He leaned against the rail. "Of course, when it is safe to return, I will. It is my duty as a member of the royal family. He was my brother."

I realized quite unexpectedly that I had been conversing with Ku Po and understanding most of his words. And my own words seemed to become comprehensible to him. I reeled back from the rail as that realization hit me.

"I understand you, Ku Po. And you seem to understand me. How could this happen?"

"I do not know either, Quetzalcoatl. Perhaps that part of you that is the god has endowed you with gifts you did not expect."

Shocked that he referred to me as Quetzlcoatl, I nearly fell into the sea at the impact of his words. I had admitted to him that I was only a man, like himself, with a man's limitations, yet he continued to call me by the name of the god. I did not know what to say in any language. Did he not understand?

Helpless to think what to say to Ku Po and filled with confusion I looked to where we had been and saw a sight more bloodcurdling than I could have imagined. Worse even that the terrifying killings of the sacrificed people came the horror of the mountain that produced the river of fire.

With no warning, some unbelievably powerful and violent force lifted the entire mountain and threw it into the air causing it to break apart as it came back down. Fire spilled from what had been its peak and poured like fast running water across the whole landscape around it.

As far from me as it was I saw it as clearly as if it had sat on the near shore. One moment the mountain sat where it had always been, down river from the city and the next it flew into the air and crumbled like a piece of badly made mortar.

In that same moment a loud noise rushed from it toward our ship. The crashing booms pounded my ears until it became actual pain. I looked around. I saw Helen on the other side of Ku Po. She bent over from the waist and had both hands pressed to her ears. All across the deck others held hands over their ears to protect them from the sounds of the great mountain's death throes.

As if the loud crashing noise had taken on a life of its own it spread across the land and pursued the ship to the sea. Behind the tumult came water. More water than I had ever seen before in one place pursued us like a multitude of demons bent on our destruction.

A huge wave hit the ship broadside. Higher than our highest mast and seeming to reach into the sky, it pushed us along with it as though we were weightless. It lifted our vessel, large as it had seemed to us before, like a wood chip of no consequence. We rocked back and forth furiously as we rushed up one side of the wave and hung there suspended between the heavens and the earth like debris imbedded in the powerful wave that overwhelmed us. I saw the rest of our ships suffering the same brutal treatment from the great wave. I could do nothing except to yell for everyone to hold on as tightly as they could and pray for mercy.

I had great confidence in our ships. Had they not weathered the greatest storm I had ever encountered on our way to this new and strange land? I had watched them being made and personally oversaw the builders and their adherence to the techniques I demanded of them. Now, for the first time, my faith in my ships foundered on the terrible reality of the vast wave that bore us north at this unbelievable speed.

Never, anywhere, had I encountered such rapid movement. Even some of the great cats I had watched run at top speed could not have kept up with this rushing water. So fast were we traveling that I did not have time to see if we all remained on board. With spray constantly in my eyes and the need to use all my concentration to hold on to a mast nothing was left for checking the people on board.

As suddenly as it had pulled us into its grasp, the wall of water dropped us down into what appeared to be its very heart.

"We are falling!" I cried out to the others. "Be alert! We do not know where we will end up."

The end of those words got lost in the screams and shouts of all my people as the great wave dropped us behind it and kept moving on, fleeing from where it left us, its magnificent power diminished not at all. I watched as it roared away from us in a continual northeasterly direction.

The ship hit the bottom of the trough with a loud crash that sounded as if we had surely lost the vessel and we would shortly be dropped into the sea itself by its death throes. I waited for the inrushing water to overtake us. I forced my body to turn as I searched for Helen in the frenzied shudder of our vessel. I saw her, still safe, though terrified almost to distraction.

When the water wall passed it left what looked like a hole in the sea which now filled up from behind us. As the new water arrived and filled in the cavity left by the great passing, my wonderful ship was raised onto the crest of this newly filled trough. Once again the sea sat beneath us and the ship lived.

Exhausted and relieved, the sailors went to work repairing the damage from the adventure. Surprisingly, the abuse left us with little injury, either to ship or men. For the men, a few rowers got tossed around violently before we steadied and a little leakage occurred in their sector. But all in all it was incredible how wonderfully our floating home survived.

I instructed the sailors to slow down our forward progress and let the ship float into a harbor I could already see ahead. There we would find what was required to patch the parts made weak from the tossing about.

In this town we would have to leave Ku Po. Despite his lack of experience at sea, he came through with great courage. I felt certain he would do well as he picked up torn edges of his life after the tragedies he had suffered.

"You do understand, do you not, that the presentation

of me as the god was intended to deceive your people? That I am not a god or anything like one. I am but a man like you, only from a different world than yours."

Ku Po smiled as he stood with me once more at the rail, this time surveying a town just coming into view. The wave, while not treating the town with gentleness, had restrained its greatest violence by the time it arrived there. Considerable damage could be seen but nothing to compare with what happened south in the city.

"I do not truly understand who you are, Quetzalcoatl. But I have experienced the many miraculous things you have done. Therefore I still believe you to be Quetzalcoatl."

People crowded the beach area and watched as we arrived. I gathered that most of them had never seen a seagoing vessel before. Their fascination was obvious.

Ku Po recognized other members of Tu Topiltzin's court, all of whom greeted him joyfully, respectfully throwing themselves on the ground the moment they saw him. Senmut and Rem-Na assisted him ashore. He had no experience with the roughly made raft we had available to carry him to the land. I strongly felt his loss as he receded from my sight and became a distant image burned forever on my memory, his hand lifted toward me before he turned to accept the welcome of his colleagues and certainly future subjects.

When we cast off once more the ship was as well repaired as we could make it. All our other vessels arrived intact and the crews praised their various gods for their assistance in our safe arrival.

Isaac came to me and pleaded that he be relieved of the responsibility of navigation.

"I am not truly a navigator, Ari, you know well. I cannot even say truly that my work had anything much to do with our safe arrival in this place."

His face twisted as he recalled the fear he experienced when faced with foreign stars. "For all I know, we may have ended up far from where we ought because of my ineptitude. Is there no one else?"

"I want none other, Isaac. It is upon you that I bestow my trust in this matter." I smiled and hit him lightly on a shoulder. "You only can lead us rightly. Of that I am sure."

He grimaced but ceased to argue.

"I can only try my best."

He stopped then began to talk about the strange stars and their potential meaning.

I interrupted him. "Come with me and we will look back to where we just left. Despite all the fury and power of the devil mountain and the great surge it generated, we have traveled only an amazingly short distance from the city."

Looking back to whence we came on this fateful day, we could only perceive the mountain as through a heavy fog. It squatted like a toad on the landscape, a massive hole in its middle as though its heart had been torn from it. Smoke nearly hid it from our sight but we could see enough to realize that there were still remnants of the temple standing. A few partial columns stuck up from the carnage as if defying death and destruction.

I wondered how many people had survived the mountain's destruction. From our distance I could still see rivers of fire pouring out of its heart. Somehow the mountain appeared to have moved north several miles, but I knew that could not be. I shuddered. I no longer believed I really knew what might happen in that strange world, both so beautiful and so cruel. It looked thoroughly burned and I could not believe anything could have survived that holocaust. I felt tears try to escape my eyes as I continued to gaze on what was left of the city. I do not know how long I might have stayed there, engrossed in what was and what was no longer.

My musings ended when Helen joined me on the deck.

"I have not seen you since we arrived at this town."

"No. My whole mind has been stayed on the destruction behind us. The deaths. The ruin of a civilization. Even Theon. All gone as if they never existed."

"It was not your fault. You are not the one who called upon the demons. If Theon has perished, so be it. He awoke sleeping spirits that were better permitted to slumber." he passed her hand through my hair and I drew her close, grateful that she was no longer in danger. Pressed against my side her heart joined mine in a rhythm that I felt sure I could set to music. Several minutes passed before I pulled away. I thanked whatever gods had helped us survive this journey and I trusted them to bring it to completion.

"Very soon we will see our children again. It has been so long. Will they still remember us?" "Yes. Deirdre is old enough to remember on her own and I trust our family to keep alive Ben-Namen's recollection of us. It may be awkward at first, but they will remember. Do not fear, my wife."

Even as I reveled in the nearness of her and in the close escape we had, I kept looking back to what remained of the city. Once, I imagined I caught a glimpse of a sail on the horizon but it was only a mirage skating over the water. It was over. No more playing god. No more battles against the dark spirits from within the flaming mountain. I turned my back to the horror we had left. My whole body ached with weariness and my knife wounds began to throb with every beat of my heart.

Helen, always sensitive to my needs, took my hand.

"It is all behind you now, except for the wounds on your body. Let me take care of those."

She led me into our tiny cabin. I stretched out on the sleeping mat and readied myself for her ministrations. I could see the feathered cloak and headdress, folded neatly and set among our personal possessions.

As Helen began to care for my wounds I felt

exhaustion overcome me and I drifted away.

I dreamed of vast seas stretching into the distance and populated with dolphins and other sea denizens all eager to lead us home. Even in my sleep I felt the joy of arriving among my family as our children reached out to welcome us. I dreamed that just beyond my ability to see, some god was holding out a trophy I was not yet ready to claim.

I woke wondering what the dream might mean. I went out on deck and in the fading light of the day I saw the sea roil with the dances of dolphins and other creatures I could not name.

I smiled. I was going home. And I trusted I would arrive safely.

Chapter 29

My flagship sailed for many days, north along the coastline, stopping overnight in tiny bays where we obtained fresh water, meat and fruits. Once in a while we saw people and animals through the dense foliage which pressed against the beaches, but none approached us. They no longer seemed like the friendly people of our mutual past. Neither did they show as hostile.

I could not resist wondering if my friend Ku Po might be among them. Especially when we sailed closer to land, I once or twice thought I caught a glimpse of him on the edge of a forest, watching us sail by. Almost certainly, it had to be my imagination. Even if, unlikely as it would seem, he remained in one of the villages we passed, he would be occupied with plans to restore or possibly replace the capital city so destroyed by fire mountains and earthquakes.

One day as Isaac and I relaxed on the ship and

watched the small jungle villages pass by, I asked him, "Are they afraid of us? In particular, have they lost all trust of me? Or perhaps they do not recognize my ship. Surely it is the only one in this part of the world with such beautiful sails. Our supply ships offer much less color and are basically utilitarian. Have you any thoughts about that?"

His reply consisted only of one of his Hebrew shrugs that served him so well.

Obviously, he decided not to speculate. I turned back to the mysterious water the gods wanted to show me. I guessed that Isaac had some contemplation of his own to deal with right then, and did not question him further. There would be time later for all that.

Despite the slow progress we made, it was steady, with little need for the rowers, except to maintain our course. It felt as if we had found some kind of river in the sea which moved us in the direction we wished to go, however slowly, and I felt grateful.

We had been away from the destruction of the capital about two weeks when the giant sea creatures we knew as whales reappeared. Our mysterious underwater river had carried us farther away from shore than we travelled previously, and now we could only view the headlands. They appeared as dark, eccentric lines against the water.

Some of the smaller dolphins gambolled about and between our ships as they had done during our journey to the land. Others maintained a discreet and dignified distance, coming near only occasionally as though to welcome us with their sprays of water. Exotic scents continued to come our way whenever the winds shifted from the land, weaker daily as we sailed farther from the stricken city.

I experienced some lethargy during this relaxed time of sailing. I spent many hours with Helen, the two of us getting to know each other all over again. We spoke of the early days, the time when she nursed me back to health. We wondered how much the children had grown in Etruria while we had been away. We became friends again as we had been in Byblos.

We settled on the deck, in a little space with rugs and pillows and another rug to separate our spot from the rest on board. A canopy on top shielded us from both sun and rain.

Isaac, Senmut and Rem-Na lived on my flagship with Helen and me. After our unusual experiences which had led us to the new land, I dared not trust that our ships would remain in sight of each other. Isaac slept below while the others made their nests nearer the prow than ours. It was so peaceful with the sea and the sun and the heavens above us that it felt more like a pleasure voyage on the Nile than an escape from death and destruction.

Our ocean river kept moving us north then inexplicably turned us to the east. We still felt the current strong against the keel while the water grew rougher, the wind blew against us, and our men had to row again. Their powerful strokes now proved necessary to keep the ship upright. The colder air spoke to us of a whole unfamiliar weather pattern, much removed from the hot and steamy place where we had been.

Our idyllic cruise was obviously over and the real work of sailing began. Isaac, who was not a true sailor and the oldest of us, was the first to have problems with increasingly frantic waves and chilling winds. As thin and emaciated as he was, he had little flesh to cover his bones. He shivered constantly each time he came on deck and began once again to spend his entire day below. I knew he would come to me if I requested, but I chose to visit him in his little nest beneath the deck.

"If I die on this voyage, Ari, will you take my bones and bury them with those of my ancestors? Surely, my family will accept them, if not me, alive."

I tossed my hair, grown long, back from my face and captured it into a knot against the wind that penetrated in gusts even here.

I laughed at his words, knowing well that it sounded hollow, even to my own ears.

"You will not die, friend Isaac. You are made of stern stuff."

He smiled, in a melancholy way. "Yes. I have survived much, Ari. But everything has its time and its ending. I feel mine is near."

"Perhaps it is near for us all, Isaac. We have no assurance that we can survive many days on this rough sea. And if we do, we may well run out of water and expire from the elements. Could this be what you fear?"

"Perhaps."

He stood up and said, "Let us go on deck. I have a need to look out on the width of the sea. It may clear my head and give me a broader view of our situation."

I helped him up, noting again how little there was left of Isaac, and it worried me. At moments like this, it seemed that nothing but his indomitable will kept him alive. We went up on deck, me watching his every move in an attempt to anticipate his need. We leaned on the hard-worked boards and watched the endless movement of the water, saying little, just enjoying each other's company.

After a fair time, Isaac repeated, his voice sounding desperately fearful, "Should God not sustain me this voyage, will you please promise that at least my bones will return to my land? That I will not be lost in the depths or buried on strange soil?"

"If it is within my power to do so, Isaac, I will get you back to your homeland one way or the other, preferably alive and well."

"You think I am mad to worry thus about my God and my hope of his ultimate acceptance of me. You cannot understand my fear and my need to be reconciled once more with him and with my family."

I shrugged. "I admit I find it difficult to believe in one god only, despite the comfort of having one person to worship, one only to entreat. So much easier than trying to determine which of many gods is the best one for a particular need and how to appeal to that one without angering an entire pantheon of gods and goddesses in competition with each other."

He laughed. "I can see how having many gods could become a kind of dance among them as you try to determine which of them would be most efficacious at the time, and how to avoid offending the one as you appeal to the other."

His words prickled me like the tiny thorns on a cactus plant. It was as if my devotion had been fragmented like a child's among his friends, and thus found wanting. Part of me wished to counter his amused concept of the many gods, but I knew I could not. How could I, when the past years had taught me so much that was unspeakable about the gods I had been raised to worship and those I had found elsewhere? I chose to let his disrespectful words pass while I considered them and their import for my life.

He sighed then turned once more to gaze at the now chill green waves which surrounded us totally so that it appeared we had returned to the bottom of a cavern of water. Nothing could be seen except an expanse of gray-green which met at the horizon and merged with a sky of nearly the same color. He turned his head and gestured to the north.

"I think we ought to go that way. It will deliver us from the danger of the jungle still so near to us."

"I have no strong conviction about our route. If this is what you believe we must do, so be it."

I signalled the rowers to make the course change. The ship moved to change direction. Isaac shivered and said he wanted to go back to his small cabin.

I left him to his reading in the now fading light and went to join Helen. She sat on a heap of mats and rugs, combing her wind tousled hair and trying to tie it down to keep it from tangling again. She smiled at me and gestured me to sit beside her. I did and watched her for a while, marvelling at her resilience and ability to adapt to whatever situation life handed her.

Early, as a slave, she had been acquiescent and obedient. Later, she was wife to me and mother to Deidre, happy foster-mother to Ben-Namen. Then, in the land of the Olmec, when the people made her a goddess, she received the worship and the adulation with the same aplomb with which she accepted the previous states of her life. I realized for the first time how truly extraordinary she was.

She looked at me now, puzzlement in her green eyes. "You are staring at me, Ari. Why?"

"I think I bewitched myself. How could I have forgotten how lovely you are and how completely you love me?"

She smiled. "Because there was Nikkal, of course. Her grace, her beauty and her independence captivated you totally, as she enchanted so many others. And that she loved you above even Pharaoh, who offered her much. How could you see another? It would be unreasonable to demand that."

She bent her head with its coppery hair. "She was good, too, Ari. Another woman who could achieve so much would gladly have ruled over one such as me. But she never did. She treated me with respect and recognized my right to you, as well."

Helen looked up at me.

"She was a sister to me and I will never forget her."

I pulled her to me and we relaxed there a short time while the daily work of the ship continued around us.

"I will be a mother to Ben-Namen", she said. "But I will keep his memory of Nikkal fresh all his life. I promise you that."

"First, my dear, we have to return to him and to Deidre." I said wryly. "Right now it appears that the chances of our making it are less than encouraging. Isaac is convinced he will die out here on the sea, my Egyptian friends are becoming distressed and fearful and I have no idea where we are headed, as everything around us is unfamiliar."

"You will know, Ari, what to do. Have you not been guided always, and spared even the fire of sacrifice? You are beloved of the gods."

I laughed bitterly. "I no longer know the gods. I no longer know to whom to make sacrifice and in whose name to cry out my need. I have been cast adrift by the gods and have none to serve as anchor."

"Then you will find the way. I know that and never doubt it."

Isaac joined us, his face fretful and his body restless. He walked about a while near us then went to lean looking out over the waves. Almost, it appeared he sought wisdom and an answer to all of life's questions in the rhythmic movement of the water. Perhaps, I thought, he succeeded.

"Are our food and our water holding up, Ari?" he asked. "How much longer can we travel before supplies become a serious problem?"

"I have never before known you to worry about such things, Isaac. Why are you so anxious?"

His face wrinkled the way a young child's does when it is deeply troubled.

"I am worried, but I do not know by what. It is just a sense of unease which permeates my very essence." He stalked in frustration up and down the crowded deck a few times then returned to us. "There is a sense of doom I feel as we travel this sea, Ari, as if something evil guides us."

I could not dispute him, as the entire journey was full of unknowns for me, as well as for Isaac. All that I could do was consign us all into the hands of whatever gods there truly were, and hope for the best. I told him so. He sighed. "Yes. Ultimately, we are in God's hands. He is the one who will determine the length of our days." He stared out over the greasy looking waters a while. "Perhaps tonight the clouds will clear enough for me to study the star patterns. If so, I can at least learn if any are familiar either from home or from our journey in this direction."

He remained watching the water a moment or so longer, then turned and went back to his place in the cabin.

Helen and I rested quietly side by side a while after Isaac left us then she said, "Isaac's question was a legitimate one, Ari. Do we have adequate supplies?"

"I cannot even answer that. How can I know how many supplies we will need when I do not know where we are, or how far from landfall?"

I shrugged impatiently.

"Does everyone expect me to read the minds of the gods? Am I a sorcerer or an oracle? Bah!"

I leaped to my feet and stomped away from her. I knew fully that a show of temper would heal nothing, but I had held so much inside me for so long that it was as if I were about to burst with it. I paced the deck, carefully skirting the containers and impedimenta of the ship as I did so. At last, when my fit of pique had been assuaged by the stomping about, I stopped and stared out to sea.

Far out on the water, I could see the dolphins and other sea creatures as they appeared to play in the waves as before. Slowly, and by a circuitous route, they neared our ship. One of the largest of the creatures came very close to us, leaped from the water onto its tail then disappeared beneath the waves. Shortly, it surfaced again, in an easterly direction. It moved that way for a while then returned to our ship, as though it were trying to communicate with us. It dove once more and again came up to the east of us. I watched its maneuvers for several minutes then, as if it had spoken in language, I knew what we must do.

"Senmut, Rem-Na, Isaac, come here!" I cried. Isaac came running from the cabin with more strength than I could have anticipated and my Egyptian friends arrived from the stern where they had been playing at swords to pass the hours.

"We will head due east. Watch the huge creature."

As though it heard and understood, the massive sea animal raised its head that was as big as our ship then raced away from us a short distance, dove, and once more surfaced to the east.

"The creature is telling us something. This is the third time it has come close then swum off to the east. We will turn east."

Senmut immediately sprang into action, quite obviously delighted at having something real and helpful to do. He called out to the man on watch above and the watch called out to the other ships. As one, we turned and moved toward the east, even as the setting sun began to fight its way through the clouds and shine its blazing glory on our sail, turning it to flame. I did not know who among the many gods I had sought decided to answer my pleas, but I was certain one had done so.

Isaac claimed, as usual, that it was his God who

directed us, and who was I to dispute that? I, who had lost

all spiritual contact with the gods of both my childhood

and my manhood, had little reason to question anyone

else's convictions.

I laughed aloud as our ship, with a small tug, got

picked up by a wind that propelled us east. Whatever

awaited us, I was grateful to have direction and assurance

that we were going somewhere. All I could hope was that

the place would prove safe and somewhere near my family

at Etruria. I spoke to my unknown god, uncomfortable at

acknowledging the possibility of such a one, and asked that

favor of him.

Chapter 30

It is impossible to relate how beautiful the coast of Etruria looked after we finally passed through the narrows and arrived at Caere, Hiras' capital city. It had grown mightily since we left and I could only admire my uncle's diligence and determination when I thought that, while feeling an eternity to me and my crew, it had been only three short years in actual time.

The territory surrounding the city had been covered with small, scraggly vines when we left. Now, even on such a hot and dusty day those vines hung heavy with richly scented grapes. The hills where they grew rose up behind them, peppered with olive trees knobby and lush, their silvery leaves shivering in the sun washed breeze. The city proper, with its municipal buildings of white and varicolored marble, now took on an air of permanence.

A new temple rose on a hill behind the marketplace, its façade sparkling in the bright sunlight. I turned my head away and looked elsewhere. I wanted no more to do with temples and gods, despite the possibility there was such thing as a god in the background, influencing my life in a strange way. Even as I turned aside, I could see a procession of priests, priestesses and acolytes with censers as they passed along the colonnaded porch. For one brief moment I imagined I saw Theon leading a procession. I shrugged away what could only be a hallucination based on evil memories.

I shuddered, recalling Theon and those priests who made sacrifice of human beings and tossed the remains into the dark wells of the Olmec. But there was no need to think about that. It was behind me now, and my life had developed beyond that nightmare. I cast one more glance over my shoulder as I prepared to anchor at Caere's extensive cothon. I felt grateful to be back in my uncle's civilized country. In fact, the power of my gratitude nearly overwhelmed me.

As we fixed our ships to the long cothon a delegation came down to greet us. In the lead was my cousin, Ribidda. From a distance, as he moved toward us, I could see that Ribidda had acquired an aura of stability, even as had Caere herself, and this showed in the gold-sashed tunic he wore and the way he carried himself. Behind my cousin walked his wife and several children, and they were followed by a number of evident worthies of the city and the usual retinue of armed soldiers who always made up part of any welcoming party for strangers. They hailed us then Ribbida stopped as if he had been yanked hard from behind.

"Is it you, cousin?"

He bent to look up into my face.

"Aribaal, it is you."

He sounded choked as if he had been given a blow to his throat that paralyzed his voice.

I rushed to him and gathered him and his wife Taseus

into the circle of my arms.

"We thought you dead." Ribbida said incredulously.

"As you can easily see, we are not." I glanced around me. "But where is my uncle?"

"He is off on a trading trip, of course, following his great love, the sea."

He smiled and added, "Except I think he planned to remain near the coast this time, trading with the small cities he himself has established. He rarely ventures out into the great sea anymore, but prefers the kinder waters along the borders of the peninsula."

"And, wise man, he appears to leave the administration of Caere in your hands."

He nodded modestly then stepped aside.

Helen came hurrying from behind me.

"Our children. Where are our children?" she cried breathlessly.

Ribidda and Taseus both laughed then culled from

the considerable group of children two who had pulled back from the knot of youngsters.

"Right here, cousin. These are yours."

Both Helen and I stared. The girl's great blue eyes and her russet hair held tenuously in check by a wide gold band which crossed her forehead and clamped the unruly tresses over her ears were all we needed to identify her to us. She was tall and as beautiful as her mother, nearly full grown. And Ben-Namen, too, was tall for one so young. His sturdy body clad in the Etruscan tunic and his curls, as golden as his sister's locks were russet, assured that he bore a look slightly foreign to the other little boys.

I watched Helen's eyes fill with tears which threatened to escape and pour down her face. My eyes, as well, filled and spilled slightly. I could not totally stop the slow flow of tears.

At first Deidre seemed reluctant to approach her mother but when Helen opened her arms to her daughter

Deidre flung herself into her arms, sobbing and laughing at one and the same time.

I sought for signs of Nikkal in Ben-Namen's face but, other than the almond shape of his intensely blue eyes, so extraordinary in his northern countenance, saw none. Perhaps, I thought, it was as well. If he were more like his mother, the pain would be too great. I leaned down and grasped his small hand in mine. We remained like that a few moments then I lifted him in my arms. It was pleasant to hold him thus, and I regretted the few years that my son had already lived without his father's presence. Had I been the trader my father intended Ben-Namen would already be accompanying me on my voyages.

Helen and I quickly settled into an elegant suite in my uncle's newly constructed mansion. Looking around me it was easy enough to see that my uncle Hiras had not abandoned his Phoenician trading ways, for the whole apartment was furnished in artefacts from every known country. It was comforting to see this, to touch the various woods and marbles and bronzes, the fabrics from exotic and remote cities.

The main room of our new home was gloriously decorated with a floor mosaic of a Phoenician ship tossed about by waves and surrounded by a plethora of fabulous sea creatures, among which I recognized our friends, the dolphins and the massive water-blowing whales, whose presence had so purposefully guided us where we needed to go. What god, I wondered, had sent us those wonderful creatures, and would I ever see them again?

Despite knowing I was welcome in my uncle's city and equally so in my lost sister's Carthage, I enjoyed no certainty that either place offered me the life I wanted or should have. A return to Egypt was another possibility. By now, a new Pharaoh wore the double crown and would gladly welcome my Egyptian friends and me. Yet again I hesitated. I did not believe that Egypt held my future.

Thinking about home and what that meant for me reminded me of Isaac. My good friend was a great worry. The voyage back had not been kind to his already disease wracked body. It did not seem possible that more flesh could melt from his bony frame, but it had done so. Skin hung on his face and neck and chest like fabric tossed down casually for perusal by a potential buyer. I did not see how he continued to survive. Was it only because of his desire to return home that he remained so long in this world? As soon as I got my land legs, I would have to find out what Isaac wanted and needed.

As for my noble Senmut and Rem-Na, I assumed they would wish to return to Egypt and pick up the lives they abandoned to accompany me on our very precarious voyage to the new land. They could readily resume their military lives and join with others from the Academy. It would grieve me to allow my little band to be broken up, but I could not in good conscience hold them to me.

Men-el, of course, would remain with me. Even if I so commanded him he would not leave. It was not in him to abandon me after the many years he had been my caretaker, my confidante and my friend.

I shook myself clear of these depressing thoughts. It would be as it should. Whatever god or gods were real, I knew that my life was not random, that there was purpose and direction, even though I had no clear vision of it.

That first evening, Helen and I spent with our children, reacquainting ourselves. We watched while Ben-Namen exhibited his fledgling skill with a tiny blunted sword of soft wood that had been made for him by my uncle's armorer. Deidre led her mother off to her own room to show her all the lovely clothes and jewellery she had accumulated. It was with a great sense of shock that I realized she was now nearly as old as I had been when I reached my majority. Helen and I needed to talk about Deidre's future.

When the children returned to their own rooms, we

marvelled in them and in our safe arrival at Caere. It seemed that, for the first time, we could have a life together, as a family. The thought held great appeal, even if I could not fathom how it would come about.

The next weeks passed quickly for me as I dwelt in a haze of contentment and peace. I had forgotten how pleasant it could be to pass my hours in the comfort of knowing I was safe and established where I was. I did not deceive myself that this idyllic life could continue indefinitely, as there were still many decisions to be made about the future. But, for the moment, all was well indeed.

Chapter 31

While our ships were in dry dock, being refurbished under the watchful eyes of my Egyptian friends, I travelled with my cousin Ribbida up the coast to visit the new cities of my uncle's rapidly expanding kingdom.

Ben-Namen travelled with me, cared for by my forever friend Men-el with the same fervor and kindness he had always shown me.

"Surely you never expected to be overseeing yet another generation of my family after all the care you gave me and my siblings."

"It is a pleasure to help direct Ben-Namen's growth into childhood and, hopefully one day, into maturity."

All I could do was laugh at my friend's devotion to me and mine. In some small way I felt I was reliving my own childhood. I could but hope that Deidre would bless his youth as Elissa did mine.

I sighed in nostalgia and regret for what was no more then I turned my attention to the water beneath our hardy vessel.

It was a perfect time to be aboard ship. The seas were as calm as a quiet inland lake and I was overjoyed to find that a group of dolphins chose to accompany us. I held Ben-Namen over the side of our ship so he could better see these marvellous creatures as they danced and gambolled among the gentle wavelets, their silvery backs glistening in the intense sunshine. He laughed joyously as water splashed him in the face as the elegant creatures ventured very near the ship.

"Look, Father, they want me to go play with them. May I, please?"

"You are too young. Later that may happen for you. But not yet."

His little face fell sadly for a moment but very

quickly he recovered his customary good nature. It was not easy for him to sustain a sorrowful demeanor. As quickly as the pout came, it disappeared into delight.

His joy was pleasant to watch and the dolphins showed considerable evidence that they were eager to entertain him for a time. Too soon, they moved away from us into deeper water and were gone from our sight. Although Ben-Namen grieved at their passing, he permitted Men-el to distract him.

The settlements north of Caere ranged from one fairly established city to a medium sized town to a rough village still being carved from the land. We visited them all and were introduced to the leading citizens, many of whom were related to me in some degree. In each settlement some sort of temple had been erected, from a primitive one of random field stones to a vast hilltop edifice complete with columns and porches. I visited none of them and did not reply to my cousin's questioning looks when I refused his invitations.

Although it was impossible not to see these buildings, I did not have to enter one. Ribidda, good man that he was, chose not to comment on my attitude.

Our journey lasted several weeks, enough time for me to establish myself with Ben-Namen and grow accustomed to a return to civilized life. By the time of our return to Caere, my whole inner being had settled down a great deal, helped by the peaceful voyage and even more so by my small son's company. I deemed myself ready to consider the future. Perhaps, I thought, I would return to my background of trading and forget the Egyptian warrior that resided within my soul. Had he not exercised his expertise enough for one lifetime? I decided the answer was yes.

Chapter 32

My uncle Hiras had already returned home when Ribidda and I got back from our little trek. His ship rode gently against the cohon and looked as if she had faced some real weather in her travels. Paint speckled by marine growths and partially worn off by the abrasive action of the waves and rocky shore testified to that. Her sail wore patches, a testimony to fierce winds wherever my uncle had travelled.

Because I had expected his journey to have been much like mine with Ribidda, I felt confused. How could such damage have been done during a coastal sail such as ours? Unless, of course, Hiras ran into severe weather farther up. But then, would we not have experienced at least some of that? My curiosity about his ship's condition could have overcome my respect for my uncle's privacy but, in the end, courtesy prevailed. I decided he would tell me when he was ready.

However, restraint did not satisfy my curiosity and each time I neared his battered ship I had to force myself to remain silent and wait for Hiras to tell me himself where he had been. However, unusually for him, Hiras chose silence.

It is rarely that am troubled by curiosity that could cause me to ask inordinate questions of anyone, family or friend. But after a full day of watching my uncle's battered ship sit at the end of the cothon with no one approaching it to repair any part of it, I decided to question my uncle even against my strong principles against prying.

Hiras had not hung around the cothon as I would have expected him to do so I had to locate him at home to assuage my curiosity.

"Uncle", I said, when I finally ran him down at his midday meal, "I would like to talk with you for a while. Is this a good time?"

He sighed mightily.

"You want to know about my ship."

I nodded.

"As you probably surmise, I did not go north along the coast as I said."

He gave me an almost surreptitious nod.

"I tried to resist my curiosity but here I sit, clearly unable to do so any longer. You are not usually secretive. I finally could not restrain my wish to learn where you went."

He sighed mightily.

"Yes. I knew it would happen one day soon. I was not and still am not ready to confront all that transpired in these weeks. The events have left me in a great turmoil."

He rose from his chair and began to pace the room

"You know you can trust me with any problem, Uncle. I will do anything I can to help you."

"Unfortunately, that is the problem, not the solution."

Now it became my turn to pace.

"How can our close relationship be a problem?"

He returned to his chair and pored us each a glass of wine.

"It is clear that I sailed the great sea past Etruria and along the coast." He cleared his throat. "The results of my battle against storms and great rocks show themselves clearly. Several times I doubted I would survive." He paused. "Perhaps it would be better had I not done so."

He hung his head as if to hide from my eyes.

"You may as well tell me everything, Uncle. I cannot believe you did anything evil or even particularly foolish. Whatever is your problem I will do anything to help you."

His face now appeared agonized.

"Yes. And that is my problem." He turned to look me straight in the face. "Perhaps if you were less willing I could wriggle out of this mess I am in."

"I have no idea what caused you such trouble, but I can try to relieve your pain."

"I had a sudden desire for at least one more sea trip

before I confine my travel to the peninsula. So, on impulse, I decided to go trading in Syria. I have stopped there many times before. In fact, it has long been one of my favorite places to trade. Over the years I have developed an unusual friendship with King Ben-Hadad and his father before him. Unfortunately, on this occasion my friendship proved a curse."

"Did Ben-Hadad turn you away?

"He did not. Contrarily, he wanted me to stay longer.

"I unloaded my goods and took on others in the port there. When nearly ready to cast off, he told me he wanted to honor my friendship with a big celebration before I sailed. I felt thrilled that the king wanted to so honor me.

He certainly outdid himself. It turned out to be far more luxurious than I would have expected. When the festival neared its end, he called me aside and told me he had a proposition for me. He got that foxy look that Syrians so often do, which made me edgy. He was never above playing tricks. In fact, he loved doing such things. Straightforward is not a word I would apply to him. "

Hiras shifted in his seat as if the upholstery had failed and the chair caused him pain.

"Even while I considered the devious way of Syrians, I felt so excited and flattered by my reception and the luxurious salute to our friendship I refused to doubt his bounty but accepted all at face value."

His face twisted in an expression of anger at his folly.

"At last he spoke his wishes. He said he had heard of my nephew's great prowess at war. I nodded, remembering that I myself had spoken about your achievements in battle. Perhaps I permitted the wine to loosen my tongue more than wisdom permitted. And now I realized I had no hope of evading the question."

My uncle stopped his discourse suddenly, as if gagged by a massive hand.

"And what did you tell him?" I asked.

His words had shaken me badly. I strongly sensed that some sort of agreement had been forged between them.

"He told me he had great need of a powerful and trustworthy leader of his army."

Hiras stopped briefly then added, "But only long enough to train a Syrian leader able to take over from you and lead his forces against Ben-Hadad's many enemies. He was adamant that it would not be a long time before you could return home and live as you wish."

"And what did you promise him?"

"Nothing, really, other than to assure him I would approach the subject with you and offer you this opportunity to lead many warriors again. That's all I did, Ari. I tell you the truth."

"And if I decline?"

His face paled.

"He said he would refuse to let us continue trading in Syria. He added that he always favored our family, but he could not guarantee that would continue."

I looked into his eyes. All I saw was pain and humiliation. I stood and walked around the room a few minutes while I considered his dilemma and mine.

When had I ever sought him and been rejected? Never. And now I had to decide whether or not to pull his fingers from the fire and lead the Syrian army against their foes, for however long they needed me. I could imagine no more ludicrous a situation. That I might lead Syria, the cruellest of nations, against its enemies challenged everything.

I tamped down my rising anger against my uncle. There could be no point in punishing him for his folly. He appeared quite able to do that for himself.

"Before I give any answer I must consult with my wife and your sons. Helen and my children are reconciled to a life in Etruria and I do not believe I could ever trust a Syrian king."

"Did not Nikkal come from Syria? Surely you could use some of your time there learning more about her."

"I know all I wish about the mother and elder brother who sold her. I doubt I would enjoy meeting them."

"Well, you never know. If they still live they may regret getting rid of Nikkal and would cherish news of her."

"Your words do nothing to tempt me to Syria. But I promise to consider your dilemma and talk to my wife about it."

Hiras laughed.

"Never have I known another man, especially a great man of war, who consulted his wife as you do. If I did not know you so well I might question your manhood. But, fortunately, I am well aware of what you are."

"Someday I hope to be able to tell the whole family about our recent past. But not quite yet."

"You are a true man of mystery, my nephew. I shall be patient."

"You are a great man, Uncle. I am fortunate indeed to have you as the titular head of our family."

I thought he might choose to persuade me to a decision, but he did not. Rather, he made no further mention of his situation. I knew he had spoken to his sons who also illustrated by their demeanors a patient attitude that most men could not achieve. I greatly admired their restraint as well as appreciated their close relationship to me.

Chapter 33

From my first talk with Hiras I could find no reasonable option. I would go to Syria. It didn't matter why or how long. I could not leave my uncle abandoned in so precarious a situation. Knowing the cruelty and pride of Ben-Hadad I feared that Hiras and his sons could suffer greatly if they lost the king's favor.

In the end, I left my children with my family once again and journeyed to a land strange to me. Helen insisted she accompany me and I could not bring myself to refuse her.

King Ben-Hadad welcomed me as if I were an old friend or relative. After formally introducing me to his court we were permitted to retire to a private suite. The king's curiosity about me was clear from the beginning.

"As a Phoenician, how did you end up with an

Egyptian name, Na-Amen?"

"My Phoenician name is Aribaal, but circumstances forced a move to Egypt when I was a very young boy. It was my adopted father who gave me the name Na-Amen, a family name from previous generations. Gratitude and a need to feel a part of the family encouraged me to accept the change."

I shrugged and added, "What use would my Phoenician name be in Egypt? From the day my family adopted me my whole life and even my past life underwent a great change."

Ben-Hadad appeared to accept my explanation but I sensed his curiosity about me had not been totally assuaged. However, he chose not to ask more.

"I look forward to how you will train my troops and handle the leadership among them. It is time you met them."

"My pleasure."

I bowed to the king and excused myself.

On meeting his leaders it became clear where his problem lay. The leader of the army, bearing the ancient name of Ashur, turned out to be a large man, as tall as I and much heavier. His lack of discipline showed clearly in every gesture. He did not rise to welcome me even though he had to know why Ben-Haddad had brought me to his nation.

He said, "Come, have some wine with me. I have sent for sweetmeats."

I glanced quickly past Ashur, hoping to see his army. Unfortunately, the scene that met my eyes offered me neither comfort nor hope. Instead of a well-trained army of tough soldiers across the whole field where I expected war games to be in progress lounged hundreds, possibly thousands, of men in partial uniforms or none at all.

At my request Ashur consented to delay our talk until later. I wanted to settle things with the king before I bestowed my hopeful expertise on his army. I turned on my heel and marched back to Ben-Haddad's throne room. After

I bowed and offered homage to the king, I requested audience.

Waving a weary looking hand the king invited me to speak.

Bowing reverently, I said, "Your highness. I have looked briefly at your army and General Ashur who commands them. I saw, not soldiers ready to overcome your enemies or even to protect your eminent person, but a slovenly mass of lazy men under an equally disinterested general. Do you seriously call them an army?"

His shocked look and those of his courtiers spread throughout the throne room showed me the reality of this job I had accepted on behalf of my uncle.

Ben-Haddad appeared propelled from his throne, he moved so quickly.

"How dare you to speak to your king in such a manner? I will have you beheaded immediately, you bold fool."

"If you must." I replied. "But do remember that you sent for me because your huge army had become unruly and an embarrassment to you. If you kill me you may never find another as experienced as I and will end up losing all that your father, the great Ben-Haddad the First left to you."

His face grew red and looked to burst into flames then, instead of calling for my death, he broke out into peals of loud laughter.

"I believe I can truthfully say I have never met any other man who dared speak to me in that manner."

"Perhaps I am the first man to challenge your word. You claimed you wanted me to change your army and now I hold you to it. Surely, your promise is good and your heart truthful."

He laughed again.

"If it is not I am convinced you will do your best to change that."

"I am happy that we truly understand each other,

Your Majesty. I promise to restore the mighty army your father left you. In fact, I have taken the liberty to command General Ashur to set an example and have placed him under my friend Senmut, an Egyptian warrior decorated by Pharaoh's own hand. His battle skills are beyond almost any warrior I have ever met."

"How did Ashur react to this command from a stranger?"

"With threats until I explained my position with you. I think he was well impressed and ultimately agreed to follow the program Senmut arranges for him."

"And your other warrior?"

"I have put him over all the army, to select the men he senses he can trust to run the daily oversight of the new officers he will appoint."

I chose not to go on. It was early yet and my program needed to be tested, especially by the king.

Ben-Haddad invited me to a banquet he intended to

give for some of his closet followers. I declined, pleading tiredness and work needing done before the morrow.

I bid him a good night and left him laughing. I hoped his good humor would remain as long as I did in his country and that eventually we would part as friends.

That very day I met with Senmut and Rem-Na to discuss our plans to apply what we had learned at Nyto's academy in Egypt. None of us had ever known another war leader with the subtlety and determination of Nyto, a truly great general. It became our determination to mold General Ashur into as full a model of Nyto as possible. It was not easy as the head warrior tried a number of tricks to put off our plan but, in the end, he became a real general and leader of warriors. The lazy, undisciplined soldiers and their lieutenants underwent a change, as well, with very few of them requiring strict discipline.

Ben-Haddad changed my name once again. I became known as Naaman, a designation more compatible with Syrian names. It mattered little to me. I now had acquired so many names that even my family became confused.

Using the disciplines and techniques of Nyto made it possible for Senmut and Rem-Na to cut through months, and even years of training for the Syrian army.

"My friends, it astounds me how much progress you have already made with the Syrians."

Rem-Na replied for both of them.

"It is not as if these men had never encountered military disciplines. Before the old king died Syria had a decent standing army. But this young king has no background in warfare. Thus far he enjoys the fruits of his father's work."

"And", he continued, "they lost the chief general of the old king's warriors and their own leader. This has left them like a rudderless ship. There has been no-one to guide them. But, with our experience and intense training in Egypt, they are ready for just about anything."

"I believe it is timely." Senmut added. "There are whispering among neighboring countries that the Greeks seek another opportunity to destroy Syria. The enmity between these countries has not died by any means."

I grew thoughtful as I considered my friends' words. Knowing them as well as Isaac, who had joined us, I had confidence that their words had not been based on rumors alone. It was time we decided to break in our army.

I did not have long to wait. The Israelis decided to come from the mountains and attack one of our outposts. It was a relatively small raid, one my army found easy to push back over the hills. Blood got shed, bones broken and soldiers died, despite the unimportance of the battle. As well, our soldiers marched a string of captives behind them for sale in the slave market of Damascus.

One slave caught my eye. A girl child, about Deidre's age, trailed at the rear of the column. Her youth and her pretty face recalled my childhood, when Men-el cared for me and became my closest and lifelong friend. He had been purchased for that purpose.

Perhaps this child would possess a similar temperament and serve my daughter as Men-el, now his own man, did me. I decided to take the thought to Helen. Her wisdom and graciousness could determine the girl's suitability.

The child's name was Sarah, a very popular name among Isaac's people. Isaac had taught me that it was the name of their patriarch's wife, much revered in Israel's history. Very soon, Sarah joined our family. She exhibited a sweetness that reminded me of Deidre herself. From the first day the two girls forged a friendship that joyed Helen's and my heart. She was like another daughter to us.

Helen permitted Sarah freedoms she would refuse to grant another slave. Very quickly, the little slave girl joined our family conferences and added her wisdom on more than one occasion. She played a musical instrument quite different than anyone in our family possessed.

When she sang her young voice sounded almost like a dirge despite her usual happy disposition. Isaac explained that her songs were ancient ones that had been played and sung for many generations. She had learned them when she still remained with her family and had heard them from a very young child.

Chapter 34

The new Syrian army continued to indulge in conflicts against other lands which either actually or potentially threatened ours. Very quickly, my fame as general spread among the lands bordering the great sea. Victory appeared inevitable each time I led the army into battle. I began to revel in all the glory offered me by friend and foe alike. I had found my true mission, and while still a young man. Yet, even as I found myself riding high like a Phoenician ship upon the crest of the waves of fame, my world changed again.

Several times, Helen had noticed a small sore place on the side of my head and another near my heart. At first I paid no attention to them.

"It is nothing, Helen. Do not fuss over a couple of small sores. Consider the many injuries I have received in war and they all healed quickly."

I had much to do and a reputation to enhance. Helen stopped speaking of the sores, but clearly she continued to fret over them.

"I have never seen any such thing before." Her brows creased with concern. "They are more like bites from strange insects."

Things might have continued like that forever had the sores not continued to spread. One reasonably quiet afternoon Helen noticed the increase and asked me if she could send for a physician. At my consent she arranged the visit.

The physician examined me carefully then said, "Noble sir, I must tell that you have become leprous and those sores are the proof."

I stared at him in disbelief.

"That cannot be so", I yelled at him. "There has never been any such plague in my background or that of my family. You must be mistaken. There is no way I could have been overtaken by such a horror."

The physician cringed and moved away as I grabbed my sword and waved it around. Then he threw himself at my feet.

"Please. I can say no more than what is true. You are now a leper."

I could only stare at him in fear. I felt he had killed me with his words. Strength left me and I collapsed on my couch. My glory, my family and even my very life now had abandoned me.

Even at the moment of such a curse, I thought of Helen, of our children. I could not inflict this upon them.

"My wife, I will have to leave our home immediately. I dare not expose our family to such a threat. All of you must be protected from me."

Page538

Helen began to weep.

"I cannot lose you, Aribaal. We have sacrificed too much. We must find a way."

I laughed and my voice sounded dry and harsh, as if already scarred by the disease.

"The only way is to let me go to a hermitage. Even though I believe King Ben-Haddad would retain me as head of the army I cannot. No one knows how the curse comes so I must be put away."

Helen and I called a family meeting that very day. I left none out, including my Egyptian warriors, Isaac and our Jewish slave Sarah, now part of the family. I explained everything to them and watched as horror overtook each beloved face, followed by tears and supplications to their gods.

Strangely, only Isaac and Sarah appeared at peace with the horrible words.

Isaac said, "I believe that some spell was laid on you

by that evil priest Theon while we resided in the jungle we so recently escaped. Leprosy was a major threat in the towns and even the capital of the land. You may not have noticed at the time, but I recognized the sickness from memories from my youth in strange places. That affliction added to my desire to get away from that land, but at the time such a thing bore little import against the larger threats against us.

Therefore, I did not speak of it."

His eyes showed agony as he spoke. Could a warning have saved me? I doubted it. With the number and variety of spells that Theon and his followers laid on me in that accursed place I would never had noticed one more.

"As an unsuspecting man you could not have stood against such power. Theon dealt with secret incantations and the calling forth of evil against you, me and any others who displeased him. I cannot name the malevolent spirits working with him, but I do not doubt their presence. Now we must learn how to deal with this nightmare. We must find a way."

Even as he spoke those bold words, in my heart I accepted the inevitability of a lifetime of advancing corruption, pain and rejection.

As we remained in stunned silence a small voice in front of me spoke words of unexpected consolation.

"There is a prophet in Samaria."

It was Helen who first responded to Sarah's words. She said, "What use is that to us? How can a prophet help my husband?"

Sarah seemed to gain strength from those words, despite her underlying temerity. She leaned against me and looked into my face, showing no fear of the disease.

"I just know he can heal you even of leprosy. He is a great man of God."

Sarah sounded much like Isaac as she spoke of her God. She asked, "Do you understand me, Isaac? Do you know of what I speak?"

Isaac's face paled at her words as he replied to her.

"I used to understand such things. But that was very long ago when I was but a child. Not much older than you. Very long ago. Then everything changed."

"God has not changed."

"No. I am the one who changed." Isaac's face grew sad as he spoke those words.

Sarah turned to me again.

"My Lord, if you ask the king of Samaria I am sure he will arrange for the prophet to heal you."

Convinced that the child believed strongly that her God reigned supreme over all other gods I chose to honor her entreaty.

I told Isaac, "Find a scribe to write a message to the king of Samaria. I must plead with him for mercy."

Since Syria was presently at war with Samaria, I promised to lift the deadly siege of his city and even provide food for its people, if he healed me through his prophet. It

Page542

seemed only courteous to approach the king rather than attempt to plead with the prophet directly.

After some days I received a response from the king of Samaria. He offered the services of a prophet named Elisha for whom he claimed great power.

So we arranged a visit to that beleaguered city whose citizens my officers had brought to almost total destruction. As proof of my sincerity I sent vast amounts of food and water to relieve the remaining residents of the city and then took Sarah, my Egyptian friends and Isaac to Samaria.

We were met outside Elisha's house by the servant of the prophet, who their king said would heal me. Quite naturally, I anticipated a ceremony of some sort to welcome me but the prophet's door remained closed. The man of God did not open his door to me but left me waiting outside.

"Isaac. What do you think the man of God is doing? Why does he leave us here outside his house instead of coming forth receive me?"

"I confess I have little knowledge of these prophets who dwell in the presence of the Lord. They are infamous for stepping aside and often disappear before the eyes of the people. We can only wait and see."

This strange behavior confused me and I fidgeted while I awaited a response from the prophet. Clearly, the man had no manners if he kept me waiting in this manner.

Suddenly, the door opened and the servant of the prophet came out to us. Instead of inviting me inside he said, "Elisha says you are to go to the Jordan River and wash seven times in its water and you will be restored to health."

Had I not travelled long and hard to present myself to the prophet? Did I not free the people of his city from the siege I had laid upon them? Did I not send food and water to the starving citizens? And all in honor of this same prophet?

I yelled at the servant.

"Does your master think we have no rivers in Syria?

If washing in a river was all I needed to do I could have done that near my home and returned clean to my family. But this demand that I must wash in the Jordan, that small and unimpressive dribble, is ridiculous. And is it necessary to do it seven times in order to acquire enough water to effectively bathe my body?"

What kind of wonder worker was this man? A pretender? A charlatan?

As I began to turn my entourage around for the return journey to Damascus little Sarah approached me.

"Master Aribaal, why will you not obey the man of God who can save you? What great thing is it to dip in the Jordan seven times? Surely it is a small work of faith for a great reward."

My wrath subsided and feeling like a fool I turned my chariot and began a slow move to the Jordan. Once there I stood down from my chariot and, throwing off my garments, stepped into the water. Seven times I immersed myself and seven times I emerged from the chilly water with its mud now stirred from the riverbed.

When I emerged I heard cries of joy and excitement and Isaac announced that I was again clean.

Senmet cried out, "You are healed, Ari. Your flesh is like that of a babe and all trace of disease left you. May the gods be praised!"

When I dressed and prepared for an encounter with Elisha I presented myself and my friends before his house once more. This time he came out to greet me.

I bowed before him and proclaimed. "Now I know there is no other God in all the world, save in Israel. Please accept a gift from your grateful servant."

"Keep what you have. I can accept nothing. Go home and be blessed."

Slowly and still confused by the prophet, I turned away and joined my entourage. After I traveled a short distance from Elisha's house, his servant Gehazi ran to me and said that the prophet changed his mind and wished to accept some gold and clothing for two of his impoverished disciples. Gladly I gave him what he asked and sent him on his way.

****

Later I learned that Gehazi actually claimed the gift for his family and was punished when the leprosy God had lifted from me was given to the unfaithful servant and to his progeny forever.

Chapter 35

Ben-Haddad expressed his pleasure when he learned how Samaria's God and the prophet delivered me from the horror of leprosy. Clearly, he felt vindicated by the success of his suggestion. To me, it felt like a bad dream that turned around and became a joyful gift.

The king's pleasure in seeing me clean again superseded even his anger when he realized that I had freed the captured city from siege and fed the starving citizens. He had good enough reason for his disappointment, as it had taken months to triumph, not an easy victory.

"You have given away all you achieved in the siege. I should punish you for that, but my joy in your healing makes me overlook the other." He began to make plans almost before I finished my tale of deliverance and I had to interrupt his colloquies before he had the chance to declare a ruling to pursue more battles.

"O great King Ben-Haddad. I have done all that you asked of me, and with great enthusiasm. I have trained an army for you that can stand against host you might encounter. My fighting spirit has been transmitted to the generals, other officers and charioteers who lead and cover your soldiers wherever they go. In your honor I have captured cities, ravaged nations and directed your navy to successful battle against your enemies. None of them has prevailed over your forces for more than a few months before you savaged them and made them helpless. It has been my honor to serve you and care for your fighting men."

I hesitated for now was the moment I dreaded.

"I wish to remind you that when I became your servant and agreed to raise an army for you it was understood that my success would be rewarded by being freed from my commitment. The time has come. Now I wish to return to my family and follow my own destiny."

"You want to leave?"

He shouted and leapt from his throne as he pulled his sword in a threatening manner.

I stood firm before his sudden rage and held my ground before his onslaught.

"I must. I have done all you asked, all I agreed to and more. And now it is over."

I permitted my gaze to cover all present. Shock appeared on the faces and in the eyes staring at me, disbelief seeming to overpower the whole court.

Then as suddenly as he had plunged into anger, Ben-Haddad's demeanor altered. He turned and walked back to his throne.

"I do not wish this, Naaman, but I will not play you falsely. You have met your obligation, fulfilled your promise and now it is my turn."

He hesitated and drew a deep breath. His doing that disclosed determination to treat me honestly.

"You are free to return to your home and family. I will not prevent."

I bowed low before him.

"You are a good and honest man, King Ben-Haddad. I hope your fame will spread and that your reputation will grow. My honor now is to my family. I long to stand upon the deck of a Phoenician ship again. When the ugly disease held me in thrall I thought often of the movement of water beneath my ship and I wanted to live again and feel the sturdy boards under my feet as they bore me over the waves. I am eager to fulfill this as soon as possible."

Ben-Haddad showed grace and spoke no more about my remaining in his land.

I did not procrastinate in my preparations to go back home. As I oversaw the packing of my minimal property, as sparse as that of any common soldier except for the ceremonial garments required in the court of Ben-Haddad, I felt a great weight flee from my shoulders. My debt to my uncle Hiras no longer held thrall over me and when at last I sailed into harbor and saw again my family I knew it all had been worth it.

In the front a few steps from Helen stood Isaac, his face filled with joy.

As soon as I could I spoke to him.

"I am happy you still live, my friend. But I am sorry I could not help you find your family. I am convinced you will one day and be reconciled with your God. As willing as he was to care for me, he has also watched over you all these years."

I reached out and pulled him to me.

"Thank you, my friend, for your prayers and your strong trust in the true God. Without that I should be isolated from my family forever."

Tears formed in his eyes and I felt his pain.

"Do not be afraid, Isaac, you will never be alone again."

I turned away and took Helen's hand as we entered our home.

****

Three days later a bedraggled ship drew up to the cothon, its paint now almost non-existent and the remnants peeling in brilliant curls and long tails of dried paint changed into shabby reminders of what once was beauty. It made me think of the fate of a beautiful but wayward woman turned into naught but a memory of her glorious past beauty. Suddenly recognizing it, I found my legs weak from the shock. There could be no doubt. This was Theon's ship. But how? I was certain I had watched the volcano destroy it.

"Theon!" I cried. "He still lives and has found his way here."

I waited to learn how this could be and how the true God wanted me to deal with it.

I did not have to wait long. From the bowels of the ship Theon reached the deck. Supported on both sides, he stumbled to the walkway and onto the cothon itself. As soon as his feet hit the cothon he shrugged away his supporters and stood precariously without help.

"Aribaal," he said, "how fortunate that you are here to welcome me. I could not have asked for better."

Ignoring him, I spoke to Ribbida.

"Please find a place to seat him or a cot he can lie upon, but do not offer him hospitality."

Ribbida nodded but I could see he felt confused. It was against family policy to reject a guest and he had never seen me to do so before.

He gestured to a servant behind him. He spoke quietly so that none could hear. The servant bowed and approached Theon. Taking the priest's arm he attempted to lead Theon wherever Ribbida had commanded.

With his usual haughtiness Theon refused to be led.

Ribbida looked at me in some confusion. It was as if he asked aloud what he should do with that arrogant man.

I stepped forward and said, "You are not welcome anywhere here or throughout Phoenician territory. Neither will we permit you to travel freely to some other land."

Proximity to the evil priest incited no fear nor showed me any essence of power. What remained was a wreck of a man who stubbornly grasped his memory of power and still expected obedience.

I signaled Senmut to me.

"He must be totally isolated from all mankind. Until we can build a fortified cell for him he will remain incarcerated in a strong room and all communication blocked from him. No one may speak to him or engage him in any manner."

Senmut nodded.

"Take him then."

Theon was dragged off screaming in fury. He

Page555

struggled but was no match for the strength of Senmut. I did not know where my Egyptians would keep him and I did not wish to know.

I learned later that he spent the remaining months of his life in a cell tunneled out of a standing rock in the desert some distance from town where he remained until his death. I never saw or spoke to him again. His once beautiful ship was burned in the harbor and any ash or other remains scattered.

With my family together at last and kept free from harm by Israel's and my God I returned to the role of trader and father of my own family.

The end

10300901R00314

Made in the USA
San Bernardino, CA
11 April 2014